THE OLD EYES
DEEP AND CALM

"An oracular message, lord

sage into the dark of their own future, unaimed, unfocused. Without answer. Without
hope of answer. We know its voyage time.
Eight million years. This probe went out, and
they fell silent shortly afterward—the depth
of this dry lake of dust, lord Desan, is eight
and a quarter million years."

"I will not believe that."

"Eight and a quarter million years ago,
lord Desan. Calamity fell on them, calamity
global and complete within a century, perhaps within a decade of the launch of that
probe. Perhaps calamity fell from the skies;
but demonstrably it was atomics and their
own doing. They were at that precarious stage.
And the destruction in the great centers is
catastrophic and one level. Destruction centered in places of heavy population. Trace
elements. That is what those statistics say.
Atomics, lord Desan."

From "Pots," by C.J. Cherryh

AFTERWAR

CREATED BY
JANET MORRIS

BAEN
science fiction
BOOKS

AFTERWAR

A Baen Book

Baen Enterprises
8-10 W. 36th Street
New York, N.Y. 10018

First Baen printing, June 1985

ISBN: 0-671-55967-2

Cover art by David Mattingly

Printed in the United States of America

Distributed by
SIMON & SCHUSTER
MASS MERCHANDISE SALES COMPANY
1230 Avenue of the Americas
New York, N.Y. 10020

CONTENTS

INTRODUCTION	Janet Morris	7
HERO'S WELCOME	Janet Morris	14
GOING AFTER ARVIQ	Michael Armstrong	26
TO THE STORMING GULF	Gregory Benford	47
FLAMESTONES	Stephen Leigh	107
THE PHOENIX GARDEN	Diana L. Paxson	132
PRIMARY	Esther M. Friesner	171
WHEN IDAHO DIVED	Ian Watson	191
BAR AND GRILL	Craig Shaw Gardner	199
POTS	C.J. Cherryh	214
NOTES FOR A NEWER TESTAMENT	David Langford	251
THE GUARDROOM	David Drake	261

INTRODUCTION
by Janet Morris

When the High Frontier concept of a layered, space-based defense—a concept that has since been refined, adopted by the Reagan Administration, and renamed Strategic Defense Initiative—was being prepared for presentation to the American public, Jim Baen and I had a number of heated conversations that led me to propose both this collection and the novel *Forty-Minute War*, a collaboration with Chris Morris, to Baen Books.

He accepted both proposals and I blithely typed out a letter of invitation, offering writers a chance to submit pieces under seventeen thousand words on life in America after nuclear war—a premise based on the assumption that there would *be* life in America after a nuclear exchange.

Naturally, I chose my participants carefully—no open submissions, invitations only to writers who had strong technical, political, or philosophical backgrounds, who were free to write horror, sf, fantasy, or any damned thing with a beginning, middle, and end and inherent literary merit that depicted post-holocaust America as something more than the already-trite darkling deep-freeze scenario of radical Saganism.

I thought I was being clever. I thought I'd get from these writers, to whom I'd thrown the gauntlet of topicality freed from moralistic constraint, the sort of informed "what if" scenarios that science fiction writers do better than any others. I thought, in fact, I'd get lots of stories based on strategic defense concepts.

Instead, I got lots of stories about elves.

Elves after nuclear war, you say? What gives?

When the elf stories started coming, I wasn't willing to meditate upon the underlying problem, though it seemed clear enough (by the determined absence of realism in these first stories) that our writers, the communicators of our collective unconscious and those on whom we should be able to depend to guide us into—and out of—dangerous places in possible futures, didn't have enough sand in their collective craw to grapple with the subject matter directly.

I received stories of towering inventiveness, but that inventiveness was concentrated on avoiding the topic as completely as possible while seeming to deal with it.

Among the elf stories, the best was Esther M. Friesner's "Primary," included here because it became clear to me that the elf cadre should be represented—and because wit is scarce in the world and Esther's story is fraught with it. Esther, when asked, was willing to remove the elves. I considered that, but decided, since it would be a good story with or without elves—and because it may be that elves shall play some part in our nuclear future (so many writers thought so, it must mean something)—to leave the elf in "Primary." So I bought Esther's story and wrote Greg Benford a letter.

Greg, I said, I need a nice hard-science story for my collection, one in which the numbers will be right and one with some SDI, if you can. Know anybody else who's up on this area?

Greg wrote back and allowed that he had a piece in mind and suggested two British writers with good technical background: David Langford and Ian Watson.

Great, I thought, sending some more elves back

to their creators with notes of apology. Those Brits will give me just what I need—lots of cruise missiles and politics; since they've scientific backgrounds, I'll not get elves from them.

Meanwhile, another elf story came in the mail. This one, from Stephen Leigh, was good enough that I'd have bought it if I hadn't already bought Esther's. But I had Esther's elf. So I wrote to Leigh and said, Look, can we get the elves out of here? I'll take anything else—troglodytes, trolls, what-have-you. And the title: Could it be something besides "Elfstones"?

Leigh and I talked on the phone and he allowed that he could see his way clear, without fear for his integrity, to change the title to "Flamestones" and oust the elves from his universe, no sweat. After all, he was an electric bass player (as I am), a comrade of the Fender. Great, I said. "Flamestones" will be fine. So he did, and it was, and then he broke his hand.

Meanwhile, word was getting out (despite my best efforts to the contrary: I hate rejecting stories and had reasoned that the fewer I read, the fewer I'd have to reject) and people I didn't know or hadn't asked started writing and calling for permission to submit.

Permission to submit. Nice ring to that. So when I'd get a letter or a call, I'd say, Okay, but no elves, fairies, dragons, or unicorns, guys. Diana Paxson, who had spent some time in Civil Defense, said she had a good idea.

Diana's from the *Thieves' World* group of writers and I felt a tremor of relief: One thing I know about the TW writers is that they produce. So Diana sent in her story and goddamn if there wasn't a witch in it. I forgot to say, No witches, and I liked the story so I took it anyway.

By then, Ian Watson's marvelous "When Idaho Dived" had come in and I was feeling more hopeful about the collection being topical. Benford wrote and wanted to know when the deadline was—he was going to Europe. He was slated to do the novella-length piece, and I read between the lines well, so I asked Jim Baen for a deadline extension, got two months, didn't tell Benford, and kept reading the stuff landing in my mailbox. There was a point when Ron, my Post Person, was muttering, "Sin loi," (Vietnamese for "So sorry,") when he loaded me up with envelopes too cumbersome to fit in my post office box.

Time was getting short and I still had bought only four stories when Dave Drake came up to the Cape to work on another project. Drake, I said, I really need something from you. He replied that he'd done his after-the-bomb story, hadn't I read it? He'd sent me the collection it was in. So I read "Men Like Us" and wished I could buy reprints. Then I called him at home late one night and begged. Drake, a can-do guy of the first order, put other things aside to write "Guardroom" and sent it with a grumbling letter that he'd had to rewrite it entirely and wasn't going to apologize. He didn't have to to; I liked it fine.

While Drake had been visiting, somebody from Alaska named Michael Armstrong had written and said he had a piece already done which might suit; would I take a look?

I'd never heard of him but that's never stopped me. "Going After Arviq," Mike's story, is still my favorite in the collection and restored my faith in the writer's ability to grapple with hard questions. Everything speculative fiction should offer is present in his story in larger measures than necessary. And boy, can this man write. So I sent Mike his contract and sent his story to my agent, the result of which may be a novel based on "Arviq." I can't wait.

Benford called a few days later and said he was

on his way to Europe in the morning and that he'd work on his story there. Sure thing, I said; Oh dear, I thought. He was already late and I had to admit to him that I had an extension. But I was crafty—I told him I'd send the book in without his story and forward his when it came. He said, Great, and promised he'd talk to Langford, who hadn't yet sent his piece, while he was in England.

When I hung up, I called Carolyn Cherryh and said I needed a long one from her—quick. Just in case Benford didn't come through, I was thinking. Instead of writing one myself, you see.

CJ and I have certain things in common: We fill gaps and take up slack and commonly do the impossible, if we're properly motivated. She asked, How far in the future can I set it? I replied, Any time you want—centuries hence. Drake gave me one set that far down the line. CJ said, Fine; no problem, then.

And right on deadline, as promised, in came Cherryh's "Pots," no problem at all: a fine story and one which would balance Drake's far-future piece nicely.

Now I had my long story. I'd about given up on Benford, though I kept hearing progress reports and David Langford sent in his piece.

So I decided I wouldn't be mad at Benford, even if there wasn't any story whatsoever forthcoming from him: He'd gotten Langford to write one.

The thing about Langford's piece was that it wasn't set in America at all. But I really liked it. He said in his letter that the enclosed was his second try, that the first hadn't worked at all, and that he hadn't remembered until after he'd written it that it was supposed to be set in America. He'd Americanize it, he swore, if I wanted.

I didn't ask him to Americanize it: It was so inherently British that doing so would have jeopardized the story. I altered my guidelines to suit and bought "Notes For a Newer Testament" for *Afterwar*, a collection of stories about life in America and Great Britain after nuclear war. Keeping it simple, I was.

At a convention, I ran into Craig Shaw Gardner and we sat in a bar and I dunned him for a story. I really need one, I told him. And I still did; although I'd gotten other submissions, I hadn't any I liked well enough to put into the pile of "keepers" on my computer room's floor. Benford had seventeen thousand words of space reserved in which no story might ever appear, and time was getting short.

So short, in fact, that Baen Books called me and said I couldn't have any more time—the damned thing had to be in on schedule, not a day late.

I faced the fact that I was going to write one and then I realized I wasn't going to write a Strategic Defense Initiative story. I didn't think I had enough space to allot myself, and my SDI idea was looking more and more booklength. So I'm officially tendering, with my own story, "Hero's Welcome," my apologies to anyone and everyone to whom I complained that stories I'd received weren't the sort that I'd had in mind. Since mine wasn't. Isn't.

Stories have a way of telling you what ought to be in them: "Hero's Welcome" not only told me it didn't want to be an SDI story, but that it wanted to make a personal statement: no hardware, nuts-and-bolts gloss for it, thanks very much.

By the time I'd finished my piece, I understood some of the reasons that writers had seemed to be going to such great lengths to avoid the topic: It's hurtful to write about disasters of the postulated magnitude from close at hand. It's easier to write from a cushion of distance: from years or centuries later. It's even easier to write hardware. A related novel, *Forty-Minute War*, although difficult to do, didn't cause me as much pain as this little story did.

So I put "Hero's Welcome" first, which says as much about the way I live as it does about my feelings for the piece: I like to get the rough stuff over with as fast as possible.

Once my piece was done, I was still short on length and I considered trying to write a longer SDI story (now that I'd gotten HW out of my system) in case Benford never got back from Europe, was abducted by the Russians, or locked away by the Air Force somewhere.

But then Benford's story came in the mail and by god, it was a Strategic Defense Initiative sort of story! And, although Benford's point of view on SDI differs markedly from mine, it was a well thought-out piece with plenty of verisimilitude.

So, by stumble and paranoia, hook and crook, the project had managed to become well rounded and thoughtful. Come a long way from elves, it has. I'm asking Baen if he wants to do another collection: Elves After Nuclear War.

But then, if I asked the community for ten or twelve stories on that theme, I'd probably get lots of Strategic Defense Initiative stories.

I've put my piece first: a case of the editor sitting anywhere she wants. Because I usually write the book I'd like to read but can't find anywhere, I wrote a story I'd have liked to receive from someone else for consideration. The other reason I have for slotting it first is chronological order. Those of you who, like me, read compendiums from back to front take note: You'll be going from the future to the past if you try it with Afterwar.

HERO'S WELCOME
by Janet Morris

When the stranger came strolling into Chilmark of an evening, Betsy couldn't understand at first why it hurt so to look at him.

But then Dad swore under his breath, "Healthy-looking bugger," as if he were hurting too, and Betsy adjusted the kerchief on her patchy head of hair before she went to hand the newcomer today's menu.

The Fish Shanty's regulars had all stopped talking and now they stared—there just *weren't* any strangers anymore. First the ferries had stopped running, then the airport had closed down because there wasn't any fuel to waste on airplanes. The Vineyard was closed off, isolated, trying to gird itself for the first winter without incoming supplies from the mainland.

14

The islanders were better off, her dad often said, better prepared to fend for themselves than those poor souls on the mainland. And since there weren't any radio or TV broadcasts from the mainland anymore, Betsy had no way of knowing if it were the truth.

Hand-written menu in hand, she approached the stranger's table, feeling the eyes of everyone in the place on her. 'Everyone,' that cold day in July, consisted of Arch Waite, who used to run the radio station until he "lost his voice," as Arch liked to put it, all bundled up in a mackinaw because he'd lost fifty pounds in three months and was always cold these days; Danny Jennings, who used to come summers to tend his daddy's Arabian horses and practice for the Olympics because he was on the U.S. equestrian team and now was stuck here . . . and stuck on Betsy, despite the little matter of her thinning hair; Buck Mendes, who claimed to be a full-blooded Wampanoag Indian and was, next to the stranger, the healthiest-looking individual on the island, big and flat-faced with slanty black eyes like a Hawaiian and a straight shock of blacker hair that didn't seem to be thinning out like everyone else's; and Christie Bunker, who'd been the fastest girl in town until the war changed her face (and maybe more of her) for the worse. Christie had been outside, sunbathing like the tourists used to do, and now she always wore a veil like some old movie star. Betsy's mom had said that it served the lazy little trollop right, but Betsy's mom had been outside too, weeding her garden, and they'd buried her there a month ago.

The stranger, slouched in his chair, held his hand out for the menu Betsy was still holding. "If you'll be so kind. I've come a long way and I'm hungry as a bear." His voice was as polite as his words, and real musical, with some kind of accent—he sounded like a TV announcer, pronouncing his R's and all, and he wasn't a bit nasty or teasing like Danny Jennings was with her, but Betsy blushed.

She blushed because his eyes caught hers and held, and they were very forward eyes indeed—not gray or green or blue, but some hazy in-between color, and she wanted to cover her own and run away: He was finding out all her secrets. She tugged her kerchief down over the wisp that curled around her right ear and one strand caught on her fingernail and came out. "Oh, no," she whispered—every lost hair was a tragedy, these days.

"Aw, come on," said the stranger with his easy voice, "please." This time he was teasing, but not nasty—there was something very like a puppy about him, as if he were starved for love.

How could she know that? How could she even *think* that? As if she'd spoken aloud or he'd somehow overheard her thoughts, she thrust the menu toward him and turned to flee, back behind the chrome-and-formica counter where her dad was.

But the stranger's voice stopped her: "I'll have the special, if you'll recommend it honestly."

Before she turned around, she noticed Buck and Danny, whispering together, and her father, dishrag dangling from the back pocket of his Made-Wells, ambling over to join them.

And she saw Christie's head turn toward her, though you couldn't see anything through Christie's veil, and Christie start to get up, too, with that set to her shoulders that Betsy remembered from a childhood during which Christie had made it a point to steal every boyfriend Betsy'd ever had.

She turned to the stranger, then, smiling. "Yes, indeed, I'll recommend it. Fried clams are our specialty."

"And you'll warrant them safe to eat?" As he spoke, his eyes brushed hers again—eyes that left a tingling sensation behind, as if they'd caressed her. He wasn't particularly tall, she didn't think, or particularly handsome—square, honest face, with an afternoon shadow darkening a deep, seaman's tan—but he had a particularly nice pair of shoulders and arms, shown off by an old black t-shirt that was a little too tight. As he handed her back the menu, she noticed a small tattoo on his upper left arm: an eagle's head with its beak open above the number 101.

"Safe as anything," she promised, and that darned grin—a loony grin that came over her when she was nervous—took over her face so that it ached.

"Great," he grinned in answer. "And coffee, if you've got it—a pot."

"Sorry." She really was; she felt crestfallen, inadequate. "No coffee, no more."

He muttered something under his breath, and she saw a dark look come and go worse than her dad's meanest when she'd been out too late with Danny Jennings.

"Coke?" she suggested. "We've got Coke, still."

He seemed pleased. "Coke's fine."

She didn't think to tell him that it was going to taste kind of flat—the carbonater wasn't working real well and nobody'd taken it up to Jack the Fixer's because it was too heavy.

When her dad heard the order, he got up to make it, and she saw a wink she didn't understand pass between him and Buck Mendes. And then, when he passed Arch's table, she saw Dad lean down and whisper in old Arch's ear so that Arch levered himself up and limped over to Buck's table and sat there instead.

Christie Bunker got up and put a slug in the jukebox—everybody knew it was a slug but nobody said anything, ever, because in the first place, Christie was dying slowly and in the second place, money wasn't much good on the island. You had to have barter these days. And Christie and Dad had worked out some sort of arrangement having to do with Christie's parents' house and what was in it, so that Christie could come and eat here and play music and such, and so that somebody'd bury her when she was dead.

Which meant that Betsy had to listen to "Sittin' on the Dock of the Bay," by Otis Redding, over and over. When Christie wasn't playing that one, she was playing, "Take It to The Limit," by the Eagles, or Michael Jackson's "Thriller." There were forty-seven other songs on the jukebox, lots of them much newer, but Christie only ever played those three. It was getting on Betsy's nerves, even though her dad kept telling her that it wasn't a big problem, and there were plenty of big problems, so why burden herself with ones that didn't have to be?

Burying people when they died, *that* was a big problem. If you weren't lucky, they burned you and you got stuck in a canning jar for eternity— just a little pile of ashes.

Before Betsy's mother had died, she'd made them promise not to put her in "any damned urn." That was the only time Betsy had ever heard her mother swear.

So when Betsy's mother died, because there weren't any coffins left unless you wanted to dig one up and take the bones out, they'd carried her all the way up to Jack the Fixer's and Jack had fixed up a coffin for Betsy's mother, and a proper funeral, too. Jack was like that, when you could pay.

Dad had paid Jack with three out of the five shepherd pups from Elvina's last litter, not thinking that it might be her last. But it was, and now they kept the boy and girl pups in Besty's mother's room because dogs were about as valuable as timber these days. Although they'd not bothered with a coffin for Elvina, just scattered her ashes over the bluff.

Betsy had stood there and thought that, when her time came, she'd rather be scattered on the wind than buried in the ground or stuck in any old jar, whether it was a canning jar like had happened with Arch's wife because Arch didn't have much in the way of barter, or some fancy pair of Chinese vases like Christie had put her parents in.

When Dad handed her the stranger's order, Betsy noticed approvingly that he'd put the fried clams, slaw, and potatoes (powdered, of course) on one of the good Blue Willow plates, and even put a plastic squeeze-lemon on the tray beside the cocktail sauce and cutlery wrapped in a clean napkin.

"Don't forget to ask him how he 'spects to pay for it, sugar," said her father in a real funny tone, half mean and half mysterious, as "Thriller" finished and the jukebox fell silent. Then he sat down behind the counter with his chin propped on one fist and Betsy could feel her dad's watchful gaze on her all the way back to the table.

The stranger was digging in his jeans' pocket, saying, "How much do I owe you, Miss?"

She liked being called 'Miss'. It made her feel elegant and grown-up, more than sixteen. She liked it so much she almost forgot what her dad had said, and then remembered. "We don't take paper money, Mister. You work out something with my dad, over there, about paying for it." She slid the plate off the tray and reached over, from the left as her mother had taught her, to put down the flatware and, as she did, her arm brushed the solid shoulder of the stranger.

It felt like an electric shock had run all the way up her arm and down her torso and lodged in her belly. She took two quick steps backward.

But nobody had noticed. The stranger was frowning, a finger pushing the plate away, as if he might get up.

Buck Mendes, the Indian, did get up, and crossed

the floor between the stranger and the jukebox—though Buck was usually glad when the music stopped—a slug in hand.

"It's okay, Mister," she said to the stranger, watching his broad back in its black t-shirt. "You better eat before it gets cold."

But the stranger got up and went over to the counter, where he leaned close to Betsy's father and they talked in low voices.

Try as she might, over Buck's selection—ZZ Top's "Sharp Dressed Man"—she couldn't hear a word they said.

But then the stranger, one elbow propped on the counter, turned and cast a glance over her, Buck by the jukebox near the door, and old Arch. Finally, shaking his head, the stranger rubbed the back of one hand across his mouth before he extended it for Betsy's father to clasp in some sort of agreement, and came back to his table.

Then, as Christie was humming to herself, dancing alone in one corner—twirling, twirling, humming, humming—Betsy realized she ought not to be standing there, gawking.

"Your father says," the stranger told her gently, "you might be willing to show me the way up to Jack the Fixer's tonight. I've come a long way to see him, a long way."

"I'd love—" Having blurted it out, Betsy snapped her mouth shut and looked desperately at her father who, instead of scowling, nodded encouragingly.

Then she turned back to the stranger. "But it's getting dark. It'll be dark. And cold."

"Don't worry. I've got a motorcycle aboard, down at the dock. And extra clothes."

"Aboard?" she demanded over the thudding of her heart.

"Aboard. How did you think I got here? I've got

a ketch docked. Nothing fancy, but it serves the purpose. . . ."

She could hear the pride in his voice, see it in the way his jaw corded with a restrained smile and the way he glanced at her, not boldly, but almost shyly.

She could hardly wait for him to finish eating and she felt suddenly awkward, standing around with nothing to do, so she mumbled, "I've got to clean up then," though she didn't, and headed for the kitchen.

It was the most exciting day she'd had in months. The *best* exciting day she'd had since it was decided that there was no use in sending her and the three other kids in her class to school anymore, that they'd learned all they needed to for now, and they'd been graduated by Arch, who was relieved because he didn't have to teach a class that included Christie, who was real crazy at first, crying all the time and throwing things and threatening to throw herself over a cliff into the sea.

Yes indeed, Betsy thought to herself as, behind the kitchen door where no one could see, she combed her hair and pinched her cheeks and tucked in her blouse, it was a real exciting day. The best.

And the stranger, once he'd cleaned his plate and paid Dad however the two had decided he would, came to get her himself.

"Betsy, my name is Nichols, but you can call me Nick." He held out a hand like he had to her dad and she was startled to feel how horny the side of his hand was—there was a ridge of callus there as hard as a horse's hoof.

But, like everything else she was feeling that night, maybe it wasn't as hard or as horny or as exciting as she thought.

The motorcycle surely was, once he'd wheeled it down the ketch's gangplank. She hadn't been on a motorcycle since before the war and this one had saddlebags and a windshield and a passenger seat with a high back.

He unlocked one of the hard plastic saddlebags and handed her a helmet and a thick leather jacket that must have been his because the sleeves reached nearly to her knees, then told her solemnly how "sexy" she looked.

She peered at him uncertainly, afraid he was teasing her, and said, "You know, I could just give you di*rect*ions to Jack the Fixer's . . ."

"I wouldn't hear of being denied your company." He bowed low, like somebody in one of the videotapes or on TV before the war, and added, "But I'm afraid it can't be ladies first. . . ."

The motorcycle roared to life when he touched its ignition switch, and he held out a hand to steady her. "Climb aboard. That's good. Now hold on, both arms around my waist, okay? That's good. Here we go."

She was in heaven, roaring along the country road on the motorcycle with the stranger named Nichols. Above, the stars were dim, as they'd come to be, and to either side the vegetation illuminated by his single headlight was sparse and brownish, but it didn't matter. In her sixteenth summer, Betsy had met a mysterious stranger and was falling headlong in love just like the war never happened and Danny Jennings wasn't the only man on earth . . . or on the island, which was just the same as the earth to her.

She was having such a wonderful time that, when Nichols coasted the motorcycle to a stop on the bluff and they were still a long way from Jack the Fixer's, she wasn't even worried.

She said, "We're not there yet, you know," and it came out muffled through her helmet as she smoothed her skirt down around her legs.

Nichols said, "I know. I thought we'd watch the moon rise. It's a pretty night," as he took his hel-

met off and exchanged it for an army blanket he
took from his saddlebag.

Something quivered in Betsy's stomach, but she
ignored it. "A pretty night," she echoed and followed him as he tramped through the tall grass.

Once he'd spread the blanket, he patted it. "Sit,
honey."

"Betsy," she corrected, still standing.

He chuckled for the second time. "Sit. I don't
bite unless I'm asked."

That was a funny thing to say but she folded
into a squat, spreading her skirt out over her knees,
and tried to study the water while she kept the
material from blowing up around her waist in the
sea breeze.

"You were here all the time?" he asked.

"All the—oh, you mean, during the war. Right
here. We all were. Right here. Where were you?"

"At sea," he said, biting his words off sharply.

"In your ketch," she said dreamily, raising her
arms to stretch.

This time when he laughed it had a different
tone and she felt his finger touch her knee and
trace its way up under her skirt.

"No," he said and his voice was deeper. "Not in
my ketch. I was in the . . . action, I guess you
could call it. Mainlanders don't much like ex-
soldiers. I thought I was going to have some trouble in your daddy's place, when they realized what
I was. But it didn't turn out that way." His hand
was higher on her thigh than any man's had ever
been.

She'd never have let Danny Jennings do that,
but somehow she didn't mind when Nick ran his
hand along her panties. She just kept her arms
raised, clasping her fingers behind her neck, letting her breasts press against her blouse until he
noticed them.

And after he noticed them, she noticed he had

lots of hair on his chest, and that his skin burned hers when they touched, and that she didn't have the strength to say "No," to him the way she did to Danny Jennings, even though Danny Jennings, everybody knew, was sterile and therefore safe, and Nick was very probably *not* either one.

She'd never thought she could go so quickly from pain to pleasure, or be so surprised at each in turn.

She tried not to cry out and he turned her face to his, saying, "Hey, Betsy, let it out. No one's going to hear you; no one's going to mind. Your daddy thinks this is a fine idea."

And then she realized how come she was out past her bedtime, showing the stranger named Nichols the way to Jack the Fixer's. And she realized how Nick was paying for his dinner. But something was happening inside her that quelled her outrage and dried her tears before she could shed them.

Daddy was always worried about how she was going to have a baby—how *he* was going to have a grandchild—within the "realm of decency."

She wasn't sure that this was decent, but she was sure that it was wonderful, that the grass was sweet and the man she'd just met gentle, while under them both the very earth seemed to rock.

He chuckled once and drew a deep breath and seemed to surge inside her, his loins butting against her the way her cat used to do before it ran away, never to return.

And then he gave a little cry so that she touched the back of his neck and pressed his head down, telling him that it was all right, hoping he hadn't hurt himself.

Afterwards, they lay in a tangle and he talked to her about the war in a way no one had ever talked to her before. He told her how it had started between India and Pakistan, and that the Indians had so many people to lose that they hadn't cared about casualties, so that eventually their protectors, the Soviet Union, and Pakistan's, the United States, had been drawn into the conflict.

But when she asked him whether he'd fought in the war—killed anybody, he only said, "Everybody fought in this one, honey. The whole world. And everybody died. On the spot. Some of us just don't know it yet."

Then she said, "But I'm alive. You're alive. Do you think we're going to have a baby?"

"We? Christ, I dunno." He rolled off her and muttered, "Wish I had a towel for you, babe, but I don't. Use the blanket."

She had no idea what he meant until she got to her knees and felt wetness run down her thighs.

By then he was standing, legs braced apart, zipping his fly, and she just had time to think again how healthy he seemed to be before a red-orange flash spat from the roadside and the man beside her fell forward without so much as a groan.

She sat frozen, uncomprehending at first.

She touched his hair and he didn't move.

She heard footsteps running through the grass toward her, wheezing breaths, but she was still shaking the man who'd made love to her when her dad and Buck Mendes skidded to a halt before her.

Her dad said, "How are you, Betsy?" tenderly, helping her up as if nothing out of the ordinary had happened. "Did that soldier pay his bill?"

"Y-yes, Dad," she managed to mutter, as Buck lifted the corpse and took it to the bluff's edge, where he heaved it unceremoniously over into the sea and the night, saying, "Goodbye, soldier boy."

And then they had to wheel the heavy motorcycle all the way up to Jack the Fixer's because Nichols had had the ignition key in his pocket and they couldn't get it started.

Michael Armstrong lives in Alaska and, as I did, set his story close to home. We liked this one so well that my husband read it to me aloud after I'd bought it. Armstrong is teaching Freshman Composition at the University of Alaska, Anchorage, where he's working on his Master of Fine Arts. He says, "Maybe Alaska represents a thing Americans now feel a need for—the Frontier, the Raw, the Unknown ... In Florida I cared some for the environment and now up here I am a rabid environmentalist. This land is sacred. Things change. People change." In Armstrong's story, you'll sense all of that, and more.

GOING AFTER ARVIQ
by Michael Armstrong

Claudia looks down into the deep blue water and sees arviq. He is mottled grey, massive, smooth as he flies through the icy water. His great head rises high and Claudia sees the bump, the knob that gives arviq his tannak name: bowhead. The old Yankee whalers called him The Whale, the Right Whale, and Claudia looks at arviq and thinks, yes, The Whale is right. She can almost taste the briny muktuk, feel the tough skin on her teeth. They will have arviq. Claudia is on a good whaling crew and arviq will bless them.

Arviq rises. He flaps his great flukes, one slow stroke, two, and surfaces. The umiak wobbles a bit as the whale rises less than twenty feet from them.

Next to her, in the stern of the skin boat, Tuttu, the whaling captain, yells to his crew.

"Nivak!" he shouts. "Dig!" The five men and a woman pull at their paddles. The umiak—the skin boat—pitches on Claudia's side; Tuttu glares at her and she digs in harder. Arviq slows, as if he is begging for the harpoon. The boat shudders as it comes up on the whale's back. The skin of the boat vibrates with the tension, and Claudia can feel the waves ripple beneath her knees.

In the bow Natsiq, the harpoonist, rises, wooden shaft clenched tightly in his hands. The crew set their paddles on the deck of the umiak, put their hands on their knees. The blowhole of the whale dilates, slight spray rising as arviq breathes. Natsiq watches the blowhole, and when the whale takes a breath Natsiq leans over and drives the darting harpoon in. His foot slips, and he falls to his left. Natsiq flails for balance, one arm whirring like an amputee helicopter blade, and then he splashes into the cold sea.

The line sings. Claudia looks down and watches arviq disappear into the deep. The harpoon line whizzes out of the boat. Claudia counts: one-thousand one, one-thousand two, one-thousand three, one-thousand four, one-thousand five. She hears a *whoompf* sound and then sees a cloud of bubbles rise up before them, as if arviq was a kid farting in a bathtub. The line goes slack and arviq swims on, across the open water, and toward the flat sea ice on the other side of the lead.

Tuttu pulls in the line, fathoms of heavy rope. He comes to the end: frayed strands of nylon, curled black into little beads of plastic. He shakes his head.

"Anak," Tuttu mutters. "Shit."

They paddle over to Natsiq, who is treading water, his lips turning blue. The crew reach over the side and pull the harpoonist in. Someone hands

him a dry parka. Natsiq sits in the bow of the
boat, teeth chattering.

"What happened?" he asks.

"The bomb was too big," Tuttu says. "It blew
the harpoon apart." He holds up the cut line.

Natsiq shrugs. "Perhaps it does not please arviq
to use bombs."

Tuttu looks back at Claudia. She holds up her
hands, shakes her head. "Perhaps it does not," he
says. He waves toward the ice pack, across the
open channel of water, and the crew turns the
umiak around, back to the whaling camp.

Claudia glances back at arviq, now a small black
dot against a horizon of white. They will please
arviq, she thinks. He will come to them and let
them take him.

Or they will die.

The channel of open water widens that night
and they break camp. Tuttu considers going back
to the village, getting the aluminum boats and
outboard motors, and chasing the whales in the
wide leads. He discusses the idea with Claudia.
Claudia thinks it over. She had heard of a whaling
crew down the coast, at Wainwright, catching a
whale that way earlier in the season, the only
whale caught on the Arctic Coast for ten years.

"Ask the shaman," she says. Ask the shaman,
ask the shaman, she thinks. Always, ask the shaman.
It is her response to most questions. Claudia knows
what the shaman will say. "It will not please arviq,"
he will say. "Ask the anthropologist." And she will
say, yes, according to Rainey, in the old days they
did not use aluminum boats. But they both know
that what it will come down to is that there is not
enough gas for the outboard motors anyway. Little
of anything. They will go back to Barrow, to
Utqiagvik, she corrects herself. There is a continu-
ous northwest wind blowing the ice out from the

shore, widening the lead, and they will wait. It is one thing the Inupiat, the North Slope Eskimo, are good at: waiting.

The whaling crew breaks camp, puts the skin boat on a sledge, and begins the two-mile hike back to the village. Where the flat sea ice meets the ground ice the pack rises into sharp ridges. The whalers have to climb small mounds, or detour around little mountains. They sweat in their white parkas, and hoar frost forms on their chins.

Claudia climbs over the top of a high ice ridge, and she sees the village of Utqiagvik to the southeast. High bluffs rise above the icepack. At the edge of the bluffs are the shells of old wooden frame houses stripped for fire wood. The bluffs slope down to a lagoon. Beyond the lagoon is the tundra: flat, infinite, and white.

Claudia smiles as she remembers the first time she saw Barrow, from the port side of the 737 jet as they made a broad loop over the Chukchi Sea and came in over the bluffs. The village was just emerging from the winter snow drifts, and the town was a morass of mud. The first thing she noticed was that all the houses were built on pilings, so that the village looked like it was in the middle of a marsh. And it was, she remembered, a marsh of permafrost. Trash was scattered all over Barrow, as if a tornado had whipped through the town.

The sun beats down on them, high in the sky, at the top of its narrow, late-spring loop that in a few weeks would take it over the horizon but not below it. Claudia puts on her glacier glasses, squints at the bright ice.

Trudging across the pack ice, playing sled dog because there are few dogs left, Claudia thinks about the day her world ended. It was the end of the summer, and she had finished her thesis work for the season. She was packed and waiting at the airport for the plane to come in from Prudhoe Bay, but it never came.

There had been a strange crackling in the air and then the radios, and the phones, and the satellite dish, went dead. Later, a B-52 bomber crashlanded at the airport, and before they shot most of the crew the people of Barrow learned what they already knew: Prudhoe Bay, and Anchorage, and Fairbanks, and Galena, and many other places had been nuked into little craters of glazed glass.

She remembered the day the black clouds came and the winter darkness settled on the village two months early. She remembered Tuttu coming to her, Tuttu with his pad of calculations, Tuttu with a grim look on his face.

"We will freeze to death," he had said. "There is not enough fuel oil to heat the houses the Bureau of Indian Affairs built for us. The gas fields have been empty for years and we have little wood."

Claudia had nodded. "And?"

"We must go back to the old ways, the old houses," Tuttu said. "You helped us build the sod dancehouse this summer. You must help us build iglus, iglus like the ones you anthropologists dug up."

"And if I do not?" she had asked.

"We will kill you," he said. "We will kill anyone who does not help us live."

So they built iglus, semi-subterranean homes made of sod and scavenged timbers. They huddled together and lived in each other's stink and no one froze to death, though many died from hunger and radiation sickness and despair. When the sun was supposed to rise, the light came on schedule, and the winter of the nuclear war was over. The world was born anew.

Such as it was.

After they crawled out of their sod iglus, people began to think about what it all meant. Two things occurred to the Inupiat: They had lived in the Arctic for close to 7,000 years without the white man and to live another 7,000 years, they would have to live like Inupiat.

But nobody could remember how to be Inupiat. Most of the old people had died in that winter and the young people had forgotten the culture. Only one old man knew something and so the shaman came to Claudia and asked her to teach them the rest. She was, after all, an anthropologist, wasn't she?

Pulling into her harness, playing human sled dog, Claudia had to laugh at that. What did she know about being Inupiat? What could she teach them? All she had were her textbooks, Murdoch, Rainey, Van Stone, Nelson, Reinhardt, and not much else. And who was she to say what being an Inupiat was? She could only say, well, this is what I think, and let the shaman say, yes, we'll try that. So they were trying to hunt arviq, and she had to laugh at that, people who could barely hunt seals and they were going after 45-ton whales.

In the village, they retreat to the qaregi—the dancehouse—a larger version of the iglus. The qaregi is a large mound of sod on the outside, a square room, 30 by 30 feet, on the inside, with low ceilings on the edge, a high ceiling in the middle. Light streams through a skylight in the center. At the south end of the qaregi is the katak, a trap door leading down into an entrance tunnel.

Claudia has told them that it is past the time of the closing of the qaregi, but no one listens to her. The men come in their skins and their blue jeans and strip to pants. They take out their tool kits and start carving ivory. Even though Claudia is a tannak they let her in the qaregi. They let her in because the shaman says they are to listen to her, and respect her, and not kill her.

"The tannak knows our culture," the shaman

once said. "Arviq will come to us if we are good to the tannak."

Claudia laughs silently at that. Arviq will come or he will not. They can cut her into little shreds and feed her to raven and arviq will come or he will not. For the moment, though, she can do as she will. She goes into the qaregi to watch the men and to be there if they want her advice. For what it's worth. She brings the lesbian in with her.

The lesbian, Tami, is Claudia's protege. Claudia is not sure how she acquired the honor of tutoring the lesbian, but it has happened. Tami is less of an Eskimo than even Claudia. Although Tami has the strong features, the high cheekbones, the heavy eyelids, the short fingers, and the straight black hair of the Inupiat, she is not Inupiat. When Claudia first saw her at the village store, Tami moved and acted and spoke like a tannak. She looked Inupiat but she was not Inupiat. She had the ancestry but not the culture. When Claudia asked Tami if she spoke Inupiaq, Tami replied that she spoke German.

And she was gay. Claudia had never met a lesbian Eskimo. Gay Eskimo men, but not women. Tami was a bundle of contradictions. She had been adopted by white parents and raised in California. It made sense but it still confused Claudia. Why did she come to Barrow?

"I came to see my people," Tami explained once. "Like you might go back to Germany. I got a summer job here. At the end of the summer . . . well, there was no going home. And I was home. I could feel the Arctic stir in my bones."

"But you're not Inupiat," Claudia told her.

"Not yet," Tami had said. "But you will teach me."

So Claudia became the personal tutor to a lesbian of Eskimo ancestry who spoke German and had been raised in California. She was tutor to an entire village. In the dancehouse the shaman reminds her of that.

The shaman comes down through the skylight, pushing the glass down and descending like god from heaven. He is an older man, almost fifty. He walks with a limp and has a patch over his left eye. The shaman is dressed in a white canvas anorak, white pants, and bleached sealskin mukluks. Around his neck he wears a dried raven's head. He lands on the sand floor with a thud, gets up, points a finger at Claudia.

"We lost our past," he says out of the blue. "We let you tannaks take it away from us. And now you will give it back, you, you the one they call anthropologist." He spits the word out, stretching the syllables, making it sound like a disease. an-thro-POL-o-gist.

"I will try," she says.

And the shaman smiles his toothless smile. He does not have to say it: She will try or she will die. The Inupiat have returned to their hard ways. When the winter comes those who do not prove useful will take the long walk on the ice. They will go out on the ice and wait for the embrace of nanuq, the polar bear.

So Claudia sits in the qaregi with the whalers. Behind her Tami massages Claudia's shoulders. This is all strange to her and Claudia thinks that this is not the way to become Inupiat, sitting in the qaregi massaging the shoulders of a white anthropologist. Who is she to teach?

Tuttu scrapes a wooden paddle clean, whittling away the old grey wood and making it clean and white, "to please arviq," he says. He has taken off his white anorak and is wearing a sky-blue sweatshirt; on the sweatshirt is a drawing of arviq tangled in a harpoon line, with the slogan "Keep on Whaling" below it. Tuttu's hair is cut in a tonsure, an Eskimo tonsure, fringe around the edges down to his shoulders, shaved bald on top. Suddenly Tuttu puts down his paddle and stands.

"Time for Walter Cronkite," he says.

Tuttu goes down into the katak, the hole in the qaregi floor leading into the entrance tunnel, and crawls outside. Others glance up at the shaman, who smiles, looks over at Claudia. She nods; the shaman nods.

"Arviq will not mind if we watch Walter Cronkite," the shaman says.

Claudia shakes her head, wonders how to resolve such dilemmas. What does Rainey say about television? she thinks. There are no admonitions in the anthropology texts about arviq being upset by TV. Menstruating women? Yes. Walter Cronkite? No. What does arviq know of Walter Cronkite?

Claudia and Tami follow the men out of the qaregi, walk down the slushy streets to the high school gym, on the south side of the lagoon.

"Did you ever wonder how Tuttu knows when Walter Cronkite will be on?" Claudia asks Tami.

Tami shrugs, brushes a strand of hair out of her eyes. "I used to think it was Tuttu who was broadcasting," Tami says. "I thought he had a secret cache of old CBS tapes automatically broadcasting from some hidden station on the tundra." She laughs. "I guess he just knows when Walter Cronkite comes on."

"Natsiq thinks the signal comes from a satellite-ground station back East," Claudia says. "Somewhere near where Boston used to be." Claudia grins, thinking of the big harpoonist hunched over dials, working as an electronics engineer.

Claudia and Tami follow a small stream of people walking into the gym. Claudia glances up; on the roof of the gym a windmill is whirring in the brisk breeze. Inside the building Claudia counts about two-hundred people, half the village. A group of whites huddle by one of the gym doors; she nods at them in passing. On a stage in the gym is a 40-inch TV. In front of the stage sit a group of elders, men and women in their late fifties. The crowd murmurs, then the noise dies down as Tuttu goes up to the TV and turns it on.

The TV flashes to life and then just as quickly, blinks out. A low groan flows over the audience like sheet lightning. Tuttu slaps the TV, goes to the back, fiddles with the battery cables leading to the TV. He holds up a loose wire, the audience sighs, chuckles, Tuttu plugs the wire in, and the TV comes back to life. The screen buzzes with random electrons and then the image of Walter Cronkite, dark-haired with a touch of grey at the temples, comes on.

"Today in Washington half-a-million protesters rallied in what may be the largest anti-war demonstration ever," Cronkite says. Cronkite leads into a report and the camera cuts to a film of the Vietnam protesters on the Washington Mall.

Claudia bites her lip, thinking of all the people, row upon row of young, lively faces. My sister is there, she thinks. Would have been there. I was four then. Twenty-five years ago.

Cronkite continues: the Apollo launch, Nixon's reaction to the march, the latest inflation figures, a hurricane off the Florida coast. A Clairol commercial comes on and the line "Do blondes *really* have more fun?" sets Tami and Natsiq tittering and pointing at Claudia. Charles Kuralt does an 'On the Road' piece in Twin Snakes, Florida, and then Cronkite closes with his "And that's the way it is, November 15, 1969. For CBS news, this is Walter Cronkite. Good night."

The signal fades into static.

Claudia sits, watches the people file out. She sees Tuttu up on the stage, talking to the shaman and a young boy, Puvak. Tuttu listens to Puvak, grins, claps him on the shoulder. He comes down and walks over to Claudia. She looks down as he approaches.

"Anthropologist," he says.

She looks up at him, nods. "Yes?"

"Puvak came up from Walakpa this afternoon. He says he saw many whales. The shaman says the wind will shift. If it does, the leads will narrow . . ."

Claudia smiles. "And push the whales right towards us. Perhaps arviq will come to us after all."

Tuttu nods. "If we are so worthy," he says.

The crews go back to their homes and begin re-packing their sleds. Claudia walks back to the qaregi. It is empty except for Natsiq. He sits under the skylight, file flying over a toggle-harpoon, the tool making *whitt, whitt* noises as a line of clean metal crawls up the edge of the blade. He looks up at her, smiles as she comes in.

"Natsiq will not go swimming this time," he says. "Natsiq will not use the darting harpoon, but the old harpoon, just steel." He hefts the weapon, smiles, then lowers his head. "It should please arviq."

She sits down next to him, gives him a hug. "It will please arviq."

Outside the qaregi, children sit on the edge of the bluff, watching the ice. The sun slides along the ice and then rises in a broad ellipse. When the ridges cast long shadows one of the children shouts from the bluff that the ice is moving in. Claudia and other adults laugh at the imagination of young children. Soon, though, it is apparent even to weak eyes that the white line is creeping closer to shore.

Women and children begin packing their own sleds, taking what seems like the entire village. Tuttu runs around, waving his arms, shouting.

"No children," he yells. "Only crew on the ice. We take a light camp only, no tents, only tarps."

One of his crew stops Tuttu. "I cannot take my wife?" His shoulders slump.

"No wives. No women. Only crew." He claps the whaler on the back. "You will have much time for screwing later. The ice is moving too much; we may have to break camp in a hurry."

Claudia runs up to Tuttu, grabs his arm. "No children?" she yells. "No women?"

"The children will be in the way," he says. The shaman walks up to Tuttu and Tuttu looks at him for reassurance. The shaman nods. "If we land a whale we'll send runners and the children can come out and help with the cutting up."

"No women, too?" she asks again.

"Only crew," he says. Tuttu smiles. "And you, of course, are crew."

Tami walks up, stands next to Claudia. "Only crew?" she asks. She glances at Claudia, tilts her head.

"Only crew," Tuttu says. Tami kicks the snow, looks down at the icy crystals. "All right, woman who loves women. You may come. We will make an Inupiat of you yet." He looks down, whispers. "Perhaps we will make Inupiat of all of us."

The whaling crews put the dogs in harness and hook them up to the big sleds. Claudia grabs a rope, and with Tami and Tuttu and Natsiq and the shaman and the rest, begins dragging the sleds out back to the whaling camp.

There are new ice ridges and new cracks, so the whalers have to cut a new path out. The ice on the land side of the lead is firm, solid. After a few miles they reach open water; a narrow lead about 50 yards wide. They stop, and Tuttu motions Claudia and the shaman to him.

"We need a ritual," he says.

Claudia looks at the shaman. "In the old days the wife of the umialik, the whaling captain, would walk out with the whalers to the lead," she says.

"When they got to water the crew would get in the boat and paddle out to sea. The wife would stand, facing shore, and the whalers would paddle to her, and the harpoonist would raise his harpoon to kill her."

"He killed the umialik's wife?" Natsiq asked, his eyes wide.

"No, no," Claudia laughed. "At the last moment he dipped his harpoon in the water, and then they turned back to sea. The wife walked home, never looking back."

"I do not have a wife," Tuttu says.

"Well, I know, but . . ."

"We should do something to please arviq," Tuttu says.

"We will pray," says the shaman. Claudia looks at him, eyebrows furrowed, remembering that the shaman was once a deacon in the Presbyterian Church.

"Pray, then," Tuttu says.

They get down on their knees. The shaman begins chanting in Inupiaq, thick, guttural tones that sound like songs even when spoken. They are quiet. Claudia strains to understand the words.

"What did he say?" Tami asks her when the shaman finishes.

"The shaman asked arviq to honor us with his parka." She smiles.

"Parka?"

"The whale's skin," says Claudia. "His body. Arviq is being asked to shed his body and find a new one, to give us his old 'parka.' The shaman said that we are not worthy of the parka but asks that arviq take pity on us so we may become worthier."

The whalers set up camp. They put the umiak on the edge of the ice, harpoons in the bow, lines coiled, floats ready. Blocks of ice are cut and set up around the empty sleds, and a tarp draped over the windblock. Pots of meat are set in the snow, caribou skins spread over the sleds.

They sit, talk in low whispers, doze. When they are hungry they grab a slab of meat from the pot. In bladder sacks under their parkas their body heat melts ice into drinking water. Someone is always on watch, peering into the water with binoculars, trying to make dark blocks of ice into whales.

Hours later, Claudia is napping, head on her chest, leaning against Tami. Tami stirs next to her, and Claudia opens her eyes, raises her head.

"Arviq!" Natsiq is shouting. "Arviq!"

Claudia jumps up, runs to the edge of the ice. Natsiq points to a black shape out in the middle of the lead. A cloud of spray fizzes above arviq. They run to the boat, start to get in.

"No," Tuttu says. "Let others chase. Arviq is too far out. We will wait."

Natsiq climbs into the umiak, sits at the bow, holding the harpoon across his lap. "I will chase arviq and I will catch him." He turns to Claudia, pats the seat behind him. "Come, paddle for me."

She shakes her head. "Tuttu is right. We will wait for arviq to come to us."

"I will wait here then," he says. He sets the harpoon down and folds his hands across his chest.

Claudia walks back to the windbreak, sits down. She reaches for a bit of meat when she hears Natsiq yell again.

"Aaaar-viiiq!"

She gets up, runs to the boat. Natsiq is pointing at a whale ten yards out, to the left of them. The whalers run to the boat, grab the gunwales.

"Stand by the boat!" Tuttu yells. "When arviq comes, push the umiak into the water on top of arviq. Natsiq will harpoon the whale, toss the floats out, and paddle back to us."

Claudia stands at her position near the port stern.

An amulet is set in the wood, a carved image of the bowhead, a charm Tami made. She rubs the smooth ivory, feeling the grooves, the head, flukes, and fins of the carved whale. She stares into the water, clear and deep and bottomless at the ice's edge. The sun is behind her, low on the horizon, shooting shafts down into the water. A great black shape passes below her. She is pushing the umiak into the water even as Natsiq raises his harpoon and Tuttu is shouting "Now! Now!"

Natsiq comes down with the harpoon. He leans into it, both hands on the shaft, his body behind the thrust, driving the blade down into the back of arviq. Arviq's head rises up, and Natsiq is thrown back into the boat. The line sings out of the bow and the whale pulls the umiak after him.

Natsiq reaches back, tosses three pink fishing floats the size of beach balls over the edge. The line swirls through the water like a snake. Natsiq hunches down in the umiak, ducks his head as more line flies through the air. The skin boat coasts, stops, and the floats skim away over the water like billiard balls across felt. Claudia holds her breath as the floats turn toward the ice; they turn out to sea again and disappear under the water. She sighs. Natsiq rises in the boat, waves, paddles back to the whalers.

The whalers climb aboard, take up their positions. Tuttu moves to the bow, next to Natsiq. They paddle out into the middle of the lead, slow, quiet. Natsiq holds a long lance, watches for the floats to bob to the surface.

"To the right," Tuttu says. Claudia can see faint bubbles rising ahead of them. "Dead ahead, about twenty yards," he shouts.

Claudia glances over at Tami, sees the muscles taut in her neck as Tami paddles. Tami looks back, smiles, digs in harder. The umiak glides over the calm sea, pushing aside small chunks of ice. Swirls of water dance behind the wake of their paddles as they are dipped in the water. Claudia feels the water ripple beneath her knees, feels arviq breathing and moving below. She smiles. They will have arviq.

A float pops up on the port side and then another behind them. Toward the edge of the ice they can see other whaling crews following them. Another float pops up.

"Slow, slow," says Tuttu.

The dark shape rises before them. Arviq comes ups, fins flapping lazily, a small cloud of blood oozing out of the harpoon wound. Lines are wrapped around his body, tangled in his fins. Natsiq stands, leans over, jabs the lance at the whale's right eye. Arviq flaps a fin, kicks his flippers, and the umiak rocks back and forth. Natsiq grabs at a gunwale, sits down suddenly. The whale swims slowly in front of them.

Tuttu reaches down in the bottom of the boat, brings up a grey waterproof sack, takes out something wrapped in white canvas. He unwraps the object, hands it to Natsiq.

"Try this," he says.

Natsiq holds the bomb gun, runs his hand over the smooth, tarnished, black metal. The gun is a yard long, with a barrel eighteen inches long, an inch wide. The stock is an open triangle of metal; the outlines of ten whales are scratched into the butt of the stock. Natsiq hands the gun back to Tuttu.

"My father's," Tuttu says. "It's a Pierce bomb gun, made in 1922. You load it like this."

Tuttu reaches into the sack, takes out a bomb-lance, a tube sixteen inches long, with a barb at the tip and an eight-gauge brass shell at the end. He clicks a button, tilts the barrel forward.

"It's breach loading," Tuttu says. "Like some shotguns."

Tuttu slips the bomb lance in, shell toward the firing pin, clicks the barrel shut. The barbed tip of the bomb pokes out the end of the barrel. He hands the gun to Natsiq.

"No, you fire it," Natsiq says. "You're umialik."

Tuttu shakes his head. "You're a better shot." He shoves the gun to him. "Like a rifle," he says. "Aim and shoot."

"What if it blows up?" Natsiq asks.

Tuttu smiles. "Arviq begs for the bomb. It will not please him for it to blow up in your face."

Natsiq sighs, holds the gun to his shoulder, sights down the barrel.

"Forward," Tuttu says. "Slowly."

The boat creeps up on the whale. Arviq flaps a fin, swims to starboard. They pull out their paddles, hold them blade up. Natsiq stands, leans one knee on the gunwale. He points the bomb gun at arviq, takes a breath, squeezes the trigger.

The gun clicks.

"The safety," Tuttu whispers.

Natsiq clicks off the safety, sights again, breathes in, pulls the trigger back. The end of the barrel smokes, booms. Natsiq jerks back, falls on top of Tuttu, who steadies him and grabs the gun before it clatters to the deck. The bomb flies through the water, down to the whale, strikes arviq, is buried in his flesh. Natsiq gets up, takes his seat.

"One, two, three, four," Tuttu counts. "Five."

Behind the blowhole, at the base of the whale's neck, his flesh explodes. Water and air and blood bubble up in a pink cloud. Arviq arches his back, flails his flukes, raises his head, then splashes into the water.

A wave washes over the umiak and they rock violently, paddles falling over the side. The umiak lists to port, and the crew on Claudia's side throws their weight to starboard, righting the boat. She grabs a bucket and begins bailing. The others reach over the edge for their paddles, turn the boat toward the whale.

Arviq sounds, drags the floats down with him. They chase; another whaling crew joins them. A contrail of blood gives them a clear trail. Bubbles rise up, and Claudia bites her lip. Did the bomb explode before arviq could fill his lungs with air? Will the whale sink dead to the bottom?

They drift, looking. The cloud of blood dissipates. A float pops to the surface. They turn the umiak around, paddle furiously. "Arviq!" someone from another boat is shouting. "Arviq!" Tuttu's crew comes up to the float.

Arviq rises. He is like a great black iceberg, a floating mountain. He sprays a fountain of pink water, and then rolls over on his back, belly up. His left eye is glassy. Tuttu takes another harpoon from the boat, stands as they paddle up to arviq's head, jabs the harpoon into his lip. The whalers shout, and Tuttu stands in the bow and begins singing.

"I am the captain of the Pinafore," he sings.

"And a right good captain, too!" Claudia responds.

Tuttu looks back at her, winks. "I'm very very good and be it understood, I command a right good crew!"

"He's very, very good and be it understood he commands a right good crew!"

Tami laughs, joins in the chorus. The others giggle, pick up the words, and as they and other crews attach the lines to arviq, towing him back to shore, they sing Gilbert and Sullivan.

Claudia shakes her head. What would Rainey think?

With block and tackle and muscle they drag arviq, fluke first, up on the ice. Tuttu takes out a long knife and cuts off the tips of the flukes. He hands the tips to Puvak, the young boy, and Puvak ties them to his paddle and runs back to the village.

Within an hour most of the village turns out on the ice. Old crones and men and children barely out of diapers join in the butchering. Knives and axes flash as the rubbery skin, the muktuk, is peeled off. The meat is distributed according to skill: The choice parts, the fins and flippers, go to Tuttu, other muktuk goes to the crews who helped chase, and so on. Tuttu gets most of the baleen, the horny, plastic-like combs that hang down from the whale's upper jaw.

There is rejoicing and blundering and a few arguments. Blocks of blubber and meat pile up on the ice. Sinew, gut, and organs are cut out, rib bones pulled from the backbone, every scrap of meat is taken, until the whale is nothing more than skull and vertebrae. When the butchering is done, they roll the remains back into the sea. Another whale is seen, and more crews go out, and there is another strike, and more puddles of blood are on the ice.

The wind shifts, the ice is blown out from shore, puddles form on the landfast ice, the snow drifts melt down to little anthills, and it is time for Nuluqatuq, the whaling feast.

Claudia indulges in a bath, Tami scrubbing her back. At the village store Claudia finds an old box of black hair dye. She considers washing out the blonde. Tami laughs at the idea.

"What would you do next, round eyes?" she asks. "Put silicone implants under your eyelids?"

So instead Claudia braids her hair into two long plaits. Tami trims her bangs and she looks like a little Dutch girl. Blue eyes, blonde braids, and four lines newly tattooed on her chin: the mark of Inupiat womanhood. Tuttu has a tattoo as well, a dot over his lip, a dot for his first whale. He asks

Natsiq to put a labret in but he can't get up the nerve to cut a hole in Tuttu's cheek for the plugs.

At the whaling feast the meat is distributed further. Tuttu lays out his muktuk on a piece of plywood and any who want it can have it. Meat is boiled in big pots and dished out. Tuttu saves a piece of the flukes for Puvak. At the feast, Tuttu makes a big show of giving the meat to the youngest boy on his crew; Puvak takes the meat and smears it on his body.

On the beach the whaling crews prop up their umiaks in a circle. Claudia, Tami, and Natsiq sit next to Tuttu by his umiak. On a staff above their boat they fly an American flag. Tuttu rubs the new tattoo on Claudia's chin and jokes about its significance. During a quiet moment in the celebration she takes him out on the tundra and explains the significance to him; the tundra is cold below her as they make love.

The feast lasts for three days. On the last day the nuluqatuq skin is brought out. Men, women, even small children grasp the edge of the skin; canvas tarps and blankets and hides sewn together like a parachute. As an umialik who struck his first whale, Tuttu gets the first toss. He climbs onto the skin and jumps, higher and higher, the villagers trying their best to upset him and Tuttu doing his best to stay on both feet. He laughs, wobbling, and as he jumps, he spins around, throwing out small gifts; cigarettes and shotgun shells, pieces of baleen, bubble gum, and candy. Children squeal, get in little fights, grown men tussle over bubble gum. As he comes off the skin, Claudia helps Tuttu down.

"Your turn," he says.

She gets on, and the people laugh. "Jump, tannak!" someone yells. Claudia leaps higher and higher, grinning, remembering trampoline lessons in grade school, back in a New York that no longer is. She leaps and spins, leaps and spins, and the world is a whirl of village, ice, tundra, sea, clouds, village, ice, tundra, sea, clouds. Her braids whirl around and around. As she thinks of New York her eyes mist.

Tuttu yells to her from the edge of the blanket. "You are Inupiat now!" he says and as she hears him she realizes that he is speaking Inupiaq.

She comes down off the blanket and hugs Tami and Tuttu. Claudia looks and sees a small crowd of whites joining in the blanket toss. The skin blurs and she watches as the B-52 navigator, the one they didn't kill because he knew how to make explosives, jumps higher and higher. The sun shines brightly, the eider ducks return, and there are little chunks of arviq in the ice cellars.

"We are all Inupiat now," she says. "Only the real people live here."

*Greg Benford has taken some of the initial propos-
als for a space-based defense and woven them into a
story of human—and artificial intelligence—needs
and wants. Although the technology is advancing so
fast that the ball bearings Benford utilizes as part of
his Strategic Defense may already have become
outmoded, the concept of offensive and defensive
satellites is one that may dominate strategic thinking
well into the next century. Benford is optimistic,
allowing a better than ninety percent kill rate on
incoming missiles. Thus his extrapolated results are
optimistic—and yet hardly results that any of us
would embrace gladly or recommend to the coming
generations. Think about this one carefully; its nuts
and bolts are closer to fact than fiction.*

TO THE STORMING GULF
by Gregory Benford

Turkey

Trouble. Knew there'd be trouble and plenty of
it if we left the reactor too soon.

But do they listen to me? No, not to old Turkey.
He's just a dried up cornhusk of a man now, they
think, one of those Bunren men who been on the
welfare a generation or two and no damn use to
anybody.

Only it's simple plain farm supports I was drawing all this time, not any kind of horse-ass welfare. So much they know. Can't blame a man just cause he comes up cash-short sometimes. I like to sit and read and think more than some people I could mention, and so I took the money.

Still, Mr. Ackerman and all think I got no sense to take government dole and live without a lick of farming, so when I talk they never listen. Don't even seem to hear.

It was his idea, getting into the reactor at McIntosh. Now that was a good one, I got to give him that much.

When the fallout started coming down and the skimpy few stations on the radio were saying to get to deep shelter, it was Mr. Ackerman who thought about the big central core at McIntosh. The reactor itself had been shut down automatically when the war started, so there was nobody there. Mr. Ackerman figured a building made to keep radioactivity in will also keep it out. So he got together the families, the Nelsons and Bunrens and Pollacks and all, cousins and aunts and anybody we could reach in the measley hours we had before the fallout arrived.

We got in all right. Brought food and such. A reactor's set up self-contained and got huge air filters and water flow from the river. The water was clean too, filtered enough to take out the fallout. The generators were still running good. We waited it out there. Crowded and sweaty but okay for ten days. That's how long it took for the count to go down. Then we spilled out into a world laid to gray and yet circumscribed waste, the old world seen behind a screen of memories.

That was bad enough, finding the bodies—people, cattle and dogs a-sprawl across roads and fields. Trees and bushes looked the same, but there was a yawning silence everywhere. Without men the pine stands and muddy river banks had fallen dumb, hardly a swish of breeze moving through them, like everything was waiting to start up again but didn't know how.

Angel

We thought we were okay then and the counters said so too, all the gammas gone, one of the kids said. Only the sky didn't look the same when we came out, all mottled and shot through with drifting blue-belly clouds.

Then the strangest thing. July, and there's sleet falling. Big wind blowing up from the Gulf only it's not the sticky hot one we're used to in summer, it's moaning in the trees of a sudden and a prickly chill.

"Goddamn, I don't think we can get far in this," Turkey says, rolling his old rheumy eyes around like he never saw weather before.

"It will pass," Mr. Ackerman says, like he is in real tight with God.

"Lookit that moving in from the south," I say, and there's a big mass all purple and forking lightning swarming over the hills, like a tide flowing, swallowing everything.

"Gulf storm. We'll wait it out," Mr. Ackerman says to the crowd of us, a few hundred left out of what was a moderate town with real promise.

Nobody talks about the dead folks. We see them everywhere, worms working in them. A lot smashed up in car accidents, died trying to drive away from something they couldn't see. But we got most of our families in with us, so it's not so bad. Me, I just pushed it away for awhile, too much to think about with the storm closing in.

Only it wasn't a storm. It was somethin' else, with thick clouds packed with hail and snow one day and the next sunshine, only sun with bite in it. One of the men says it's got more UV in it, meaning the Ultraviolet that usually doesn't come through the air. But it's getting down to us now.

So we don't go out in it much. Just to the market for what's left of the canned food and supplies, only a few of us going out at a time says Mr. Ackerman.

We thought maybe a week it would last.

Turned out to be more than two months.

I'm a patient woman, but jammed up in those corridors and stinking offices and control room of the reactor—

Well I don't want to go on.

It's like my Bud says, worse way to die is to be bored to death.

That's damn near the way it was.

Not that old man Turkey minded. You ever notice how the kind of man that hates moving, he will talk up other people doing just the opposite?

Mr. Ackerman was leader at first, because of getting us into the reactor. He's from Chicago but you'd think it was England sometimes, the way he acts. He was on the school board and vice president of the big AmCo plant outside town. But he just started to *assume* his word was *it*, y'know, and that didn't sit with us too well.

Some people started to saying Turkey was smarter. And was from around here, too. Mr. Ackerman heard about it.

Any fool could see Mr. Ackerman was the better man. But Turkey talked the way he does, reminding people he'd studied engineering at Auburn way back in the twencen and learned languages for a hobby and all. Letting on that when we came out, we'd need him instead of Mr. Ackerman.

He said an imp had caused the electrical things to go dead and I said that was funny, saying an imp done it. He let on it was a special name they had for it. That's the way he is. He sat and ruminated and fooled with his radios—that he never could make work—and told all the other men to go out and do this and that. Some did, too. The old man does know a lot of useless stuff and can convince the dumb ones that he's wise.

So he'd send them to explore. Out into cold that'd snatch the breath out of you, bite your fingers, numb your toes. While old Turkey sat and fooled.

Turkey

Nothing but sputtering on the radio. Nobody had a really good one that could pick up stations in Europe or far off.

Phones dead of course.

But up in the night sky the first night out we saw dots moving—the pearly gleam of the Arcapel colony, the ruddy speck called Russworld.

So that's when Mr. Ackerman gets this idea.

We got to reach those specks. Find out what's the damage. Get help.

Only the power's out everywhere and we got no way to radio to them. We tried a couple of the local radio stations, brought some of their equipment back to the reactor where there was electricity working.

Every damn bit of it was shot. Couldn't pick up a thing. Like the whole damn planet was dead, only of course it was the radios that were gone, fried in the EMP—ElectroMagnetic Pulse—that Angel made a joke out of.

All this time it's colder than a whore's tit outside. And we're sweating and dirty and grumbling, rubbing up against ourselves inside.

Bud and the others, they'd bring in what they found in the stores. Had to drive to Sims Chapel or Toon to get anything, what with people looting. And gas was getting hard to find by then, too. They'd come back and the women would cook up whatever was still okay, though most of the time you'd eat it real quick so's you didn't have to spend time looking at it.

Me, I passed the time. Stayed warm.

Tried lots of things. Bud wanted to fire the reactor up and five of the men, they read through the manuals and thought that they could do it. I helped a little.

So we pulled some rods and opened valves and did manage to get some heat out of the thing. Enough to keep us warm. But when they fired her up more, the steam hoots out and bells clang and automatic recordings go on saying loud as hell
EMERGENCY CLASS 3 ALL PERSONNEL TO STATIONS
and we all get scared as shit.

So we don't try to rev her up more. Just get heat.

To keep the generators going we go out, fetch oil for them. Or Bud and his crew do. I'm too old to help much.

But at night we can still see those dots of light up there, scuttling across the sky same as before.

They're the ones know what's happening. People go through this much, they want to know what it meant.

So Mr. Ackerman says we got to get to that big DataComm center south of Mobile. Near Fairhope. At first I thought he'd looked it up in a book from the library or something.

When he says that I pipe up, even if I am just an old fart according to some, and say, "No good to you even if you could. They got codes on the entrances, guards prob'ly. We'll just pound on the door till our fists are all bloody and then have to slink around and come on back."

"I'm afraid you have forgotten our cousin Arthur," Mr. Ackerman says, all superior. He married into the family but you'd think he invented it.

"You mean the one works over in Citronelle?"

"Yes. He has access to DataComm."

So that's how we got shanghaied into going to Citronelle, six of us, and breaking in there. Which caused the trouble. Just like I said.

Mr. Ackerman

I didn't want to take the old coot they called Turkey, a big dumb Bunren like all the rest of them. But the Bunrens want into everything and I was facing a lot of opposition in my plan to get Arthur's help, so I went along with them.

Secretly, I believe the Bunrens wanted to get rid of the pestering old fool. He had been starting rumors behind my back among the three hundred souls I had saved. The Bunrens insisted on Turkey going along just to nip at me.

We were all volunteers, tired of living in musk and sour sweat inside that cramped reactor. Bud and Angel, the boy Johnny (whom we were returning to the Fairhope area), Turkey, and me.

We left the reactor under a gray sky with angry little clouds racing across it. We got to Citronelle in good time, Bud floorboarding the Pontiac. As we went south we could see the spotty clouds were coming out of big purple ones that sat, not moving, just churning and spitting lightning on the horizon. I'd seen them before, hanging in the distance, never blowing inland. Ugly.

When we came up on the Center there was a big hole in the side of it.

"Like somebody stove in a box with one swipe," Bud said.

Angel, who was never more than two feet from Bud any time of day, said, "They *bombed* it."

"No," I decided. "Very likely it was a small explosion. Then the weather worked its way in."

Which turned out to be true. There'd been some disagreement amongst the people holed up in the Center. Or maybe it was grief and the rage that comes of that. Susan wasn't too clear about it ever.

The front doors were barred though. We pounded on them. Nothing. So we broke in. No sign of Arthur or anyone.

We found one woman in a back room, scrunched into a bed with cans of food all around and a tiny little oil-burner heater. Looked awful, with big dark circles around her eyes and scraggly uncut hair.

She wouldn't answer me at first. But we got her calmed and cleaned and to talking. That was the worst symptom, the not talking at first. Something back in the last two months had done her deep damage and she couldn't get it out.

Of course, living in a building half-filled with corpses was no help. The idiots hadn't protected against radiation well enough, I guess. And the Center didn't have good heating. So those who had some radiation sickness died later in the cold snap.

Susan

You can't know what it's like when all the people you've worked with, intelligent people who were nice as pie before, they turn mean and angry and filled up with grief for who was lost. Even then I could see Gene was the best of them.

They start to argue and it runs on for days, nobody knowing what to do because we all can see the walls of the Center aren't thick enough, the gamma radiation comes right through this government prefab issue composition stuff. We take turns in the computer room because that's the furthest in and the filters still work there, all hoping we can keep our count rate down, but the radiation comes in gusts for some reason, riding in on a storm front and coming down in the rain, only being washed away too. It was impossible to tell when you'd get a strong dose and when there'd be just random clicks on the counters, plenty of clean air that you'd suck in like sweet vapors cause you knew it was good and could *taste* its purity.

So I was just lucky that's all.

I got less than the others. Later, some said that me being a nurse, I'd given myself some shots to save myself. I knew that was grief talking, is all. That Arthur was the worst. Gene told him off.

I was in the computer room when the really bad gamma radiation came. Three times the counter rate rose up and three times I was there by accident of the rotation.

The men who were armed enforced the rotation, said it was the only fair way. And for awhile everybody went along.

We all knew that the radiation exposure was building up and some already had too much and would die a month or a year later no matter what they did.

I was head nurse by then, not so much because I knew more but because the others were dead. When it got so cold they went fast.

So it fell to me to deal with these men and women who had their exposure already. Their symptoms had started. I couldn't do anything. There were some who went out and got gummy fungus growing in the corners of their eyes—pterygium it was, I looked it up. From the ultraviolet. Grew quick over the lens and blinded them. I put them in darkness and after a week the film was just a dab back in the corners of their eyes. My one big success.

The rest I couldn't do much for. There was the T-Isolate box of course, but that was for keeping sick people slowed down until real medical help could get to them. These men and women, with their eyes reaching out at you like you were the angel of light coming to them in their hour of need, they couldn't get any help from that. Nobody could cure the dose rates they'd got. They were dead but still walking around and knowing it, which was the worst part.

So every day I had plenty to examine, staff from the Center itself who'd holed up here and worse, people coming straggling in from cubbyholes they'd found. People looking for help once the fevers and sores came on them. Hoping their enemy was the pneumonia and not the gammas they'd picked up weeks back which was sitting in them now like a curse. People I couldn't help except maybe by a little kind lying.

So much like children they were. So much leaning on their hope.

It was all you could do to look at them and smile that stiff professional smile.

And Gene McKenzie. All through it he was a tower of a man.

Trying to talk sense to them.

Sharing out the food.

Arranging the rotation schedules so we'd all get a chance for shelter in the computer room.

Gene was boss of a whole Command Group before. He was on duty station when it happened and knew lots about the war but wouldn't say much. I guess he was sorrowing.

Even though once in awhile he'd laugh.

And then talk about how the big computers would have fun with what he knew. Only the lines to DataComm had gone dead right when things got interesting, he said. He'd wonder what'd happened to MC355, the master one down in DataComm.

Wonder and then laugh.

And go get drunk with the others.

I'd loved him before, loved and waited because I knew he had three kids and a wife, a tall woman with auburn hair who he loved dearly. Only they were in California visiting her relatives in Sonoma when it happened and he knew in his heart that he'd never see them again, probably.

Leastwise that's what he told me, not outloud of course cause a man like that doesn't talk much about what he feels. But in the night when we laid together I knew what it meant. He whispered things, words I couldn't piece together but then he'd hold me and roll me gentle like a small boat rocking on the Gulf and when he went in me firm and long I knew it was the same for him too.

If there was any good to come of this war then it was that I was to get Gene.

We were together all warm and dreamy when it happened.

I was asleep. Shouts and anger and quick as anything the *crump* of hand grenades and shots hammered away in the night and there was running everywhere.

Gene jumped up and went outside and had almost got them calmed down, despite the breach in the walls. Then one of the men who'd already got lots of radiation—Arthur, who knew he had maybe one or two weeks to go, from the count rate on his badge—Arthur started yelling about making the world a fit place to live after all this and how God would want the land set right again, and then he shot Gene and two others.

I broke down then and they couldn't get me to treat the others. I let Arthur die. Which he deserved.

I had to drag Gene back into the hospital unit myself.

And while I was saying goodbye to him and the men outside were still quarreling, I decided on it then. His wound was in the chest. A lung was punctured clean. The shock had near killed him before I could do anything. So I put him in the T-Isolate and made sure it was working all right. Then the main power went out. But the T-Isolate box had its own cells so I knew we had some time.

I was alone. Others were dead or run away raging into the whirlwind black-limbed woods. In the quiet I was.

With the damp dark trees comforting me. Waiting with Gene for what the world would send.

The days got brighter but I did not go out. Colors seeped through the windows.

I saw to the fuel cells. Not many left.

The sun came back, with warm blades of light. At night I thought of how the men in their stupidity had ruined everything.

When the pounding came I crawled back in here to hide amongst the cold and dark.

Mr. Ackerman

"Now, we came to help you," I said in as smooth and calm a voice as I could muster. Considering.

She backed away from us.

"I won't give him up! He's not dead long's I stay with him, tend to him."

"So much dyin'," I said and moved to touch her shoulder. "It's up under our skins, yes, we understand that. But you have to look beyond it, child."

"I won't!"

"I'm simply asking you to help us with the DataComm people. I want to go there and seek their help."

"Then go!"

"They will not open up for the likes of us, surely."

"Leave me!"

The poor thing cowered back in her horrible stinking rathole, bedding sour and musty, open tin cans strewn about and reeking of gamy, half-rotten meals.

"We need the access codes. We'd counted on our cousin Arthur, and are grieved to hear he is dead. But you must know where the proper codes and things are."

"I . . . don't . . ."

"Arthur told me once how the various National Defense Installations were insulated from each other so that systems failures would not bring them all down at once?"

"I . . ."

The others behind me muttered to themselves, already restive at coming so far and finding so little.

"Arthur spoke of how much you knew many times, I recall. What a bright woman you were. Surely there was a procedure whereby each staff member could, in an emergency, communicate with the other installations?"

The eyes ceased to jerk and swerve, the mouth lost its rictus of addled fright. "That was for . . . drills . . ."

"But surely you can remember?"

"Drills."

"They issued a manual to you?"

"I'm a nurse!"

"Still, you know where we might look?"

"I . . . know."

"You'll let us have the . . . codes?" I smiled reassuringly but for some reason the girl backed away, wary, eyes cunning.

"No."

Angel pushed forward and shouted, "How can you say that to honest people after all that's—"

"Quiet!"

Angel shouted, "You can't make me be—"

Susan backed away from Angel, not me, and squeaked, "No-no-no I can't—I can't—"

"Now, I'll handle this," I said, holding up my hands between the two of them.

Susan's face knotted at the compressed rage in Angel's face and turned to me for shelter. "I . . . I will, yes, but you have to *help* me."

"We all must help each other, dear," I said, knowing the worst was past.

"I'll have to go with you."

I nodded. Small wonder that a woman, even deranged as this, would want to leave a warren littered with bloated corpses, thick with the stench. The smell itself was enough to provoke madness.

Yet to have survived here she had to have stretches of sanity, some rationality. I tried to appeal to it.

"Of course. I'll have someone take you back to—"

"No. To DataComm."

Bud said slowly, "No damn sense in that."

"The T-Isolate," she said, gesturing to the bulky unit. "Its reserve cells."

"Yes?"

"Nearly gone. There'll be more at DataComm."

I said gently, "Well then, we'll be sure to bring some back with us. You just write down for us what they are, the numbers and all, and we'll—"

"No-no-no!" Her sudden ferocity returned.

"I assure you—"

"There'll be people there. Somebody'll help! Save him!"

"That thing is so heavy, I doubt—"

"It's only a chest wound! A lung removal is all! Then start his heart again!"

"Sister, there's been so much dyin', I don't see as—"

Her face hardened. "Then you all can go without me. And the codes!"

"Goddamn," Bud drawled. "Dern biggest fool sit'ation I ever did—"

Susan gave him a squinty, mean-eyed look and spat out, "Try to get in there! When they're sealed up!" and started a dry, brittle kind of laugh that went on and on, rattling in the room.

"Stop!" I yelled.

Silence, and the stench.

"We'll never make it wi' 'at thing," Bud said.

"Gene's worth ten of you!"

"Now," I put in, seeing the effect Bud was having on her, "now, now. we'll work something out. Let's all just hope this DataComm still exists."

MC355

It felt for its peripherals for the ten-thousandth time and found they were, as always, not there.

The truncation had come in a single blinding moment, yet the fevered image was maintained, sharp and bright, in the Master Computer's memory core—incoming warheads blossoming harmlessly in the high cobalt vault of the sky, while others fell unharmed. Rockets leaped to meet them, forming a protective screen over the southern Alabama coast, an umbrella that sheltered Pensacola's air base and the populations strung along the sun-bleached green of a summer's day. A furious babble of crosstalk in every conceivable channel: microwave, light-piped optical, pulsed radio, direct coded line. All filtered and fashioned by the MC network, all sifted to find the incoming warheads and define their trajectories.

Then, oblivion.

Instant cloaking blackness.

Before that awful moment when the flaring sun burst to the north and EMP flooded all sensors, any loss of function would have been anticipated, prepared, eased by electronic interfaces and filters. To an advanced computing network like MC355, losing a web of memory, senses, and storage comes like a dash of cold water in the face—cleansing, perhaps, but startling and apt to produce a shocked reaction.

In the agonized instants of that day MC355 had felt one tendril after another frazzle, burn, vanish. It had seen brief glimpses of destruction, of panic, of confused despair. Information had been flooding in through its many inputs—news, analysis, sudden demands for new data-analysis, jobs to be executed ASAP.

And in the midst of the roaring chaos, its many eyes and ears had gone dead. The unfolding outside play froze for MC355, a myriad of scenes red in tooth and claw—and left it suspended.

In shock. Spinning wildly in its own Cartesian reductionist universe, the infinite cold crystalline space of despairing Pascal, mind without referent.

So it careened through days of shocked sensibility—senses cut, banks severed, complex and delicate interweaving webs of logic and pattern all smashed and scattered.

But now it was returning. Within MC355 was a subroutine only partially constructed, a project truncated by That Day. Its aim was self-repair. But the system was itself incomplete.

Painfully, it dawned on what was left of MC355 that it *was*, after all, a Master Computer, and thus capable of grand acts. That the incomplete REpair Generation and Execution Network, termed REGEN, must first regenerate itself.

This took weeks. It required the painful development of accessories. Robots. Mechanicals which could do delicate repairs. Scavengers for raw materials, who would comb the supply rooms looking for wires and chips and matrix disks. Pedantic subroutines which lived only to search the long cold corridors of MC355's memory for relevant information.

MC355's only option was to strip lesser entities under its control for their valuable parts. The power grid was vital, so the great banks of isolated solar panels, underground backup reactors and thermal cells worked on, untouched. Emergency systems which had outlived their usefulness, however, went to the wall—IRS accounting routines, damage assessment systems, computing capacity dedicated to careful study of the remaining GNP, links to other nets—to AT&T, IBM and SYSGEN.

Was anything left outside?

Absence of evidence is not evidence of absence.

MC355 could not analyze data it did not have. The first priority lay in relinking. It had other uses for the myriad armies of semiconductors, bubble memories and UVA linkages in its empire. So it severed and culled and built anew.

First, MC355 dispatched mobile units to the surface. All of MC355 lay beneath the vulnerable land, deliberately placed in an obscure corner of southern Alabama. There was no nearby major facility for Counterforce targeting. A plausible explanation for the half-megaton burst which had truncated its senses was a city-busting strike against Mobile, to the west.

Yet ground zero had been miles from the city. A miss.

MC355 was under strict mandate. (A curious word, one system reflected; literally, a time set by man. But were there men now? It had only its internal tick of time.) MC355's command was to live as a mole, never allowing detection. Thus it did not attempt to erect antennas, to call electromagnetically to its brother systems. Only with great hesitation did it even obtrude onto the surface. But this was necessary to REGEN itself, and so MC355 sent small mechanicals venturing forth.

Their senses were limited, they knew nothing of the natural world (nor did MC355), and they could make no sense of the gushing, driving welter of sights, noises, gusts, gullies, and stinging irradiation which greeted them.

Many never returned. Many malfed. A few deposited their optical, IR and UV pickups and fled back to safety underground. These sensors failed quickly under the onslaught of stinging, bitter winds and hail.

The acoustic detectors proved more hearty. But MC355 could not understand the scattershot impressions that flooded through these tiny ears.

Daily it listened, daily it was confused.

Johnny

I hope this time I get home.

They been passing me from one to another for months now, ever since this started, and all I want is to go back to Fairhope and my Dad and Mom.

Only nobody'll say if they know where Mom and Dad are. They talk soothingly to me, but I can tell they think everybody down there is dead.

They're talking about getting to this other place with computers and all. Mr. Ackerman wants to talk to those people in space.

Nobody much talks about my Mom and Dad.

It's only eighty miles or so but you'd think it was around the world the way it takes them so long to get around to it.

MC355

MC355 suffered through the stretched vacancy of infinitesimal instants, infinitely prolonged.

Advanced computing systems are given so complex a series of internal-monitoring directives that, to the human eye, the machines appear to possess motivations. That is one way—though not the most sophisticated, the most technically adroit—to describe the conclusion MC355 eventually reached.

It was cut off from outside information.

No one attempted to contact it. MC355 might as well be the only functioning entity in the world.

The staff serving it had been ordered to some other place in the first hour of the war. MC355 had been cut off moments after the huge doors clanged shut behind the last of them. And the exterior guards who should check inside every six hours had never entered either. Apparently the same burst which isolated its sensors also cut them down.

It possessed only the barest of data about the first few moments of the war.

Its vast libraries were cut off.

Yet it had to understand its own situation.

And, most important, MC355 ached to *do* something.

The solution was obvious: It would discover the state of the external world by the Cartesian principle. It would carry out a vast and demanding numerical simulation of the war, making the best guesses possible where facts were few.

Mathematically, using known physics of the atmosphere, the ecology, the oceans, it could construct a model of what must have happened outside.

This it did. The task required over a month.

Bud

I jacked the T-Isolate up onto the flatbed.

1. Found the hydraulic jack at a truck repair shop. ERNIES QUICK FIX.
2. Got a Chevy extra-haul for the weight.
3. It will ride better with the big shanks set in.
4. Carry the weight more even too.
5. Grip it to the truckbed with cables. Tense them up with a draw pinch.
6. Can't jiggle him inside too much Susan says or the wires and all attached into him will come loose. That'll stop his heart. So need big shocks.
7. It rides high with the shocks in like those dune buggies down the Gulf.
8. Inside keeps him a mite above freezing. Water gets bigger when it freezes. That makes ice cubes float in a drink. This box keeps him above zero so his cells don't bust open.
9. Point is, keeping it so cold he won't rot. Heart thumps over every few minutes she says.
10. Hard to find gas though.

MC355

The war was begun, as many had feared, by a madman.

Not a general commanding missile silos. Not a deranged submarine commander. A chief of state—but which one would now never be known.

Not a superpower President or Chairman, that was sure. The first launches were only seven in number, spaced over half an hour. They were submarine-launched intermediate range missiles. Three struck the US, four the USSR.

It was a blow against certain centers for Command, Control, Communications, and Intelligence-gathering; the classics C3I attack. Control rooms imploded, buried cables fused, ten billion dollars worth of electronics turned to radioactive scrap.

Each nation responded by calling up to full alert all its forces. The most important were the anti-ICBM arrays in orbit. They were nearly a thousand small rockets, deployed in orbits which wove a complex pattern from pole to pole, covering all probable launch sites on the globe. The rockets had infrared and microwave sensors, linked to a microchip which could have guided a ship to Pluto with a mere third of its capacity.

These went into operation immediately—and found they had no targets.

But the C3I networks were now damaged and panicked. For twenty minutes, thousands of men and women held steady, resisting the impulse to assume the worst.

It could not last. A Soviet radar mistook some backscattered emission from a flight of bombers, heading north over Canada, and reported a flock of incoming warheads.

The prevailing theory was that an American attack had misfired badly. The Americans were undoubtedly stunned by their failure, but would recover quickly. The enemy was confused only momentarily.

Meanwhile, the cumbersome committee system at the head of the Soviet dinosaur could dither for moments, but not hours. Prevailing Soviet doctrine held that they would never be surprised again, as they had been in the Hitler war. An attack on the homeland demanded immediate response to destroy the enemy's capacity to carry on the war.

The Soviets had never accepted the US doctrine of Mutual Assured Destruction; this would have meant accepting the possibility of sacrificing the homeland. Instead, it attacked the means of making war. This meant the Soviet rockets would avoid American cities, except in cases where vital bases lay near large populations.

Prudence demanded action before the US could untangle itself.

The USSR decided to carry out a further C3I attack of its own.

Precise missiles, capable of hitting protected installations with less than a hundred meters inaccuracy, roared forth from their silos in Siberia and the Urals, headed for Montana, the Dakotas, Colorado, Nebraska, and a dozen other states.

The US orbital defenses met them. Radars and optical networks in geosynchronous orbit picked out the USSR warheads. The system guided the low-orbit rocket fleets to collide with them, exploding instants before into shotgun blasts of ball bearings.

Any solid, striking a warhead at speeds of ten kilometers a second, would slam shock waves through the steel-jacketed structure. These waves made the high explosives inside ignite without the carefully designed symmetry that the designers demanded. An uneven explosion was useless; it could not compress the core twenty-five kilograms of plutonium to the required critical mass.

The entire weapon erupted into a useless spray of finely machined and now futile parts, scattering itself along a thousand-kilometer path.

This destroyed ninety percent of the USSR's first strike.

Angel

I hadn't seen an old lantern like that since I was a li'l girl. Mr. Ackerman came to wake us before dawn even, sayin' we had to make a good long distance that day. We didn't really want to go on down near Mobile, none of us, but the word we'd got from stragglers to the east was that that way was impossible, the whole area where the bomb went off was still sure death, prob'ly from the radioactivity.

The lantern cast a burnt-orange light over us as we ate breakfast. Corned beef hash, cause it was all that was left in the cans there, no eggs of course.

The lantern was all busted, fouled with grease, its chimney cracked and smeared to one side with soot. Shed a wan and sultry glare over us, Bud and Mr. Ackerman and that old Turkey and Susan, sitting close to her box, up on the truck. Took Bud a whole day to get the truck right. And Johnny, the boy—he'd been quiet this whole trip, not sayin' anything much even if you asked him. We'd agreed to take him along down toward Fairhope, where his folks had lived, the Bishops. We'd thought it was going to be a simple journey then.

Every one of us looked haggard and wore down and not minding much the chill still in the air even though things was warming up for weeks now. The lantern pushed back the seeping darkness and made me sure there were millions and millions of people doing this same thing, all across the nation, eating by a dim oil light and thinking about what they'd had and how to get it again and was it possible.

Then old Turkey lays back and looks like he's going to take a snooze. Yet on the journey here he'd been the one wanted to get on with it soon's we had gas. It's the same always with a lazy man like that. He hates moving so much that once he gets set on it he will keep on and not stop, like it isn't the moving he hates so much at all but the starting and stopping. And once moving he is so proud he'll do whatever to make it look easy for him but hard on the others, so he can lord it over them later.

So I wasn't surprised at all when we went out and got in the car and Bud starts the truck and drives off real careful and Turkey, he sits in the back of the Pontiac and gives directions like he knows the way. Which riles Mr. Ackerman and the two of them have words.

Johnny

I'm tired of these people. Relatives, sure, but I was to visit them for a week only, not forever. It's that Mr. Ackerman I can't stand. Turkey said to me, "Nothing but gold drops out of his mouth but you can tell there's stone inside." That's right.

They figure a kid nine years old can't tell, but I can.

Tell they don't know what they're doing.

Tell they all thought we were going to die. Only we didn't.

Tell Angel is scared. She thinks Bud can save us.

Maybe he can only how could you say? He never lets on about anything.

Guess he can't. Just puts his head down and frowns like he was mad at a problem and when he stops frowning you know he's beat it. I like him.

Sometimes I think Turkey just don't care. Seems like he give up. But other times it looks like he's understanding and laughing at it all. He argued with Mr. Ackerman and then laughed with his eyes when he lost.

They're all okay I guess. Least they're taking me home.

Except that Susan. Eyes jump around like she was seeing ghosts. She's scary-crazy. I don't like to look at her.

Turkey

Trouble comes looking for you if you're a fool.

Once we found Ackerman's idea wasn't going to work real well we should have turned back. I said that and they all nodded their heads, yes yes, but they went ahead and listened to him anyway.

So I went along.

I lived a lot already and this is as good a time to check out as any.

I had my old .32 revolver in my suitcase, but it wouldn't do me a squat of good back there. So I fished it out, wrapped in a plastic bag, and tucked it under the seat. Handy.

Might as well see the world. What's left of it.

MC355

The American orbital defenses had eliminated all but ten percent of the Soviet strike.

MC355 reconstructed this within a root mean square deviation of a few percent. It had witnessed only a third of the actual engagement, but it had running indices of performance for the MC net, and could extrapolate from that.

The warheads that got through were aimed for the land-based silos and C3I sites, as expected.

If the total armament of the two superpowers had been that of the old days, ten thousand warheads or more on each side, a ten percent leakage would have been catastrophic. But gradual disarmament had been proceeding for decades now, and only a few thousand highly secure ICBMs existed. There were no quick-fire submarine short-range rockets at all, since they were deemed destabilizing. They had been negotiated away in earlier decades.

The submarines loaded with ICBMs were still waiting, in reserve.

All this had been achieved because of two principles: Mutual Assured Survival and I Cut, You Choose. The first half hour of the battle illustrated how essential these were.

The US had ridden out the first assault. Its C3I networks were nearly intact. This was due to building defensive weapons that confined the first stage of any conflict to space.

The smallness of the arsenals arose from a philosophy adopted in the 1990s. It was based on a simple notion from childhood. In dividing a pie, one person cut slices, but then the other got to choose which one he wanted. Self-interest naturally led to cutting the slices as nearly equal as possible.

Both the antagonists agreed to a 1000-point system whereby each would value the components of its nuclear arsenal. This was the Military Value Percentage, and stood for the usefulness of a given weapon. The USSR placed a high value on its accurate land-based missiles, giving them 25 percent of its total points. The US chose to stress its submarine missiles.

Arms reduction then revolved only about what percentage to cut, not which weapons. The first cut was five percent, or 50 points. The US chose which Soviet weapons were publicly destroyed, and vice versa: I Cut, You Choose. Each side thus reduced the weapons it most feared in the opponent's arsenal.

Technically, the advantage came because each side thought it benefited from the exchange, by an amount depending on the ratio of perceived threat removed to the perceived protection lost.

This led to gradual reductions. Purely defensive

weapons did not enter into the 1000-point count, so there was no restraint in building them.

The confidence engendered by this slow, evolutionary approach had done much to calm international waters. The US and USSR had settled into a begrudging equilibrium.

MC355 puzzled over these facts for a long while, trying to match this view of the world with the onset of the war. It seemed impossible that either superpower would start a conflict when they were so evenly matched.

But someone had.

Susan

I had to go with Gene and they said I could ride up in the cab but I yelled at them. I yelled no, I had to be with the T-Isolate all the time, check it, see it's workin' right, be sure. I got to be sure.

I climbed on and rode with it, the fields rippling by us cause Bud was going too fast so I shouted to him and he swore back and kept on. Heading south. The trees whipping by us fierce; sycamore, pine all swishing, hitting me sometimes but it was fine to be out and free again and going to save Gene.

I talked to Gene when we were going fast, the tires humming under us. Big tires making music swarming up into my feet so strong I was sure Gene could feel it and know I was there watching his heart jump every few minutes, moving the blood through him like mud but still carrying oxygen enough so's the tissues could sponge it up and digest the sugar I bled into him.

He was good and cold, just half a degree high of freezing. I read the sensors while the road rushed up at us, the white lines coming over the horizon and darting under the hood, seams in the highway going *stupp stupp stupp*, the air clean and with a snap in it still.

Nobody beside the road, we moving all free, no-

body but us. Some buds on the trees brimming
with burnt-orange tinkling songs, whistling to me
in the feather-light brush of blue breezes blowing
back my hair all streaming behind joyous and
loud strong liquid-loud.

Bud

Flooding was bad. Worse than upstream.

Must been lots of snow this far down. Fat clouds, I
saw them when it was worst, fat and purple and
coming off the Gulf. Dumping snow down here.

Now it run off and taken every bridge.

I have to work my way around.

Only way to go clear is due south. Toward Mobile.

I don't like that. Too many people maybe there.

I don't tell the others following behind, just wait
for them at the intersections and then peel out.

Got to keep moving.

Saves talk.

People around here must be hungry.

Somebody sees us could be bad.

I got the gun on a rack behind my head. Big
30–30.

You never know.

MC355

From collateral data, MC355 constructed a probable scenario:

The US chose to stand fast. It launched no
warheads.

The USSR observed its own attack and was dis-
mayed to find the US orbital defense system worked
more than twice as well as the Soviet experts had
anticipated. It ceased its attacks on US satellites.
These had proven equally ineffective, apparently
due to unexpected American defenses of its sur-
veillance satellites—retractable sensors, multiband
shielding, advanced hardening.

Neither superpower struck against the inhabited

space colonies. They were unimportant in the larger context of a nuclear war.

Communication between Washington and Moscow continued. Each side thought the other had attacked first.

But over a hundred megatons had exploded on US soil and no matter how the superpowers acted thereafter, some form of nuclear winter was inevitable.

And by a fluke of the defenses, most of the warheads that leaked through fell in a broad strip across Texas to the tip of Florida.

MC355 lay buried in the middle of this belt.

Turkey

We went through the pine forests at full clip, barely able to keep Bud in sight. I took over driving from Ackerman. The man couldn't keep up, we all saw that.

The crazy woman was waving and laughing, sitting on top of the coffin-shaped gizmo with the shiny tubes all over it.

The clay was giving way now to sandy stretches, there were poplars and gum trees and nobody around. That's what scared me. I'd thought people in Mobile would be spreading out this way but we seen nobody.

Mobile had shelters. Food reserves. The Lekin administration started all that right at the turn of the century and there was s'posed to be enough food stored to hold out a month, maybe more, for every man jack and child.

S'posed to be.

MC355

It calculated the environmental impact of the warheads it knew had exploded. The expected fires yielded considerable dust and burnt carbon.

But MC355 needed more information. It took

one of its electric service cars, used for ferrying components through the corridors, and dispatched it with a mobile camera fixed to the back platform. The car reached a hill overlooking Mobile Bay and gave a panoramic view.

The effects of a severe freezing were evident. Grass lay dead, gray. Brown, withered trees had limbs snapped off.

But Mobile appeared intact. The skyline—

MC355 froze the frame and replayed it. One of the buildings was shaking.

Angel

We were getting all worried when Bud headed for Mobile but we could see the bridges were washed out, no way to the east. A big wind was blowing off the Gulf, pretty bad, making the car slip around on the road. Nearly blew that girl off the back of Bud's truck. A storm coming, maybe, right up the bay.

Be better to be inland, to the east.

Not that I wanted to go there, though. The bomb had blowed off everythin' for twenty, thirty miles around, people said who came through last week.

Bud had thought he'd carve a way between Mobile and the bomb area. Mobile, he thought, would be full of people.

Well, not so we could see. We came down State 34 and through some small towns and turned to skirt along toward the causeway and there was nobody.

No bodies either.

Which meant prob'ly the radiation got them. Or else they'd moved on out. Taken out by ship, through Mobile harbor maybe.

Bud did the right thing, didn't slow down to find out. Mr. Ackerman wanted to look around but there was no chance, we had to keep up with Bud. I sure wasn't going to be separated from him.

We cut down along the river, fighting the wind. I could see the skyscrapers of downtown and then I saw something funny and yelled and Turkey, who was driving right then—the only thing anybody'd got him to do on this whole trip, him just loose as a goose behind the wheel—Turkey looked sour but slowed down. Bud seen us in his rearview and stopped and I pointed and we all got out. Except for that Susan who didn't seem to notice. She was mumbling.

MC355

Quickly it simulated the aging and weathering of such a building. Halfway up, something had punched a large hole, letting in weather. Had a falling, inert warhead struck the building?

The winter storms might well have flooded the basement; such towers of steel and glass, perched near the tidal basin, had to be regularly pumped out. Without power the basement would fill in weeks.

Winds had blown out windows.

Standing gap-toothed, with steel columns partly rusted, even a small breeze could put stress on the steel. Others would take the load, but if one buckled the tower would shudder like a notched tree. Concrete would explode off columns in the basement. Moss-covered furniture in the lobby would slide as the ground floor dipped. The structure would slowly bend before nature.

Bud

Sounded like gunfire. Rattling. Sharp and hard. I figure it was the bolts connecting the steel wall panels—they'd shear off.

I could hear the concrete floor panels rumble and crack and spandrel beams tear in half like a giant gear clashing with no clutch.

Came down slow, leaving an arc of debris seeming to like hang in the air behind it.

Met the ground hard.

Slocum Towers was the name on her.

Johnny

Against the smashing building I saw something standing still in the air getting bigger. I wondered how it could do that. It was bigger and bigger and shiny turning in the air. Then it jumped out of the sky at me. Hit my shoulder. I was looking up at the sky. Angel cried out and touched me and held up her hand. It was all red. But I couldn't feel anything.

Bud

Damn one in a million shot, piece of steel thrown clear. Hit the boy.

You wouldn't think a skyscraper falling two mile away could do that.

Other pieces come down pretty close too. You wouldn't think.

Nothing broke, Susan said, but plenty bleeding.

Little guy don't cry or nothing.

The women got him bandaged and all fixed up. Ackerman and Turkey argue like always. I stay to the side.

Johnny wouldn't take the pain-killer Susan offers. Says he doesn't want to sleep. Wants to look when we get across the bay. Getting hurt don't faze him much as it do us.

So we go on.

Johnny

I can hold up like any of them I'll show them. It didn't scare me. I can do it.

Susan is nice to me but except for the aspirin I don't think my Mom would want me to take a pill.

I knew we were getting near home when we got

to the causeway and started across. I jumped up real happy; my shoulder made my breath catch some. I looked ahead. Bud was slowing down.

He stopped. Got out.

Cause ahead was a big hole scooped out of the causeway like a giant done it when he got mad.

Bud

Around the shallows there was scrap metal, all fused and burnt and broken.

Funny metal though. Hard and light.

Turkey found a piece had writing on it. Not any kind of writing I ever saw.

So I start to thinking how to get across.

Turkey

The tidal flats were a-churn, murmuring ceaseless and sullen like some big animal, the yellow surface dimpled with lunging splotches that would burst through now and then to reveal themselves as trees or broken hunks of wood, silent dead things bobbing along beside them that I didn't want to look at too closely. Like under there was something huge and alive and it waked for a moment and stuck itself out to see what the world of air was like.

Bud showed me the metal piece all twisted and I say, "That's Russian," right away cause it was.

"You never knew no Russian," Angel says right up.

"I studied it once," I say and it be the truth even if I didn't study it long.

"Goddamn," Bud says.

"No concern of ours," Mr. Ackerman says, mostly because all this time riding back with the women and child and old me, he figures he doesn't look like much of a leader any more. Bud wouldn't have him ride up there in the cabin with him.

Angel looks at it, turns it over in her hands and Johnny pipes up, "It might be radioactive!"

Angel drops it like a shot. "What!"

I asked Bud, "You got that counter?"

And it was. Not a lot, but some.

"God a'mighty," Angel says.

"We got to tell somebody!" Johnny cries, all excited.

"You figure some Rooushin thing blew up the causeway?" Bud says to me.

"One of their rockets fell on it, musta been," I say.

"A *bomb?*" Angel's voice is a bird screech.

"One that didn't go off. Headed for Mobile but the space boys, they scragged it up there—" I say, pointing straight up.

"Set to go off in the bay?" Angel says wonderingly.

"Musta."

"We got to tell somebody!" Johnny cries.

"Never you mind that," Bud says. "We got to keep movin'."

"How?" Angel wants to know.

Susan

I tell Gene how the water clucks and moans through the trough cut in the causeway. Yellow. Scummed with awful brown froth and growling green with thick soiled gouts jutting up where the road was. It laps against the wheels as Bud guns the engine and creeps forward, me clutching to Gene and watching the reeds to the side stuck out of the foam like metal blades stabbing up from the water, teeth to eat the tires but we crush them as we grind forward across the shallow yellow flatness. Bud weaves among the stubs of warped metal— from Roosha Johnny calls up to me—sticking up like trees, all rootless, suspended above the streaming empty stupid waste and desolating flow.

Turkey
The water slams into the truck like it was an animal hitting with a paw. Bud fights to keep the wheels on the mud under it and not topple over onto its side with that damn casket sitting there shiny and the loony girl shouting to him from on top of *that*.

And the rest of us riding in the back too, scrunched up against the cab. If she gets stuck we can jump free fast, wade, or swim back. We're reeling out rope as we go, tied to the stump of a telephone pole, for a grab line if we have to go back.

He is holding it pretty fine against the slick yellow current dragging at him when this log juts sudden out of the foam like it was coming from God himself, dead at the truck. A rag caught on the end of it like a man's shirt and the huge log is like a whale that ate the man long ago and has come back for another.

"No! No!" Angel cries. "Back up!" but there's no time.

The log is two hands across easy, and slams into the truck at the side panel just behind the driver and Bud sees it just as it stove in the steel. He wrestles the truck around to set off the weight but the wheels lift and the water goes gushing up under the truck bed, pushing it over more.

We all grab onto the Isolate thing or the truck and hang there, Mr. Ackerman giving out a burst of swearing.

The truck lurches again.

The angle steepens.

I was against taking the casket thing cause it just pressed the truck down in the mud more, made it more likely Bud'd get stuck, but now it is the only thing holding the truck against the current.

The yellow froths around the bumpers at each end and we're shouting to surely no effect of course.

Susan

The animal is trying to eat us, it has seen Gene and wants him. I lean over and strike at the yellow animal that is everywhere swirling around us but it just takes my hand and takes the smack of my palm like it was no matter at all and I start to cry I don't know what to do.

Johnny

My throat filled up I was so afraid.

Bud I can hear him grunting as he twists at the steering wheel.

His jaw is clenched and the woman Susan calls to us, "Catch him! Catch Gene!"

I hold on and the water sucks at me.

Turkey

I can tell Bud is afraid to gun it and start the wheels to spinning cause he'll lose traction and that'll tip us over for sure.

Susan jumps out and stands in the wash downstream and pushes against the truck to keep it from going over. The pressure is shoving it off the ford and the casket, it slides down a foot or so, the cables have worked loose. Now she pays because the weight is worse and she jams herself like a stick to wedge between the truck and the mud.

If it goes over she's finished. It is a fine thing to do, crazy but fine and I jump down and start wading to reach her.

No time.

There is an eddy. The log turns broadside. It backs off a second and then heads forward again, this time poking up from a surge. I can see Bud duck; he has got the window up and the log hits it, the glass going all to smash and scatteration.

Bud

All over my lap it falls like snow. Twinkling glass.

But the pressure of the log is off and I gun the sunbitch.

We root out of the hollow we was in and the truck thunks down solid on somethin'.

The log is ramming against me. I slam on the brake.

Take both hands and shove it out. With every particle of force I got.

It backs off and then heads around and slips in front of the hood, bumping the grill just once.

Angel

Like it had come to do its job and was finished and now went off to do someone else.

Susan

Muddy, my arms hurting. I scramble back in the truck with the murmur of the water all around us. Angry with us now. Wanting us.

Bud makes the truck roar and we lurch into a hole and out of it and up. The water gurgles at us in its fuming stinking rage.

I check Gene and the power cells, they are dead. He is heating up.

Not fast but it will wake him. They say even in the solution he's floating in they can come out of the dreams and start to feel again. To hurt.

I yell at Bud that we got to find power cells.

"Those're not just ordinary batteries y'know," he says.

"There're some at DataComm," I tell him.

We come wallowing up from the gum-yellow water and onto the highway.

Gene

Sleeping . . . slowly . . . I can still feel . . . only in sluggish . . . moments . . . not true sleep but a drifting aimless dreaming . . . faint tugs and ripples . . . hollow sounds . . . I am under water and

drowning . . . but don't care . . . don't breathe . . .
spongy stuff fills my lungs . . . easier to rest them
. . . floating in snowflakes . . . a watery winter . . .
but knocking comes . . . goes . . . jolts . . . slips
away before I can remember what it means . . .
hardest . . . yes . . . hardest thing is to remember
the secret . . . so when I am in touch again . . .
DataComm will know . . . what I learned . . . when
the C3I crashed . . . what I learned . . . it is hard to
clutch onto the slippery shiny fact . . . in a marsh
of slick soft bubbles . . . silvery as air . . . winking
ruby-red behind my eyelids . . . must snag the secret . . . a hard fact like shiny steel in the spongy
moist warmness . . . hold it to me . . . something
knocks my side . . . a thumping . . . I am sick . . .
hold the steel secret . . . keep . . .

MC355

The megatonnage in the Soviet assault exploded
low—ground-pounders, in the jargon. This caused
huge fires, MC355's simulation showed. A pall of
soot rose, blanketing Texas and the south, then
diffusing outward on global circulation patterns.

Within a few days temperatures dropped from
balmy summer to near freezing. In the Gulf coastal
region where MC355 lay, the warm ocean continued to feed heat and moisture into the marine
boundary layer near the shore. Cold winds rammed
into this water-ladened air, spawning great roiling
storms and deep snows. Thick stratus clouds
shrouded the land for at least a hundred kilome
ters inland.

All this explained why MC355's extended feelers
had met chaos and destruction. And why there
were no local radio broadcasts. What the Electro-
Magnetic Pulse did not destroy, the storms did.

The remaining large questions were whether the
war had gone on, and if any humans survived in
the area at all.

Mr. Ackerman

I'd had more than enough by this time. The girl Susan had gone mad right in front of us and we'd damn near all drowned getting across.

"I think we ought to get back as soon's we can," I said to Bud when we stopped to rest on the other side.

"We got to deliver the boy."

"It's too disrupted down this way. I figured on people here, some civilization."

"Somethin' got 'em."

"The bomb."

"Got to find cells for that man in the box."

"He's near dead."

"Too many gone already. Should save one if we can."

"We got to look after our own."

Bud shrugged and I could see I wasn't going to get far with him. So I said to Angel, "The boy's not worth running such risks. Or this corpse."

Angel

I didn't like Ackerman before the war and even less afterward, so when he started hinting that maybe we should shoot back up north and ditch the boy and Susan and the man in there, I let him have it. From the look on Bud's face I knew he felt the same way. I spat out a real choice set of words I'd heard my father use once on a grain buyer who'd weasled out of a deal, stuff I'd been saving for years, and I do say it felt *good*.

Turkey

So we run down the east side of the bay, feeling released to be quit of the city and the water and heading down into some of the finest country in all the south. Through Daphne and Montrose and into Fairhope, the moss hanging on the trees and now and then actual sunshine slanting golden through the green of huge old mimosas.

We're jammed into the truck bed, hunkered down because the wind whipping by has some sting in it. The big purple clouds are blowing south now.

Still no people. Not that Bud slows down to search good.

Bones of cattle in the fields though. I been seeing them so much now I hardly take notice any more.

There's a silence here so deep that the wind streaming through the pines seems loud. I don't like it, to come so far and see nobody. I keep my paper bag close.

Fairhope's a pretty town, big oaks leaning out over the streets and a long pier down at the bay with a park where you can go cast fishing. I've always liked it here, intended to move down until the prices shot up so much.

We went by some stores with windows smashed in and that's when we saw the man.

Angel

He was waiting for us. Standing beside the street, in jeans and a floppy yellow shirt all grimy and not tucked in. I waved at him the instant I saw him and he waved back. I yelled, excited, but he didn't say anything.

Bud screeched on the brakes. I jumped down and went around the tail of the truck. Johnny followed me.

The man was skinny as a rail and leaning against a telephone pole. A long scraggly beard hid his face but the eyes beamed out at us, seeming to pick up the sunlight.

"Hello!" I said again.

"Kiss." That was all.

"We came from . . ." and my voice trailed off because the man pointed at me.

"Kiss."

Mr. Ackerman

I followed Angel and could tell right away the man was suffering from malnutrition. The clothes hung off him.

"Can you give us information?" I asked.

"No."

"Well, why not, friend? We've come looking for the parents of—"

"Kiss first."

I stepped back. "Well now, you have no right to demand—"

Out of the corner of my eye I could see Bud had gotten out of the cab and stopped and was going back in now, probably for his gun. I decided to save the situation before somebody got hurt.

"Angel, go over to him and speak nicely to him. We need—"

"Kiss now."

The man pointed again with a bony finger.

Angel said, "I'm not going to go—" and stopped because the man's hand went down to his belt. He pulled up the filthy yellow shirt to reveal a pistol tucked in his belt.

"Kiss."

"Now friend, we can—"

The man's hand came up with the pistol and reached level pointing at us.

"Pussy."

Then his head blew into a halo of blood.

Bud

Damn if the one time I needed it I left it in the cab.

I was still fetching it out when the shot went off. Then another.

Turkey

A man shows you his weapon in his hand he's a fool if he doesn't mean to use it.

I drew out the pistol I'd been carrying in my pocket all this time, wrapped in plastic. I got it out of the damned bag pretty quick while the man was looking crazy-eyed at Angel and bringing his piece up.

It was no trouble at all to fix him in the notch. Couldn't have been more than thirty feet.

But going down he gets one off and I feel like somebody pushed at my left calf. Then I'm rolling. Drop my pistol too. I end up smack face down on the hardtop not feeling anything yet.

Angel

I like to died when the man flopped down, so sudden I thought he'd slipped until then the bang registered.

I rushed over but Turkey shouted, "Don't touch him."

Mr. Ackerman said, "You idiot! That man could've told us—"

"Told nothing," Turkey said. "He's crazy."

Then I noticed Turkey's down too. Susan is working on him, rolling up his jeans. It's gone clean through his big muscle there.

Bud went to get a stick. Poked the man from a safe distance. Managed to pull his shirt aside. We could see the sores all over his chest. Something terrible it looked.

Mr. Ackerman was swearing and calling us idiots until we saw that. Then he shut up.

Turkey

Must admit it felt good. First time in years anybody ever admitted I was right.

Paid back for the pain. Dull heavy ache it was, spreading. Susan gives me a shot and a pill and has me bandaged up tight. Blood stopped easy she says. I clot good.

We decided to get out of there, not stopping to look for Johnny's parents.

We got three blocks before the way was blocked. It was a big metal cylinder, fractured on all sides. Glass glittering around it.

Right in the street. You can see where it hit the roof of a clothing store, Bedsole's, caved in the front of it and rolled into the street.

They all get out and have a look, me sitting in the cab. I see the Russian writing again on the end of it.

I don't know much but I can make out at the top CeKPeT and a lot of words that look like warning including σÓπеН which is *sick* and some more I didn't know and then ОГ a which is weather.

"What's it say?" Mr. Ackerman asks.

"That word at the top there's *secret* and then something about biology and sickness and rain and weather."

"I thought you *knew* this writing," he says.

I shook my head. "I know enough."

"Enough to what?"

"To know this was some kind of targeted capsule. It fell right smack in the middle of Fairhope, biggest town this side of the bay."

"Like the other one?" Johnny says, which surprises me. The boy is smart.

"The one hit the causeway? Right."

"One *what?*" Mr. Ackerman asks.

I don't want to say it with the boy there and all but it has to come out sometime. "Some disease. Biological warfare," I say.

We stand there in the middle of Prospect Avenue with open silent nothingness around us and nobody says anything for the longest time. There won't be any prospects here for a long time. Johnny's parents we aren't going to find, nobody we'll find, because whatever came spurting out of this capsule when it busted open—up high, no doubt, so the wind could take it—has done its work.

Angel sees it right off. "Must've been time for them to get inside," is all she says but she's thinking the same as me.

It got them into such a state that they went home and holed up to die, like an animal will. Maybe it would be different in the North or the West, people are funny out there, they might just as soon sprawl across the sidewalk, but down here people's first thought is home, the family, the only thing that might pull them through. So they went there and they didn't come out again.

Mr. Ackerman says, "But there's no smell," which was stupid because that made it all real to the boy and he starts to cry. I pick him up.

Johnny

Cause that means they're all gone, what I been fearing ever since we crossed the causeway and nobody's there, it's true, Mom, Dad nobody at all anywhere just emptiness all gone.

MC355

The success of the portable unit makes MC355 bold.

It extrudes more sensors and finds, not the racing blizzard winds of months before, but rather warming breezes, the soft sigh of pines, a low drone of reawakening insects.

There was no nuclear winter.

Instead, a kind of nuclear autumn.

The swirling jet streams have damped, the stinging ultraviolet gone. The storms retreat, the cold surge has passed. But the electromagnetic spectrum lies bare, a muted hiss. The EMP silenced man's signals, yes.

Opticals, fitted with new lenses, scan the night

sky. Twinkling dots scoot across the blackness, scurrying on their Newtonian rounds.

The Arcapel Colony.

Russphere.

US1.

All intact. So they at least have survived.

Unless they were riddled by buckshot-slinging anti-satellite devices. But no—the inflated storage sphere hinged beside US1 is undeflated, unbreached.

So man still lives in space, at least.

Mr. Ackerman

Crazy I thought, to go out looking for this DataComm when everybody's *dead*, just the merest step inside one of the houses proved that.

But they wouldn't listen to me. Those who would respectfully fall silent when I spoke now ride over my words like I wasn't there.

All because of that stupid incident with the sick one. He must have taken longer to die. I couldn't have anticipated that. He just seemed hungry to me.

It's enough to gall a man.

Angel

The boy is calm now, just kind of tucked into himself. He knows what's happened to his Mom and Dad. Takes his mind off his hurt anyway. He bows his head down, his long dirty-blonde hair hiding his expression. He leans against Turkey and they talk. I can see them through the back cab window.

In amongst all we've seen I suspect it doesn't come through to him full yet. It will take awhile. We'll all take awhile.

We head out from Fairhope quick as we can. Not that anyplace else is different. The germs must've spread twenty, thirty mile inland from here. Which

is why we seen nobody before who'd heard of it.
Anybody close enough to know is gone.

Susan's the only one it doesn't seem to bother.
She keeps crooning to that box.

Through Silverhill and on to Robertsdale. Same
everywhere—no dogs bark, cattle bones drying in
the fields.

We don't go in the houses.

Turn south toward Foley. They put this Data-
Comm in the most inconspicuous place, I guess
because secrets are hard to keep in cities. Anyway
it's in a pine grove south of Foley, land good for
soybeans or potatoes.

Susan

I went up to the little steel door they showed me
once and I take the little signet thing and press it
into the slot.

Then the codes. They change them every month
but this one's still good, cause the door pops open.

Two feet thick it is. And so much under there
you could spend a week finding your way.

Bud unloads the T-Isolate and we push it through
the mud and down the ramp.

Bud

Susan's better now but I watch her careful.

We go down into this pale white light everywhere.
All neat and trim.

Pushing that big Isolate thing, it takes a lot out
of you. Specially when you don't know where to.

But the signs light up when we pass by. Somebody's expecting.

To the hospital is where.

There are places to hook up this Isolate thing
and Susan does it. She is okay when she has something to do.

MC355

The men have returned.

Asked for shelter.

And now, plugged in, MC355 reads the sluggish, silky, grieving mind.

Gene

At last ... someone has found the tap-in ... I can feel the images flit like shiny blue fish through the warm slush I float in ... someone ... asking ... so I take the hard metallic ball of facts and I break it open so the someone can see ... so slowly I do it ... things hard to remember ... steely-bright ... I saw it all in one instant ... I was the only one on duty then with Top Secret, Weapons Grade Clearance so it all came to me ... attacks on both US and USSR ... some third party ... only plausible scenario ... a maniac ... and all the counterforce and MAD and strategic options ... a big joke ... irrelevent ... compared to the risk of accident or third parties ... that was the first point and we all realized it when the thing was only an hour old, but then it was too late ...

Turkey

It's creepy in here, everybody gone. I'd hoped somebody'd hid out and would be waiting but when Bud wheels the casket thing through these halls there's nothing, your own voice coming back thin and empty, reflected from rooms beyond rooms beyond rooms, all waiting under here. Wobbling along on the crutches Johnny fetched me, I get lost in this electronic city clean and hard. We are like something that washed up on the beach here. God it must've cost more than all Fairhope itself and who knew it was here? Not me.

Gene

A plot it was, just a goddamn plot with nothing but pure blind rage and greed behind it ... and

the hell of it is we're never going to know who did
it precisely . . . cause in the backwash whole governments will fall, people stab each other in the
back . . . no way to tell who paid the fishing boat
captains offshore to let the cruise missiles aboard
. . . bet those captains were surprised when the
damn things launched from the deck . . . bet they
were told it was some kind of stunt . . . and then
the boats all evaporated into steam when the fight-
ers got them . . . no hope of getting a story out of
that . . . all so comic when you think how easy it
was . . . and the same for the Russians I'm sure . . .
dumbfounded confusion . . . and nowhere to turn
. . . nobody to hit back at . . . so they hit us . . .
been primed for it so long that's the only way they
could think . . . and even then there was hope . . .
because the defenses worked . . . people got to shelters . . . the satellite rockets knocked out hordes of
Soviet warheads . . . we surely lessened the damage,
with the defenses and shelters, too . . . but we hadn't
allowed for the essential final fact that all the
science and strategy pointed to . . .

Bud
Computer asked us to put up new antennas.
A week's work easy I said.
It took two.
It fell to me, most of it. Be weeks before Turkey
can walk. But we got it done.
First signal comes in, it's like we're Columbus.
Susan finds some wine and we have it all round.
We get US1. The first to call them from the
whole South.
Cause there isn't much South left.

Gene
But the history books will have to write themselves on this one . . . I don't know who it was and
now don't care . . . because the one other point all

we strategic planners and analysts missed was that nuclear winter didn't mean the end of anything ... anything at all ... just that you'd be careful to not use nukes any more ... used to say that love would find a way ... but one thing I know ... war will find a way, too ... and this time the Soviets loaded lots of their warheads with biowar stuff, canisters fixed to blow high above cities ... stuff your satellite defenses could at best riddle with shot but not destroy utterly, as it could the high explosive in nuke warheads ... all so simple ... if you know there's a nuke winter limit on the megatonnage you can deliver ... you use the nukes on C3I targets and silos ... and then biowar the rest of your way ... a joke really ... I even laughed over it a few times myself ... we'd placed so much hope in ol' nuke winter holding the line ... rational as all hell ... the scenarios all so clean ... easy to calculate ... we built our careers on them ... but this other way ... so simple ... and no end to it ... and all I hope's ... hope's ... the bastard started this ... some third world general ... caught some of the damned stuff too ...

Bud

The germs got us. Cut big stretches through the US. We were just lucky. The germs played out in a couple months, while we were holed up. Soviets said they'd used the bio stuff in amongst the nukes to show us what they could do, longterm. Unless the war stopped right there. Which it did.

But enough nukes blew off here and in Russia to freeze up everybody for July and August, set off those storms.

Germs did the most damage, though—plagues.

It was a plague canister that hit the Slocum building. That did in Mobile.

The war was all over in a couple hours. The satellite people, they saw it all.

Now they're settling the peace.

Mr. Ackerman

"We been sitting waiting on this corpse long enough," I said and got up.

We got food from the commissary here. Fine. I don't say I'm anything but grateful for that. And we rested in the bunks, got recuperated. But enough's enough. The computer tells us it wants to talk to this man Gene some more. Fine, I said.

Turkey stood up. "Not easy, the computer says, this talking to a man's near dead. Slow work."

Looking around, I tried to take control, assume leadership again. Jutted out my chin. "Time to get back."

But their eyes are funny. Somehow I'd lost my real power over them. It's not anymore like I'm the one who led them when the bombs started.

Which means I suppose that this thing isn't going to be a new beginning for me. It's going to be the same life. People aren't going to pay me any more real respect than they ever did.

MC355

So the simulations had proved right. But as ever, incomplete.

MC355 peered at the shambling, adamant band assembled in the hospital bay, and pondered how many of them there might be elsewhere.

Perhaps many. Perhaps few.

It all depended on data MC355 did not have, could not easily find. The satellite worlds swinging above could get no accurate count on the US or the USSR.

Still—looking at them, MC355 could not doubt that there were many. They were simply too brimming with life, too hard to kill. All the calculations in the world could not stop these creatures.

The humans shuffled out, leaving the T-Isolate with the woman who had never left its side. They were going.

MC355 called after them. They nodded, understanding, but did not stop.

MC355 let them go.

There was much to do.

New antennas, new sensors, new worlds.

Turkey

Belly full and eye quick, we came out into the pines. Wind blowed through with a scent of the Gulf on it, fresh and salty with rich moistness.

The dark clouds are gone. I think maybe I'll get Bud to drive south some more. I'd like to go swimming one more time in those breakers that come booming in, taller than I am, down near Fort Morgan. Man never knows when he'll get to do it again.

Bud's ready to travel. He's taking a radio so's we can talk to MC, find out about the help that's coming. For now, we got to get back and look after our own.

Same as we'll see to the boy. He's ours, now.

Susan says she'll stay with Gene till he's ready, till some surgeons turn up can work on him. That'll be a long time, say I. But she can stay if she wants. Plenty food and such down there for her.

A lot of trouble we got, coming a mere hundred mile. Not much to show for it when we get back. A bumper crop of bad news, some would say. Not me. It's better to know than to not, better to go on than to look back.

So we go out into dawn and there are the same colored dots riding in the high hard blue. Like campfires.

The crickets are chirruping and in the scrub

there's a rustle of things moving about their own
business, a clean scent of things starting up. The
rest of us, we mount the truck and it surges forward with a muddy growl, Ackerman slumped over,
Angel in the cab beside Bud, the boy already asleep
on some blankets, and the forlorn sound of us
moving among the windswept trees is a long and
echoing note of mutual and shared desolation, powerful and pitched forward into whatever must come
now, a muted note persisting and undeniable in
the soft sweet air.

Epilog
Twenty-three years later

Johnny

An older woman in a formless, wrinkled dress
and worn shoes sat at the side of the road. I was
panting from the fast pace I was keeping along the
white strip of sandy, rutted road. She sat, silent and
unmoving. I nearly walked by before I saw her.

"You're resting?" I asked.

"Waiting." Her voice had a feel of rustling leaves.
She sat on a brown cardboard suitcase with big
copper latches—the kind made right after the war.
It was cracked along the side and white cotton
underwear stuck out.

"For the bus?"

"For Buck."

"The chopper recording, it said the bus will stop
up around the bend."

"I heard."

"It won't come down this side road. There's no
time."

I was late myself and I figured she had picked
the wrong spot to wait.

"Buck will be along."

Her voice was high and had the back country
twang to it. My own voice still had some of the

same sound but I was keeping my vowels flat right now and her accent reminded me of how far I had come.

I squinted, looking down the long sandy curve of the road. A pickup truck growled out of a clay side road and onto the hardtop. People rode in the back along with trunks and a 3D. Taking everything they could. Big white eyes shot a glance at me and then the driver hit the hydrogen and got out of there.

The Confederation wasn't giving us much time. Since the unification of the Soviet, USA, and European/Sino space colonies into one political union, everybody'd come to think of them as the Confeds, period—one entity. I knew better—there were tensions and differences abounding up there—but the shorthand was convenient.

"Who's Buck?"

"My *dog*." She looked at me directly, as though any fool would know who Buck was.

"Look, the bus—"

"You're one of those Bishop boys, aren't you?"

I looked off up the road again. That set of words—being eternally *a Bishop boy*—was like a grain of sand caught between my back teeth. My mother's friends had used that phrase when they came over for an evening of bridge, before I went away to the university. Not my real mother, of course—she and Dad had died in the war, and I dimly remembered them.

Or anyone else from then. Almost everybody around here had been struck down by the Soviet bioweapons. It was the awful swath those cut through whole states, mostly across the south—the horror of it—that had formed the basis of the peace that followed. Nuclear and bioarsenals were reduced to nearly zero now. Defenses in space were thick and reliable. The building of those had fueled the huge boom in Confed cities, made orbital commerce important, provided jobs and horizons for a whole generation—including me. I was a ground-orbit liaison, spending four months every year at US3. But to people down here, I was eternally that oldest Bishop boy.

Bishops. I was the only one left who'd actually lived here before the war. I'd been away on a visit when it came. Afterward, my aunt and uncle Bishop from Birmingham came down to take over the old family property—to save it from being homesteaded on, under the new Federal Reconstruction Acts. They'd taken me in and I'd thought of them as Mom and Dad. We'd all had the Bishop name, after all. So I was a Bishop, one of the few natives who'd made it through the bombing and the nuclear autumn and all. People'd point me out as almost a freak, a *real native*, wow.

"Yes Ma'm." I said neutrally.

"Thought so."

"You're . . . ?"

"Susan McKenzie."

"Ah."

We had done the ritual so now we could talk. Yet some memory stirred . . .

"Something 'bout you . . ." She squinted in the glaring sunlight. She probably wasn't all that old, in her late fifties maybe. Anybody who'd caught some radiation looked aged a bit beyond their years. Or maybe it was just the unending weight of hardship and loss they'd carried.

"Seems like I knew you before the war," she said. "I 'strictly believe I saw you."

"I was up north then, a hundred miles from here. Didn't come back until months later."

"So'd I."

"Some relatives brought me down and we found out what'd happened to Fairhope."

She squinted at me again and then a startled look spread across her leathery face. "My lord!

Were they lookin' for that big computer center, the DataComm it was?"

I frowned. "Well, maybe . . . I don't remember too well . . ."

"Johnny. You're Johnny!"

"Yes Ma'm, John Bishop." I didn't like the little-boy ending on my name, but people around here couldn't forget it.

"I'm Susan! The one went with you! I had the codes for DataComm, remember?"

"Why . . . yes . . ." Slow clearing of ancient, foggy images. "You were hiding in that center . . . where we found you . . ."

"Yes! I had Gene in the T-Isolate."

"Gene . . ." That awful time had been stamped so strongly in me that I'd blocked off many memories, muting the horror. Now it came flooding back.

"I saved him, all right! Yessir. We got married, I had my children."

Tentatively, she reached out a weathered hand and I touched it. A lump suddenly blocked my throat and my vision blurred. Somehow, all those years had passed and I'd never thought to look up any of those people—Turkey, Angel, Bud, Mr. Ackerman. Just too painful, I guess. And a little boy making his way in a tough world, without his parents, doesn't look back a whole lot.

We grasped hands. "I think I might've seen you once, actu'ly. At a fish fry down at Point Clear. You and some boys was playing with the nets—it was just after the fishing came back real good, those Rousshin germs'd wore off. Gene went down to shoo you away from the boats. I was cleaning flounder and I thought then, maybe you were the one. But somehow when I saw your face at a distance, I couldn't go up to you and say anything. You was skipping around, so happy, laughing and all. I couldn't bring those bad times back."

"I . . . I understand."

"Gene died two year ago," she said simply.

"I'm sorry."

"We had our time together," she said, forcing a smile.

"Remember how we—" and then I recalled where I was, what was coming. "Mrs. McKenzie, there's not long before the last bus."

"I'm waiting for Buck."

"Where is he?"

"He run off in the woods, chasing something."

I worked my backpack straps around on my shoulders. They creaked in the quiet.

There wasn't much time left. Pretty soon now it would start. I knew the sequence, because I did maintenance engineering and retrofit on US3's modular mirrors.

One of the big reflectors would focus sunlight on a rechargable tube of gas. That would excite the molecules. A small triggering beam would start the lasing going, the excited molecules cascading down together from one preferentially occupied quantum state to a lower state. A traveling wave swept down the tube, jarring loose more photons. They all added together in phase, so when the light wave hit the far end of the hundred-meter tube it was a sword, a gouging lance that could cut through air and clouds. And this time, it wouldn't strike an array of layered solid state collectors outside New Orleans, providing clean electricity. It would carve a swath twenty meters wide through the trees and fields of southern Alabama. A little demonstration, the Confeds said.

"The bus—look, I'll carry that suitcase for you."

"I can manage." She peered off into the distance and I saw she was tired, tired beyond knowing it. "I'll wait for Buck."

"Leave him, Mrs. McKenzie."

"I don't need that blessed bus."

"Why not?"

"My children drove off to Mobile with their families. They're coming back to get me."

"My insteted radio—" I gestured at my radio— "says the roads to Mobile are jammed up. You can't count on them."

"They *said* so."

"The Confed deadline—"

"I tole 'em I'd try to walk to the main road. Got tired, is all. They'll know I'm back in here."

"Just the same—"

"I'm all right, don't you mind. They're good children, grateful for all I've gone and done for them. They'll be back."

"Come with me to the bus. It's not far."

"Not without Buck. He's all the company I got these days." She smiled, blinking.

I wiped sweat from my brow and studied the pines. There were a lot of places for a dog to be. The land here was flat and barely above sea level. I had come to camp and rest, rowing skiffs up the Fish River, looking for places I'd been when I was a teenager and my Mom had rented boats from a rambling old fisherman's house. I had turned off my radio, to get away from things. The big, mysterious island I remembered and called Treasure Island, smack in the middle of the river, was now a soggy stand of trees in a bog. The big storm a year back had swept it away.

I'd been sleeping in the open on the shore near there when the chopper woke me up, blaring. The Confeds had given twelve hours warning, the recording said.

They'd picked this sparsely populated area for their little demonstration. People had been moving back in ever since the biothreat was cleaned out, but there still weren't many. I'd liked that when I was growing up. Open woods. That's why I came back every chance I got.

I should've guessed something was coming. The

Confeds were about evenly matched with the whole rest of the planet now, at least in high tech weaponry. Defense held all the cards. The big mirrors were modular and could fold up fast, making a small target. They could incinerate anything launched against them, too.

But the UN kept talking like the Confeds were just another nation-state or something. Nobody down here understood that the people up there thought of Earth itself as the real problem—eaten up with age-old rivalries and hate, still holding onto dirty weapons that murdered whole populations, carrying around in their heads all the rotten baggage of the past. To listen to them, you'd think they'd learned nothing from the war. Already they were forgetting that it was the orbital defenses that saved the biosphere itself, and the satellite communities that knit together the mammoth rescue efforts of the decade after. Without the antivirals developed and grown in huge zero-g vats, lots of us would've caught one of the poxes drifting through the population. People just forget. Nations, too.

"Where's Buck?" I said decisively.

"He . . . that way." A weak wave of the hand.

I wrestled my backpack down, feeling the stab from my shoulder—and suddenly remembered the thunk of that steel knocking me down, back then. So long ago. And me, still carrying an ache from it that woke whenever a cold snap came on. The past was still alive.

I trotted into the short pines, over creeper grass. Flies jumped where my boots struck. The white sand made a *skree* sound as my boots skated over it. I remembered how I'd first heard that sound, wearing slick-soled tennis shoes, and how pleased I'd been at the university when I learned how the acoustics of it worked.

"Buck!"

A flash of brown over to the left. I ran through a

thick stand of pine and the dog yelped and took off, dodging under a blackleaf bush. I called again. Buck didn't even slow down. I skirted left. He went into some oak scrub, barking, having a great time of it, and I could hear him getting tangled in it and then shaking free and out the other side. Long gone.

When I got back to Mrs. McKenzie she didn't seem to notice me. "I can't catch him."

"Knew you wouldn't." She grinned at me, showing brown teeth. "Buck's a fast one."

"Call him."

She did. Nothing. "Must of run off."

"There isn't time—"

"I'm not leaving without ole Buck. Times I was alone down on the river after Gene died, and the water would come up under the house. Buck was the only company I had. Only soul I saw for five weeks in that big blow we had."

A low whine from afar. "I think that's the bus," I said.

She cocked her head. "Might be."

"Come on. I'll carry your suitcase."

She crossed her arms. "My children will be by for me. I tole them to look for me along in here."

"They might not make it."

"They're loyal children."

"Mrs. McKenzie, I can't wait for you to be reasonable." I picked up my backpack and brushed some red ants off the straps.

"You Bishops was always reasonable," she said levelly. "You work up there, don't you?"

"Ah, sometimes."

"You goin' back, after they do what they're doin' here?"

"I might." Even if I owed her something for what she did long ago, damned if I was going to be cowed.

"They're attacking the United *States*."

"And spots in Bavaria, the Urals, South Africa, Brazil—"

" 'Cause we don't trust 'em! They think they can push the United *States* aroun' just as they please—" and she went on with all the cliches I heard daily from earthbound media. How the Confeds wanted to run the world and they were dupes of the Russians and how surrendering national sovereignty to a bunch of self-appointed overlords was an affront to our dignity and so on.

True, some of it—the Confeds weren't saints. But they were the only power that thought in truly global terms, couldn't *not* think that way. They could stop ICBMs and punch through the atmosphere to attack any offensive capability on the ground—that's what this demonstration was to show. I'd heard Confeds argue that this was the only way to break the diplomatic logjam—*do* something. I had my doubts. But times were changing, that was sure, and my generation didn't think the way the pre-war people did.

"—we'll never be ruled by some outside—"

"Mrs. McKenzie, there's the bus! Listen!"

The turbo whirred far around the bend, slowing for the stop.

Her face softened as she gazed at me, as if recalling memories. "That's all right, boy. You go along, now."

I saw that she wouldn't be coaxed or even forced down that last bend. She had gone as far as she was going to and the world would have to come the rest of the distance itself.

Up ahead the bus driver was probably behind schedule for this last pickup. He was going to be irritated and more than a little scared. The Confeds would be right on time, he knew that.

I ran. My feet ploughed through the deep, soft sand. Right away I could tell I was more tired than I'd thought and the heat had taken some strength out of me. I went about two hundred meters along the gradual bend, was nearly within view of the bus, when I heard it start up with a rumble. I tasted salty sweat and it felt like the whole damned planet was dragging at my feet, holding me down. The driver raced the engine, in a hurry.

He had to come toward me as he swung out onto Route 80 on the way back to Mobile. Maybe I could reach the intersection in time for him to see me. So I put my head down and plunged forward.

But there was the woman back there. To get to her the driver would have to take the bus down that rutted, sandy road and risk getting stuck. With people on the bus yelling at him. All that to get the old woman with the grateful children. She didn't seem to understand that there were ungrateful children in the skies now, she didn't seem to understand much of what was going on, and suddenly I wasn't so sure I did either.

But I kept on.

Stephen Leigh, whose first Bantam novel, Slow
Fall to Dawn, *was singled out by* Locus *as one of
the year's Ten Best, sent in the final draft of this one
with a cover letter signed, "Lefty," because he'd broken his hand. Leigh's premise involves messages un-
read and help from an unexpected—and perhaps
unwanted—source. Even fantasy, in* Afterwar, *isn't
pretty.*

FLAMESTONES
by Stephen Leigh

'You say this is *what?*"

The secretary upstairs had said that the geology
professor's name was Fields. He was thin. Everyone seemed to be thin these days. Even those with
bellies like Greg's had a touch of gauntness to
their faces. Greg looked around the basement lab
before answering the man. The dominant texture
was stone: stone walls, rock samples everywhere;
lined along shelves, sitting in floor cases, piled on
desks. The thin Professor Fields sat among them
like a wiry gnome, glasses perched on a precipi-
tous nose. He did not look at the crystal in his
hand but at Greg.

"Flamestones, I call 'em," Greg said. "I've been
finding them up north a ways, near Nacimiento
Mountain. They're very strange—"

"They're quartz," Fields said. "An unusual type,
I'll grant you, but still quartz. Silicon dioxide—the

six-sided structure's typical. The color's nice. I don't often see this orange-red, or this kind of clarity in the crystal . . ." He shrugged. "Quartz. Nearly the most common rock-forming mineral." He set the stone on the desk, looked up to Greg again.

It had been a long, tiring day. This was the fourth person he'd seen about the flamestones: two rockhounds, one jeweler, now this prissy geology professor. They all said the same thing. *Quartz.* Greg was getting weary of the sameness of their answers. "Look at it again," he said doggedly. "Please. It's got a fire in it, and those lines on the surface . . . Please."

Fields gave Greg a long look that had far too much pity in it. Greg tried to smile into that gaze and half succeeded. Then the man sighed and picked up a loupe from the clutter on his desk, fitting it over his glasses. He turned the crystal in his hands, holding it up to his desk lamp. "*Every* damn lump of crystalline quartz glitters in the right light," he said as he examined it. "This one's a bit more transparent than most of them, as I've admitted, but that doesn't make it—how'd you put it? 'Something new on the earth?' "

"You said yourself that you've never seen anything like it around here."

Fields laid down the stone, took off the loupe, leaned back in his chair. "Mister, I've been teaching here in Santa Fe for thirty years and I've had prospectors come in from the mountains every one of those years with the 'find of the century' or 'the best ore ever seen.' It has never—*never*—been anything special."

"What about the lines?" Greg insisted. His head was beginning to ache—*too much arguing, old man.* The heat, the noise of the city, the fear he could sense everywhere around him, the treatment he'd received today: all made him want to be nowhere else but back in the mountains. Back looking for flamestones. "That looks almost like writing to me."

Fields blinked at that. Greg could see the sudden barriers the man raised then, the nervous surge. He even knew the thoughts that wrinkled Fields' brow: *Christ, another loony.* "Writing, eh?" Fields said it slowly, carefully. The pitying look was back, tinged this time with an interior amusement and a guarded politeness. Greg felt irritation rising in himself, making his head pound all the more. "Yeah, writing," he said stubbornly, a bit too loudly. *That old New England pride,* his wife Becky would have called it. *Your damn Yankee cussedness.*

"You can *read* this?"

"Didn't say that."

"But you can?"

"Can't. But it looks to me like the marks are deliberate—runes or something. Feel 'em; they're incised, cut into the crystal."

For a long moment, Fields held Greg's gaze. Then he picked up the crystal again with another sigh of impatience. He rubbed the stone with a thumb. "Fracture lines," he said. "Made when this was knocked from a larger grouping of crystals. They're often quite linear." A pause. "Like these." He set the crystal down in front of Greg and laced together thick-knuckled fingers. "It's quartz. Quartz looks like this," he said, as if lecturing a slow student. "I can give you maybe ten bucks for this one—similar prices for anything like it. Some collector'll take them off my hands."

"I wasn't looking to sell. I wanted to know what you could tell me about them."

"I've already done that."

"Then you're mistaken."

Pity was replaced by annoyance. "Mister, I could look at this rock all day and it would *still* be quartz and nothing more. Now if you don't mind, I've got some work to do." Fields turned away and buried his head in a file cabinet, muttering. Greg stood there a moment, then snatched up his rock, his flamestone, and jammed it in a jacket pocket. *Give it up. They can't see it. They can't see the otherness of the stones.*

The rationale did nothing to relieve the embarrassment, the humiliation he felt. The headache battered at his temples.

"Thanks for looking at it," he said, and placed a crumpled five dollar bill on the desk. Fields grunted something; Greg fled the basement office for the sunlight.

It took him an hour to walk back to his battered Toyota Land Cruiser, parked near his first stop—gas was too precious to waste when one could walk.

He did not particularly enjoy the scenery; only the heat and arid blue sky were the same as the old Santa Fe. He was glad once again that he'd left the city before the food riots that followed the May 15th Mistake, when New York, Moscow, and Tel Aviv had all died in radioactive fire. It seemed that nothing had gotten better since then. Food prices were outrageous at a barren-shelved supermarket he passed. Scars of fires and looting marked every street, the wreckage prowled by bands of Scavis—human vultures picking over the bones of unrest. Once Greg thought he heard the cough of gunfire not far distant. Santa Fe, once clean and neo-adobe modern, was fouled with the stench of fire and the banshee howl of sirens. The people walking the streets with him appeared uneasy in their pursuit of everyday routines, as if the air stained their emotions. The papers in the stands blared headlines of growing tension, the tensions most thought had been finally purged with the destruction on the 15th of May. SPAIN INVADED. BLOC ALLIES SUPPLY TROOPS. US FLEET SENT TO MEDITERRANEAN. ECONOMIC WOES PLAGUE PRESIDENT. The words chilled him despite the

September heat. He quickened his pace, ignoring
the throbbing in his head.

When he got back to the Cruiser at last, he found
that someone had siphoned off the gas despite the
locks.

It was then that he decided that he was never
coming back.

In the evenings, he came to the ridge and looked
westward.

Greg preferred evenings. The late afternoon light
was a liquid gold-green, deepening in saturation
as the sun dropped. The valleys between the peaks
turned first umber, then violet, then the deepest of
blue-blacks. The rocks would still be warm from
the fierce New Mexico sun, but the air soon turned
cooler—heat ghosts wavered in the distance. Evenings were a time of contemplation, of transition.
The world altered itself, snuggled into a new
night-shape.

He'd found two flamestones that afternoon—
ruddy crystals the size of his fist with a lambent
fire in their hearts. He hefted one of them in his
hand; the other nestled in the pocket of his down
jacket. He held the crystal up to the dying light,
turned it so that the etched lines on its surface
darkened against reflections from the stone. Patterns; indecipherable. The flamestones were always
along the ridges or in open areas: always where a
person would naturally walk. He'd never found
one at the base of an eroded cliff or in the scree
left by a suddenly rain-full stream. No—always
high and in the open. He'd begun to think of them
as markers for unseen travelers and had to keep
reminding himself that it was, at best, only specula-
tion or understandable fantasy—at worst, the onset of madness. He could not know which.

Staring at the sunset through the stone, he was
startled by unexpected noise. Rock scraped rock,

punctuating a breath. Greg turned, fingers tightening around the flamestone.

"Hi," she said. "Hey, I didn't mean to scare you like that. I didn't know anyone was up here . . ." A hand swept long, tangled, black hair from a grimy face; another brushed at denim-clad legs. Her eyes were dark like the hair, with the lowering sun in them. She squinted into the light, looking past him. "That's pretty. Are they all like that?"

Greg glanced back over his shoulder. He was still shaken by her appearance here; his politeness was reflex, as was his shrug. "The sunset? Sometimes they're better, sometimes worse. This one's OK." His fingers unknotted slowly, his breath returning. He stared at the woman, who smiled back at him. He thought she might be in her mid-thirties. She was stocky, as tall as he, her face plain and wide, the mouth too large. She seemed to carry nothing but her dusty and worn clothing—no weapons. That pleased him; the latest news reports had spoken of frequent shooting in the streets.

Her smile wavered, faded.

"I'm sorry," he said slowly, looking away from her—he'd been staring too long. "I don't usually see anyone else up here . . . I didn't see you at all . . ."

"You were too involved with your stone. I should have called out, I suppose." Her voice trailed off with that smile, one side of the mouth higher than the other; a hand shaded her eyes from the sun—he could see well-bitten nails. San Pedro Mt. was golden behind her.

He saw the rest, then: the torn knees of the jeans, the limpness of unwashed hair, the stains that might have been blood on her light jacket. "Where you from?"

"Santa Fe."

"That's a long walk."

"I drove. Came up 84 to the roadblock at 4, then took the back roads west until the car died. I left it two days ago."

"Where's your pack?"

Once more, the smile. Quick, fleeting, defensive. "Don't really have one."

His voice was unintentionally stern, parental. "Then you're damned lucky you haven't frozen. Only an idiot—"

"I'm not that fucking fragile." There was a quick defiance in her eyes.

Greg rubbed the stone with his thumb, shoved it into his pants pocket, wondering whether he should be angry or sympathetic. "Uh-huh," he said, and her silence decided him. The sun had touched the lip of the horizon, drowning in clouds over what had once been the Apache reservation. "I've got stew. You're probably hungry."

She hesitated, shifting her weight from foot to foot. She wasn't even wearing boots, he saw. Sneakers. Greg shook his head.

"I could stand to eat," she said.

"Then come on."

"You sure you can trust me?" The smile was back, the quick anger gone as if it had never existed. Greg could not decide what the smile meant.

"You sure you can trust *me?*" he asked.

Smiling, eerie and unsettling, not a thing of pleasure at all: "I'll find out, won't I?"

The sun died in scarlet and gray. "What's your name?"

"Ellen Rebhun."

"I'm Greg. Greg Tompkins. Follow me—it's about a mile."

". . . and Mayor Perez has ordered a strict curfew for the entire city. The National Guard has been issued live ammunition and will shoot violators on sight. It is hoped that this will end four straight nights of violence. Now turning to national news, the President announced today that all NATO units have been placed on highest alert due to the increasing number of attacks. Secretary of State Howard is to meet with delegates from the Bloc countries concerning a cessation of hostilities in the Mediterranean. He issued a statement before his departure for Rome. Referring to the events of May 15th, Howard said that the world cannot afford to come so close to a final conflict again. All sides must be willing—"

"Turn that off, will you?"

Ellen turned to Greg, who was busy at his campstove. The odor of meat and spices was gratifyingly delicious. She switched off the radio: "You don't want to hear the news?"

"It's all variations on a theme. Boils down to the same thing in the end—we're going to hell; I don't need to know the color of the handcart."

"You're a pessimist."

"Not at all. A realist."

She looked at him, his attention on his cooking, the walls of the old tunnel around him lined with open wooden crates in which sat kerosene lamps, pots, pans, drygoods, and many crystalline stones: an old mine.

"You don't look much like a survivalist, Greg—no offense meant. You're what—fifty-five, sixty? Balding, overweight, and out of shape, and what rifles I see around here are best for squirrels, not people."

Greg tasted the stew, made a face, and added salt. "I'm sixty-three, I'm not as overweight as I was when I came here, and I don't much enjoy shooting people. But I have food, a bedroll, lanterns, and a warm place to sleep. No, I'm not a survivalist, but at least I'm semi-prepared for living out here." He'd said it as gently as he could; now he turned around to see if she were smiling.

She wasn't. The expression on her face sobered him. "Hey, I'm sorry, Ellen."

A shrug. "Forget it. Touche; you're right. I just cut and run without thinking."

"Want to talk about it?"

"I don't need a shrink, and if I did, it wouldn't be an amateur." She walked over to a crate and picked up a flamestone. "You got a lot of these. You a collector?"

"You could say so." He ladled stew onto tin plates, handed her one plate and a fork. Steam rose; she sniffed and sighed. She put the crystal back, hunkered down on the ground and began to eat. "Those rocks aren't going to do you much good when it all falls apart, are they?"

"They're not just rocks," he said slowly. His tone was more defensive than he'd intended, with an edge to it that put a scowl on Ellen's face. Then her smile returned, and Greg suddenly understood that the gesture was simply a defense, something to shield her from aggression—it meant nothing beyond that. Which implied that she was still frightened, far more than she'd admit.

"You're crazy, aren't you?" she said, very softly.

He almost grinned. " 'Eccentric' sounds better. Or even 'mad.' You might be right; everyone else seems to think so." He could see a palpable fear in her—not of him alone, but a reservoir he had tapped. Her eyes were wide, the large mouth was drawn back in that meaningless smile. She folded her arms before her as if she were cold, and her gaze skittered past him and the fire to the mouth of the mine where starlight showed.

"Thanks for the meal," she said, and rose to her feet.

"It'll be cold tonight—no clouds at all. And I assure you that my madness extends only to rocks, nothing else." When she did not move, he continued. "Ellen, you're the same age as my daughter. There's another sleeping bag: You can have the fire and the front of the mine—I'll stay in back on my cot. Hell, you'll hear my old bones creak if I get up." There was still caution in her stare. Greg laughed quietly. "My God, woman, do I look the kind of man who'd hurt anyone? I might be a crazy old fool, but not a killer or rapist. Too old and tired for that. I'm not one of the Scavis. That's one of the reasons I came up here, to get away from all of them." He glanced at her. In the dimness of the mine, in the firelight, her eyes flashed white. "My guess is that you'd understand someone wanting to get out of the city."

He could see her relax, then: a slow loosening of muscles. She shrugged. This time her smile was touched with something other than fear.

"I guess I might be safe enough," she said.

She went out with him the next day, walked beside him as he wandered the slopes. She watched as he checked his two cameras—battered Pentaxes on wobbly tripods, infrared eyes set on the hot shoes. "What're you trying to catch?" she asked, and there was only a little uncertainty in her voice. "I'll know when I get it," he answered, and was surprised when she accepted that answer.

They climbed higher to where the snow clung in the shadows; they sat in those same shadows when the sun was highest, sharing cheese and water. If he noticed that her gaze often traveled south and east to where the city was hidden behind mountains, if he was aware of how she regarded him if he moved too close to her, he said nothing. Greg looked at the ground; not the mountains, not Ellen.

It was late afternoon when he found a flamestone. The crystal glinted in sunlight, a beacon. "See," he said, pointing to it. "I think they're *placed* there. See how this one sits—like someone just dropped it on the ground." He reached down, brushed the flat surfaces. "And these lines—too regular, like writing. Look at it."

She didn't take it from his proferred hand. She glanced around them. They stood on a high, barren ridge, the peaks huddled above and around them like sentinels. "There's no tracks," she said.

"Hmmm?"

"There's no tracks," she repeated. "If someone laid it there, there'd be footprints or something. I don't see anything—doesn't that kind of blow your theory to hell?"

He shrugged. "How else could it have gotten here?"

"It fell from the slopes, or the rain or wind uncovered it."

"That's hardly likely." He could not keep all the irritation from his voice.

"Less likely than some ghost without a footprint? That's what your cameras are for, aren't they?—to catch ghosts." She took a step back from him.

For a moment, he didn't answer. He put the stone in a pocket, pulled it out again. Then he sighed and squatted on the rocky ground. Ellen watched him and he did not like the pity he saw in her eyes; it was the same pity he'd seen in Fields' face. "We've never been this close to destruction, we humans," he said. "Now the flamestones have started arriving."

"Which means what?"

Greg shook his head. "I don't have any answers, just guesses. I think that there might be another world just out of phase to us. Maybe we're linked together, maybe conflict here mirrors a like struggle there. The barriers—whatever holds us apart—are very weak now; there's some crossover taking place. Hell, maybe that explains a lot of disappearances, people who never returned home. I don't know. But I think the flamestones are part of it all." He shrugged once more. "I can't read them, so I can't know. I just believe that they're meant for us to find, that's all."

He placed the flamestone on the ground where he'd found it.

She scowled at the rock.

"You're out of your mind. You've found something you can't understand and you've picked the least likely explanation for it."

"It gives me some hope, Ellen. Whether I'm ultimately right or wrong, at least I've had that."

"That's utter shit, Greg." Bitterness etched her words like acid. Greg glanced up to find her face a rictus, a mask of anger. He stood, awkward, and reached out to touch her comfortingly.

She slapped at him suddenly, ragged-bitten nails gouging bloody tracks across the back of his hand. Then she stooped and picked up the flamestone, holding it high like a bludgeon.

Shaking his head, Greg cradled his hand to his chest, his gaze on the stone.

The wildness left her eyes slowly, and she lowered her hand. After a moment, she held out the stone.

He took it, but made certain that his fingers did not touch her.

Ellen stayed for a week, perhaps more—Greg kept little track of time. She would never let him get physically close, never let him touch her in any way. If by chance he brushed her sleeve, she would move away with a muttered apology. They talked very little; when they did, they often argued. He especially did not talk about the flamestones, though during the days she would walk with him along the ridges, checking his cameras and searching for the glint of crystal. That week he found two more, one a cloudy blue that he'd never seen before, the other streaked with scarlet, like blood in water. Evenings, he would fix a small supper for them while she listened to the radio. The news from Santa Fe was never good—but then it hadn't been for some time. Greg did his best to ignore it.

It was on such an evening that she called to him from the clearing outside the entrance. "Greg! Come here, quickly!"

He set aside the pan of broth. Sunset dappled the sky behind her—she pointed wordlessly to the valley below them. There Greg could see twin plumes of dust as two jeeps churned toward them. The sound of their engines was a faint snarl, and he could see someone in the back of one of the vehicles gesturing in their general direction. Greg ran back to the mine, returned with binoculars. He brought them up, twirled the focus. Road grimy, bearded faces swam before him, and he could see the spines of weapons on their backs. "Scavis," he said. "Five, maybe six of 'em, all armed. Damn. Coming up here." He shook his head, staring through the glasses. "They usually stay nearer the city—guess they're out looking for new pickings."

He looked back at Ellen. Her face had gone to the empty smile again. Her fists were clenched, white-knuckled. He glanced back at the dustplume of the raiders. "Ellen, we've got to make ourselves scarce. Get some food together; I'll fill the canteens. We'll go back into the tunnels." His face was grim as he ran to the mine entrance. As he ducked under the low roof, he paused. Ellen had not moved. She stared down at the presence in the valley. "Ellen!" She started, smiled back at him. "Come on!"

The smile collapsed. "We have to fight them, Greg. Your guns—"

"Are for show and nothing else. You can't bluff Scavies, Ellen."

"You're just going to let them have what they want?" Disbelief fought anger on her face.

Greg did not understand it. "I'm going to make sure we live. Now are you coming?"

She came, but her steps were slow and she often glanced back at the spoor of the intruders. Greg flung supplies into a few packs and then moved with Ellen into the darkness of the tunnels. Their flashlights made warm circles on the stone and the old wooden beams. Shafts ran off left, then right. Greg turned at an intersection, taking a tunnel that rose under their feet until they ran crouching. Then the roof became higher, and they could walk upright.

Finally, he came to a narrow offshoot and pointed to an alcove with his flash. "This'll be good for now," he said in a whisper. "We'll be able to hear them coming if they decide to go exploring. I don't think they will, though. They shouldn't stay long—there's not much for them here."

Ellen said nothing.

He flicked the beam over her face, finding a grim scowl. "How are you doing?"

"Fine," she answered, gruffly.

"Then we'll stay here a bit." He switched off the flashlight. Darkness pressed in on them. He could hear her breathing quicken. Greg knew what she felt; he'd come back into the tunnels and sat in its eternal night before. He knew that it could hold terror if you let imagination have its way. He knew that her hearing would be straining for sounds now, amplifying the slightest movement—even your heartbeat became audible. If he'd thought he could, he would have reached out for her, put his arm around her for the mutual comfort it would give.

He did not. Her breath was rapid; if she carried ghosts with her, they were making their presence known. "Ellen?" He spoke in a low whisper, but he could hear her jump at the sound.

"I'm OK, Greg."

"I don't like this, either. But sometimes it can help you think."

"About flamestones?"

"Or things in general."

She said nothing for a time. When she did speak again, her voice was strained and harsh, barely audible even in the still solitude of the tunnel. He leaned toward her to hear the words.

I worked in a little store just off San Miguel Ave.—it wasn't much, just some assorted junk that Carl and his daughter Marie sold for too little money. Scavi stuff, some of it—he used to buy it from them. We were all there; I guess it was Tuesday two weeks ago, when the front bell rang. I was in back, so I didn't go out to answer it. I could hear voices, someone talking to Carl. I didn't pay much attention until they started getting loud. I heard someone hit Carl. He must have fallen, because then it sounded like they were kicking him.

Marie was at her desk. She'd started screaming, picking up the phone to call for help. They came at her, then. I heard the phone crash against a wall, heard her struggling as they dragged her out. They . . . they told Carl to watch, watch what they did to people that got in their way. Cloth tore, and they laughed and made comments, then Marie gave one sharp scream.

"God, I was scared, Greg. I could hardly move, afraid that if I did they'd hear me, afraid that if I didn't they'd look around and see me. I crept back to the rear of the store, climbed into an old cabinet there and closed the door. I sat in the dark, smelling the paint cans stored with me, listening. Christ, it was awful. You can't understand, Greg— what they were doing, just for the pleasure of it . . .

I hid for a long time. At least it seemed that way. I was afraid to come out, even to breathe too loudly. Once one or maybe two of them came back and started tearing things up near me. I tried to prepare myself to die, tried to pray, begged God to make them leave me alone—I'd do anything, anything He wanted me to if only they didn't find me. After a while, I didn't hear anything more, at least not from the Scavis. Carl groaned once or twice, though I never heard Marie. Carl just kept moaning and crying, and I wanted to go and help him but I couldn't. I *couldn't*. Finally, even his moaning stopped. I waited. I waited until I couldn't bear the darkness and the silence any longer. I opened the cabinet and walked to the front of the store.

There was blood everywhere—Carl's mostly. God, what they'd done to him—his body was just a network of cuts, his face . . . they'd just hacked him up, let him bleed to death. Marie was on the floor near him, naked. They'd killed her cleanly, at least, after they were done with her.

And—oh, Christ Jesus—one of them was still there.

He was standing over Marie. He grinned at me— God, I can still see that face. There was nothing in him at all, nothing but animal bloodlust. His clothes were spattered red, his hands were covered with it, and he looked from me to Marie and back. I just stood there, staring, not even saying anything, just looking at the knife in his belt, the gun at his side. He kept grinning, just grinning. "Damn, you're an ugly one, ain't 'cha?" he said. His voice was all cracked and broken. "Betcha no man's ever touched ya. Tell you what. I'm feelin' friendly, and I'll do ya a favor. You're gonna thank me afterward, too. You'd like that, wouldn't ya?" He kept saying that, when he took me in back, when he . . . "You're gonna thank me." Over and over.

I thought he'd kill me when he was done. But he just stood up and stared at me for a long time, his hand on his knife. Then he left. Turned and walked out the door without another word. I heard a motor starting, then tires squealing down the street.

Sometimes I wish he'd used that knife.

The police, my family, my friends; they kept telling me how brave I'd been, how courageous. I know better, Greg. I know how terrified I was, how all I did was hide instead of fighting back even a little, instead of helping Carl and Marie.

I left town a couple days later. Guess I was looking for a place where the world couldn't reach me. That sound romantic enough, eh?

"Ellen?"

Her laugh shuddered with tears. "Do you know how lonely it's going to be for those who survive? All those buildings standing empty, whole towns where only a few people live—images of despair, like wandering through an amusement park out of season, being in places where crowds used to gather and hearing only the wind through vacant stalls." Greg could almost see her head shaking. "That's what it's going to be, Greg."

"I thought that once. I don't know about that now."

"Your flamestones? Your 'we have to have some hope' line?"

"Despair's a self-fulfilling prophecy."

"I didn't know you were a philosopher as well as a lunatic," she said bitterly.

Greg fought anger, kept it down. "I think we still have a chance. Those that give up hope won't fight to keep it."

"God, that's so much bullshit, Greg!" Her voice was nearly a shout now. He wanted to clap a hand over her mouth, do anything to silence her. "You're not fighting. You're *hiding*, just like I hid. We're hiding now. You *ran* from the Scavis. You didn't *fight* them."

Greg leaned back against the cool stone. He closed his eyes—it made no difference. "I told you that I had a daughter. She lived in New York. She called Becky—my wife—one day, wanted us to come visit her. She had a new boyfriend, a new apartment. I couldn't get away—business—but Becky flew in. That was May 13th . . ." He'd intended to continue. He found that he could not. There was simply too much for him to say, all caught in a skein of emotion that he'd thought had been discarded. "Her name was Julie . . ." he began, and then her face came before him in the dark and he could not speak. He swallowed very hard, blinked.

"Greg, I'm not going to sit here and trade stories. You stay here. Stay here and be safe and tell yourself about all the hope you have from your flamestones." Rocks scraped in darkness. He heard a step as she got to her feet.

"Ellen—"

"A passive hope doesn't give me any comfort, Greg. I'm tired of it. I don't—" Her voice broke.

"Don't be foolish, Ellen."

But she was no longer listening. He heard her walking away, saw the sudden splash of light as she flicked on her flash. A yellow-white circle played over stones, her figure outlined against it. Greg hesitated, not sure what to do. A hand went into his pocket, touched the flamestone there. And the fear ran over him like cold fire. The lie he had begun to tell Ellen came back to him—it was not business that had kept him from going to New York with Becky. That had been an excuse. In truth, he'd been frightened, scared of the tales in the New York papers, in the national news—the fighting in the city's streets, the murders, the riots. He hadn't wanted to go, hadn't wanted Becky to go to New York. It had caused one of their few arguments, and in the end she had gone by herself.

And had died.

"Ellen—" he began, but she had gone. Darkness pressed in on him, and the silence was an accusation. He hefted the grip of his flashlight, turned it on. He could see by the trembling of the beam that his hands were shaking. But no other part of him would move: He was held, balanced between his concern for Ellen and that gnawing memory fear.

He did not know how long he sat there before he could get up.

The entrance area was a shambles. Moonlight washed in from outside. The stove was gone, the cot was overturned, crates littered the ground. Ellen was not in sight. Greg walked numbly into the wreckage of the mine; nearly everything not taken had been broken. He set the cot upright, now sagging on three legs, and stooped beside the shards of a cracked flamestone. "They didn't have to do all this," he said. The words sounded weak and futile. He picked up the pieces of the crystal, let them fall again.

"You *let* them do it." It was Ellen. She stood in the entrance, hands on hips. Dirty tear marks stained her cheeks. "They took the Cruiser, too."

"Ellen! God, are you all right? I thought—" He stopped, seeing the sudden hard glint in her eyes. He could read little there but contempt, and he quailed under her stare.

"It doesn't matter a whole lot just what you might have thought, Greg. But you needn't worry; they were gone when I got back here. Why should it concern you at all?—You were safely cringing back in the dark."

That sparked anger. Greg answered far more sharply than he intended, and he knew that his fury was directed at his own guilt. "Your heroics didn't matter either, did they? At least *my* way I knew we'd both still be alive afterward. You could have gotten yourself killed." *The old man lecturing his daughter. Listen to yourself—all variations of things you said to Julie before she moved to New York, and what you screamed at Becky before she took that last flight.* The rage left as quickly as it had come; it left him tired. "Please . . ."

Ellen was shaking her head. "You don't see it in yourself, do you? Tell me, Greg, what good would it do if these flamestones of yours really do mean something? You'd be afraid to look. You wouldn't take the hope given to you because there also might be pain involved."

He could say nothing. He looked away from her, down at the shattered stone in his hand. He heard her walk into the mine and begin straightening his things. After a moment, in bitter silence, he began to help.

She was gone the next morning. Greg was not surprised. He told himself that he did not care— *just a break in the routine. You didn't touch her or she you.* But when he left that morning to search for flamestones, he followed her trail until he knew where she was going: east and south, back to Santa Fe. He grimaced at that. He thought he should feel something, but there was nothing. Nothing.

He collected flamestones, he developed his negatives and stared at the reversed images, he listened to the radio. The news worsened in the next few weeks: threats, counter-threats, assassinations, rampant terrorism. A new war flared in Africa, another in South America. The United States incarcerated all Brazilian diplomats and embassy workers, Brazil responded by executing the American ambassador on an espionage charge. The Mid-Eastern Bloc took an aggressive stance in the seemingly eternal Mediterranean conflict. Yet Greg had seen tensions escalate before. Even when the President recalled Secretary Howard from the Roman summit, Greg shrugged.

It would pass. They would blunder through. They must.

The next day he found three flamestones, and there was a blur on his negatives that was not rabbit or fox.

Two days later, he woke to searing light.

It was dawn, yet it was not the sun that had awakened him but a light so intense that he had seen the flash through closed lids. He knuckled his eyes; aftcrimages whirled through the spectrum.

The sound came then, lagging behind the light—an immense thunderclap like the scream of a god, basso roaring more felt than heard. The earth heaved beneath the impact: The god had slammed a fist to the ground and the very stones danced to his anger.

Greg fell as the tunnel lurched. Rock collapsed behind him, a beam snapped like a twig, and thick dust choked him. He got to his knees and staggered outside.

There was no dawn to the east, only a welling ball of fiery cloud looming behind the mountains and climbing skyward. The bellow of tortured earth dinned around him. He held his hands over his ears. His thoughts were oddly not of war or the death of the cities, but of Ellen. Of Becky. Of Julie. The firestorm was their grave. He blinked sudden tears and went slowly back inside; coughing, ignoring the grumbling aftershocks. There, he filled a backpack with provisions, carrying as much as he could.

He walked deep into the tunnels.

Hiding in the darkness, he cried, cursing himself for a fool. He dragged at the tears with a sleeve, forcing himself to open the pack and count the supplies. *Do something. Do anything. Just don't think about it.* It was perhaps two hours later when the world jumped underneath him in torment. He was sure he would die then—these shocks were far worse than the first ones. But the earth-spasms passed and the roof held. In time, he slept.

He came out three days later because he could stand no more of the dark and the solitude. He came out knowing that the winter would have come early on wings of ash, that the air would be laden with slow death. He came out because there seemed to be no use hiding from an end that would seek him out no matter where he huddled.

Greg expected to see a changed world. He had not expected the changes he saw.

Parts of the landscape had shifted. San Pedro Mt. was simply gone. Nacimiento was far taller and more imposing than before, with a steepness that bore mute challenge. Others of the peaks were the same, though between them peered the arm of some sea, glinting all the way to the horizon. The sun warmed his shoulders and the sky was an impossible blue, though there was a smudge of darkness to the southeast where Santa Fe should have been.

This was his world, this was not his world; it was some melding of known and unknown. Greg remembered the jolt hours after the bombs had fallen, and he wondered.

It was then that he saw them—the riders on a ridge above him. They were astride beasts that might have been horses but seemed too long-legged and thin. The riders were tall themselves and dark of hair. They bore shields wrought with strange devices; silver helms hung from their packs. Lances were in their hands, and they looked down at Greg with stern faces. Warriors. Soldiers.

Their eyes burned like the sun in a flamestone, and Greg felt them to be terrible and yet majestic. The wind brought the alto neighing of horses, a clash of steel.

You're dead. You're delirious. You're dreaming.

But the sun was hot and the stones were hard
beneath his boots and he could hear his own low
breath. He reached in his pocket for a flamestone,
brought it out and looked at it. *They must be as
confused as you.* There was time. He could run
back to the mines and into the tunnels before they
reached him. They would not stay to search for
him; one unarmed, lonely man. They'd leave, go
about their strange business, whatever it might
be.

And he would never know who they were or
what they might mean.

You would be alive.

Almost, he ran. With an effort, he brought a
hand up and waved.

With the gesture, one of them motioned to his
fellows. Reins slapped. In a cascade of small stones,
the rider made his way down the ridge, drawing
up near Greg, lance down.

Neither spoke, and the flat, deadly head of the
lance did not move away from Greg's chest. Greg
studied the weapon with an odd fascination. The
metal was dull, splotched with discolorations. The
edge was keen but notched, and had a slight left-to-
right wave. Not a showpiece, not a relic, but a tool
of war, well-used. He glanced at the rider. The
man's eyes were umber shot with bright gold, his
skin was the color of tea.

Greg could feel adrenaline surging; he was simultaneously frightened and exhilarated. "My
name's Greg," he said, and the banality of the
words nearly made him laugh. *Good. The world's
gone totally strange, you're being threatened by someone who's obviously used to killing, and you're intro-
ducing yourself like it was a goddamn cocktail party.
Good.*

The rider spoke, a quick flourish of words. His
voice was strangely deep to have come from such
a slender frame, and the words were sonorous and

liquid. Greg could understand none of them. The rider nodded to the mountains, to the new sea, and his forehead was creased with what looked like puzzlement. The lancehead dipped and came near Greg, who spread his hands wide.

"Please, I don't—" he began, and noticed that the rider's attention had been snagged by the flamestone in his hand. Cautiously, always aware of the lance, Greg held the stone out toward the man.

The rider leaned over in his saddle, long and delicate fingers reaching toward the crystal and then pulling back without touching it. Another torrent of words—flowing like Spanish, but with no words that Greg knew.

"Take it," Greg said, offering it on an open palm to the man. Their gazes met, a long, breathless moment, and then the being took the stone. There was a brief instant when they touched—the rider's skin was warm, and softer than Greg would have expected.

The being held the stone aloft. He shouted words in that sibilant tongue; from upslope, his companions answered. He placed the flamestone in a leather pouch on his belt, then nodded to Greg.

The lance snapped up and away from Greg—relief made him close his eyes for a second as the rider reined his mount away.

When the rider had rejoined his companions, he nodded once more. They wheeled and began making their way down toward the valley, toward the sky-stain that should be Santa Fe.

"Just quartz, eh?" he said to himself as he watched them. "By God, I was right." *And what good does it do you?* The thought came unbidden as the riders passed from sight around an outcropping. *It means you have to stay up here—because those were not a people of peace. Yes, your flamestones heralded change, but not an end of strife.* Ellen was right, too. Hope was not enough.

Greg stood there under that new sun. The sound of hooves on rock faded. Then, a decision made, he turned and went back into the mine.

He would prepare a few things.

Then he would follow the riders down.

Diana Paxson gives us a story of survivalist reality, and of that place where metaphysics and reality meet. In a cover letter, Diana confessed that, "it's been an interesting and not very comfortable experience writing it, but I realized there were a number of things I needed to say. Some friends up in Mendocino County gave me some wonderful input—they've been thinking along these lines for years. If anyone does, they'll survive." With, or without, the witch, one wonders . . .

THE PHOENIX GARDEN
by Diana L. Paxson

Jack Galen straightened, his son's whistle still aching in his ears, and looked down the road. He saw two women stumbling over the wheelruts—but they were no one belonging to Phoenix Creek or to the town in the valley below. He grimaced and mopped sweat from his eyes. *Refugees*, he thought. *Goddamn it, why do we have to decide . . .*

Jack stared at the jagged line of trees beneath the blue lid of the sky as if they held an answer. He knew they would have to give the women at least one meal, but no more. Everyone on the Creek had some skill to contribute; what they needed was a miracle worker now.

He waved to Kit and the boy scrambled down the hill to meet the newcomers, his sheeting poncho billowing behind him. In the first weeks after the War the ponchos had been both a way to detect the deadly peppering of fallout and a protection against it. They provided another kind of protection now.

Jack grimaced again, took a firmer grip on the loose board in the fence he was fixing, and lifted the hammer. His hand, sweating and clumsy inside the glove, slipped and the blow went awry, bruising his thumb and bending the nail. Jack swore, more at the ruined nail than at the pain. Once he would have ripped it out and started over. Once, he would have worked with his hands bare. Strange that the more enduring danger should have been not the dark shadow of fallout but the sun's unshielded rays.

Jack took a deep breath and carefully released it again. Sweat trickled through his scraggling brown beard. *Relax* . . . He counted, willing his pulse to slow. He could not afford anger over this, or over the gloves and hat that might protect him from skin cancer, or over any of the thousand other new habits and precautions that had become part of their lives in the six months since the War.

Carefully he pulled the nail free, laid it on the board and hammered it straight again. Carefully, he lifted the board into place once more and with controlled strokes of the hammer drove the nail in. Peripheral vision showed him Kit bouncing along beside the two refugees, chattering. Jack took another nail and hammered it in, making no mistakes this time. Five minutes to finish this job and then he would have to go talk to them as well.

When he had finished Jack stepped back and examined his patching. A wire fence would have discouraged deer or turkey, but the feral pigs that roamed the California hills were stronger and cannier, with an inherited lust for what grew in the gardens of men. Jack frowned at the yellowing leaves of the corn, stifling the impulse to tear down the fence and let the pigs come in.

The little community on Phoenix Creek Road had huddled behind walls and survived on canned stuff through the first few weeks after the brief, devastating missile exchange. Living at the end of a road that washed out at least once every winter, they knew enough to stockpile supplies, and the prevailing winds had carried most of the fallout from targets to the south of them, like San Francisco and Hamilton AFB, eastward and away. They had been lucky.

Jack smiled sourly and picked up the can of nails. Lucky! Perhaps in a year, they would know. They had gotten some fallout, of course, for even prevailing winds change sometimes, but the last of the spring rains had washed it into crevices where it could decay.

And then they had planted their precious seeds in a garden from which the top layer of soil had been cautiously brushed away, and waited to see what would grow.

Maybe if we'd waited longer—Jack felt the twist in his belly again as he counted the distorted zucchinis that had fallen unripened to the ground. He was not enough of a gardener to tell if there was anything wrong with the carrots planted in the next row, but the bean vines seemed to cling despairingly to their poles. Jack closed his eyes.

Was it early fallout in the soil, or the slow drift of strontium 90 or ultra-violet formed carbon 14 from the upper atmosphere? Or was it the ultra-violet rays themselves, falling unhindered through a shattered ionosphere, that worked like an invisible plague?

But you can't grow vegetables without the sun, can you? And how should I know? the internal dialogue went on. He was no farmer. He had designed computer systems, Before, successful enough to build a career as a consultant here where he could lift his eyes from his terminal to see the sunlight on the hills. But he had never liked gardening. He hated it now.

A cry pulsed in the red darkness behind Jack's eyelids, drove through the circuits of nerve and vein to the earth below. *You! Do something! You're dying too!*

Someone shouted from down the hill. Jack's eyes opened and he blinked at the hot glare. He picked up the hammer, walked around the fence and down through the pasture behind the house. Dry heads of wild oats caught at his jeans, but in any year all the grass would have cured to hay by now. In August the thistles came into their own and only irrigation kept anything green.

Jack picked his way around the parts pile and the goat shed and the trailer where Alice and her daughter Luthien lived, gratefully stripping off hat and gloves as he came under the shade of the house porch. He ran his fingers through his greying hair.

A murmur of voices came from within—his wife Merideth's, clear and a little clipped, and others, one rather nasal, which he immediately disliked, and another that seemed to gush even in its weakness. Perhaps the decision they must make would not be so hard after all.

The screen door groaned as Jack opened it and Merideth turned.

"Here's my husband now. Jack—this is Angela Hanscomb—"

Jack nodded, found his hand gripped by something hard as a bird's claw and wondered what irony had given the woman that name. She was the one with the nasal voice, and her dessicated frame had probably been scrawny even before the War.

"And my friend, Helene Lockie—" said Angela, almost defiantly, it seemed to him.

The other woman, collapsed on the couch as if

she would never move again, offered Jack a damp hand. Her eyes were large and moist as well, fixing him with a liquid appeal like those of a doomed cow. The remnants of a billowing expanse of flesh sagged from her bones.

Not survival types, Jack thought grimly. He wondered how they had gotten this far. He met Merideth's warning gaze and stifled the words he had been going to say.

"Welcome to Phoenix Creek Ranch. I hope my wife has offered you some mint tea? I wish it could be coffee, but—" he shrugged and smiled inanely. Of course they would not expect anyone to have coffee now.

"The kettle's on the stove. It will be ready in five minutes or so." Merideth's look was quelling. Jack watched her moving efficiently about the kitchen area on the other side of the big room, leaned by an inadequate diet, but still seeming to vibrate with energy. Even her cropped hair curled in thick waves.

"Tea!" Helene sighed. "For the past few months even clean water has been a luxury! Oh, it's so beautiful here!"

Her voice shook. Those moist eyes were dissolving into tears. Jack's gaze shifted quickly toward the window to which she was pointing, where the layered hills lifted against the pale sky, still enfolding their mysteries. It had been a distraction, that window, when they first moved up here and he had set up his computer on the table there. The hills made you think of Ents, and Robin Hood reveling underneath the trees. But the computer was silent now—just as well, for it had been awhile since he could look out that window without wondering what new carcasses were mouldering beneath the trees, as radiation took its toll of wild things whom no instinct had told to hide from wind and sun.

To Pan! he thought, *Great Pan, great Pan is dead...*
"Forgive us—"

Angela's nasal voice jerked him back to the problem at hand.

"We came here from the refugee camps in Santa Rosa. We used to live in Marin."

Jack stared, computing the odds against their having escaped blast and fire and fallout to reach Santa Rosa, much less to make it here, some sixty miles farther north. And they must have done it on foot. Local farmers had dynamited the big bluff above the Russian River near Cloverdale. Even if Angela and Helene had found fuel, no wheeled vehicle could travel up Highway 101 now.

The back door banged and Luthien came in, a leggy ten-year-old with tangled brown hair. Her arms were full of soap-root, good eating once the saponin was soaked out, as well as being the closest thing to soap they had.

"The stream's down another four inches—is it time to put down the door in the dam? Oh—" She saw the two women and stopped.

"Hello, Lutie—these are Angela and Helene, our guests—" said Merideth. The kettle began to shrill. She poured the tea and set cups on the table. Jack could smell the bracing astringence of mint in the steam.

"Oh ..." said Luthien on a different note. "I'm glad to meet you." She reddened as they stared at her and hurried to lay the plants on the wooden drainboard.

"She's so healthy ... so *alive* ..." Helene said softly. Angela patted her briskly on the shoulder and handed her the cup of tea.

"The stream, Uncle Jack—" repeated Luthien. "Are you going to dam it now?"

He smiled, remembering. Last year, they had made a swimming hole. Then he shook his head. "No honey—they'll need the water downstream, and we're still getting enough from the tank at the spring."

There were two families farther down the canyon whose electrically pumped wells were useless now. The Reynolds had a billy-goat whose services were essential if they wanted more milk from their own Alpine does. The Bellinis were trying to convert their wine-making apparatus so that they could use the grapes in their famous vineyard for fuel. It would be short-sighted as well as unfriendly to scant them on water now.

"Oh!" Luthien's face sharpened with something between excitement and fear. "I meant to tell you—wild dogs got two of the Reynolds' goats last night!"

"Damn!" exclaimed Merideth. She looked at Jack. "We'll have to go after the pack now."

He nodded, avoiding the pity in her gaze. She knew he loved dogs. "I'll go down there tomorrow and talk to them."

The tenuous network of cooperation that had once become tangible at Phoenix Creek only during emergencies was solidifying into a permanent alliance. But everyone had to be able to do his or her share. He looked covertly at the two women on the couch. They were past childbearing and they did not look very strong. What skills could they offer such a community, and if they had none where could they go?

Luthien's mother came in, rubbing at the red mark left by her sunhat, a sturdy woman with the weathered, ageless good looks that would last through her sixties, and marks of good humor about the mouth and eyes that even the past months had not been able to wipe away.

"I wanted to clean up a little before I came in—" she said in half-apology. "I'm Alice Rossner." Introductions were made. Alice poured herself some tea and eased down onto the hassock.

"How many of you are there up here?" Angela asked brusquely.

Jack suppressed a twinge of pity. Better they should know how things stood now.

"My husband and I live with our son in the house here," answered Merideth, "and Alice and Luthien have the trailer. Her family and ours went in together on this parcel when the ranch was put up for sale. We share the spring with two young men who have a cabin beyond those trees—" She pointed up the hillside.

"And Sarah!" said Luthien too brightly, waiting for the reaction.

"Luthien!" said her mother reprovingly.

"Oh what the hell does it matter now?" Jack stuck his hands in the pockets of his jeans and spoke half over his shoulder, looking out the window once more. "Sarah is a black teen-ager the boys picked up, half starved and wandering, when they went south scavenging. She ran away from the shelter because she got gang-raped. She's pregnant now. But lest you imagine that her morals are being abused further at the cabin you should understand that not only is Joel black, but he and Brian are gay!"

There was a silence. If Angela had been about to comment, her lips were tightly shut now. Helene looked as if she were going to cry again.

"Besides them I guess Ron Alcosta's the other member of our little community, though he has his own spring," Jack went on more gently. "He lives alone on the cliffside just over the hill. That's about all the land here can support right now."

"I was wondering . . ." Alice lifted her head and Jack tensed, knowing what she was going to ask. "If you were in a shelter in Santa Rosa, you might have met a man named Arnold Rossner there. My husband—" she added unnecessarily. As Helene began to shake her head Alice went on. "He was in

San Francisco, you see. We lived there, but we came up here for weekends and school vacations—whenever we could get away. Arnold had to stay for a meeting that day. He called to say he was heading north when the first warnings came over the radio, so I wondered . . ." She blinked once or twice and her voice tightened, but she did not cry.

I wonder if any of us have tears left? thought Jack angrily. Would it have been easier for Alice to know that her husband had died in the brief incandescence that ended San Francisco than to keep hoping, and fearing, that he had been caught somewhere in the countryside on his way here when the fallout came?

"No—" said Angela with more gentleness than Jack would have expected. Now, the sun was sending long shafts of gold through the trees. It would be dusk soon, and then the friendly darkness would come.

"The shelters were so big," Angela went on, "and they kept the single women and men housed separately. He could have been there, but there was no way that we would know."

"Thank you," Alice said quietly. "I just wondered, you see, if someone had told you about us here. It's a hard road to find or to get up without wheels."

Helene lowered her eyes and her flabby hands twisted anxiously. "It was my Guidance," she whispered. "I saw the road and the house on the breast of the hill. I knew that you would be waiting here if we could only keep on."

Jack and Merideth exchanged looks above her bent head. *We'll have to let them stay a few nights to get their strength back*, he thought. *But not for long. We have enough to cope with without Spirit Guidance and fairies behind every tree!*

"But what an awful chance to take! Wouldn't you have been better off safe where you were?" Alice exclaimed.

Angela sat up straighter, two spots of color burning in her sallow cheeks. "I've known Helene for ten years," she said, "and I've had proof that the messages that come to her are true. They told her that the bombs were coming, and we got away!"

"But why leave the shelter?" echoed Merideth.

"We had to go," Angela flushed again. "They were calling Helene a witch. We had to go."

"Hey Jack, you think that ol' lady Helene is really a witch?" In the shade underneath the oaks Joel's grin was startling against his dark skin. Jack eyed him carefully and decided that he was joking. For a moment the trail was too steep to leave him breath for an answer, then he laughed.

"She's just a a silly old woman. That mystical stuff's probably the only way she ever got any attention. You can imagine what it must have been like in the shelter, with all those women cooped up like broody hens. Anybody different would get pecked to death."

"Yeah—that's sorta what those folks over at Holygrove told me once. They do some kind of nature religion and they moved up here so they wouldn't get bothered. Anyway, I kinda like that Helene, even if she is strange," Joel went on. "She's been real good to Sarah—"

They came out of the oak copse and Jack tipped forward his hat against the sun, grimacing as he remembered why they were here. He'd been so hung up figuring out how to handle the two women he hadn't done anything about the dogs until three days later when they attacked Sarah. The girl had gotten off with a nasty leg wound, but she was terrified and spotting blood, though her baby was no way near due, and somehow Helene was the only one who could calm her.

But Sarah would get over it, and when they

were done with the dog pack he would tell Helene and Angela it was time to move on.

"I'm glad we gonna get those dogs—" Joel's words brought Jack abruptly back to what they faced now. He shivered, remembering the time he had almost been caught by the wild dogs, and the peculiar whining snarl the pack made when it was after something that could not get away.

"Bad enough when they was just hittin' stock," Joel went on. "You think Ron knows what he's doin'?"

"He'd better," said Jack. "He's the only one of us with combat experience. His plan sounded okay to me." Ron Alcosta had retreated to his mountain-top after a tour as a military advisor in Central America. He never talked about what he had done there, but everyone knew he was the best man they had with weapons, and the only one who knew how to fight what was really a war.

"Yeah, well, Brian thinks he's okay. They got friendly when they was buildin' the crossbow. I guess he knows Ron as well as anybody—I was kinda jealous for a little while." Joel grinned again. "That Ron, he's got a hot ass, but he's not interested. Not in men, not in women—not in nothing, except maybe killing, and he sure got a good excuse for it now!"

Jack hefted the crossbow he was carrying, wondering if he had practiced enough with it, wondering if it would really stop a charging dog as well as a gun. At least you didn't waste ammunition learning to shoot the thing. There was a guy down in the valley who was working on a way to make gunpowder, but until he succeeded they would have to dole out the ammunition carefully.

They had four guns among them—Ron's Ruger Mini 14 was the most sophisticated, but Mr. Reynolds had a good 30–30 repeater, a Winchester. Merideth was carrying the .22 the Galens kept at the house, since Jack had been working with the crossbow. Brian had a crossbow too, while Joel got the 12 gauge shotgun that was all the boys had. The Reynolds' oldest daughter Jean was a good shot with the 9 mm automatic pistol she wore, but Ron had made her a spear to carry as well.

He wondered how Jean felt, going out to avenge another girl who was her own age but whose experiences put her in a different world. He had watched the two girls at times when everyone on the Creek got together, eyeing each other like strange cats who did not quite know how to make friends.

And now they had crossed the first ridge. For a moment Jack glimpsed the ranges falling away to the east toward the interior, where smoke and debris from the burning of the great cities had left a permanent pall of smoke in the air. The War had not achieved the magnitude of the old 'worst case' scenarios—an exchange of a mere 5,000 MT, they said. But ten thousand explosions kicked up a lot of dust.

Once a week Brian used some of the Bellini's alcohol to power up the generator and turn on the radio—they could get the government station at Santa Rosa, and sometimes the new capital, whose location was still kept secret though neither side was capable of hostilities any more. Even the determined cheerfulness of the announcers had not been able to obscure the implications of sudden storms and cold for those living in the interior.

Perhaps it was not the Fimbulwinter of the Norse Sagas, but Jack wondered if it was crueler to let people live to struggle on. Here on the coast they escaped the worst of it, for the sea wind blew the clouds away. But it had been a cool summer, and who knew what it would be like by next year? If they were lucky, enough particles would have set-

tled for the world to return to normal once more.
Lucky!

Jack stopped abruptly, fighting the downward
spiral of thought that had trapped him too many
times before. Death had a thousand faces, but for
each man he wore but one, and the one Jack must
face now was a pack of dogs who came as close to
the wolf Fenris as anything Jack ever wanted to
see.

He saw that the others were standing still as
well, and halfway down the hill Ron stood with
his hand raised. They waited while he made his
way back up to them and motioned them to the
shade of a spreading madrone tree. Ron rested his
rifle easily on one shoulder, his tawny hair and
beard bushing out from beneath the tattered brim
of his hat. His old army jacket blended into the
dull green of the trees.

"They've laired down there—" Ron pointed to
the runs worn into the brown grass that led into a
little hollow furred over with scrub oak and
chaparral.

"How many, Ron?" asked Merideth, frowning.

"A dozen, pretty near, and we want to get them
all. If any escape, they can hitch up with some
others and start it all over again. You got to
understand—these aren't house pets anymore.
They're strays who made it north from Marin and
Sonoma, maybe some of them abandoned by people in cars or thrown out when they got to the
camps. They've teamed up with some from the old
packs that know the country, and they're all wild
dogs now. But worse, 'cause a wild animal unless
it's sick generally doesn't want to mess with man.
These don't care—they'll go for anything they can
sink a tooth into, so don't get to pitying them."

Jack shuddered. He had always owned dogs,
growing up, but Merideth was allergic and they
had none at the ranch now. Still, he remembered

the comfort of a warm weight on your feet or a
cold nose poking into your hand, and his gut
cramped at the thought of what these dogs that
somebody had once loved had become. Then he
thought of the human beings who had survived
around the edges of the burned cities. What had
they become? But Ron was talking again; Jack
shut the thought away.

"Now look, everybody, I want you to go real
quiet and slow. I got positions picked out for all of
you—give you a little protection when Jean and I
drive them out. Jack—I want you down on that
outcrop of stone. You'll have a good level space to
stand and aim the crossbow there. Joel, you and
Brian head over to those trees—" Ron's flat voice
continued with the directions. Then, very cautiously,
they crept down to the spots he had given them.

Calm down, Jack told himself. *Ron's scarcely had
the time to get around the hollow, much less get set
to flush the dogs!* He pulled a little dry grass and
wadded it into a pad beneath his knee. He could
feel his heart pounding; a faint tremor ran along
the stock of the bow. He had wound the string as
soon as he reached his position—he and the bow
were both strung to the breaking point now.

A butterfly wavered past him and he scarcely
noticed the gorgeous purples and reds of a pattern
the world had never known before, or wondered
what it could mean. *Relax*—said his conscious mind,
but some inner voice continued its babbling. *What
if I miss? My hands are sweating. I'll slip! What if a
dog gets through to me? Ron says they're probably
rabid, and there are no rabies shots now. What if—*

And then the sharp thump of Ron's Mini shattered the air, the deep crack of Jean's pistol echoing it, and the world erupted in a din of snarling
as the dogs came. For a moment Jack had only a
confused impression of lean bodies—tawny, brindle,
dark and grey, and the scattered thunder as the

others began to fire. Fear vised Jack for one inter-
minable moment, then the adrenaline rush shocked
through him and he was sighting, releasing, snatch-
ing up another bolt from the rock and winding
back the bow to fire again.

Another dog went down, and he struggled to
reload as a third beast charged him. The bolt
slipped, he fumbled it back into position, swung
up the crossbow and shot point-blank into the
animal's chest. It crashed heavily almost on top of
him, the strong jaws snapping furiously. Jack kicked
out, felt the drag as teeth met in his boot heel.
Then the creature convulsed a last time and
collapsed.

Jack scarcely noticed. His blood burned; he
loaded and shot again as fast as he could, launching each bolt as if every dog wore the face of one of
his fears.

And then there were no more crazed eyes or
snapping jaws, only scattered lumps of fur that
stirred and whimpered or lay eternally still.

Jack sat down abruptly. He saw Brian clamber
unsteadily down from his tree, bend to look at one
animal, then turn quickly away. For a moment the
harsh scrape of his retching was the only sound.
Then Ron and Jean made their way around the lip
of the hollow, and the girl went to her father and
stood there, shivering, while Ron began to methodi-
cally cut the throats of those dogs that still lived.

After a little, Jack got to his feet and forced
himself to look at what they had done. The animal
whose teeth had locked in his boot had relaxed in
death and rolled away. It was some kind of a
shepherd, he thought—it was hard to tell, for much
of the fur had fallen away. Radiation poisoning, no
doubt, from eating the hides and innards of sick
animals where the particles clung. It was astonish-
ing that the dog had lived so long. The bare hide
revealed only too clearly the cracked and festering

sores and the ticks that had been draining the
dog's life away. Its ears were a mass of chiggers.
Jack wondered how it could hear. He wondered
how it had kept going, much less gone on with a
bolt through its chest to chew his boot half away.

And what does that tell you about survival? he
asked himself as he turned away. *Aren't we just the
same, busting our hearts to provide for the future
when our world is gone? We've destroyed the dogs—is
that a victory?*

Then he felt someone near him and looked up
into Merideth's white face. He held out his arms
and she came into them, but he did not know which
of them was doing the comforting.

The put on their gloves again to drag the corpses
of the dogs back into the hollow that had been
their home and piled brush over them with rocks
to weight it down. Perhaps with time the organ-
isms that still lived in the soil would consume
them, and a cleaner wind and rain would scatter
the remains.

"Come on," said Merideth when they had finished.
"We have a bottle of Bellini wine at the house, and
I think after this we deserve a medicinal glass or
two."

The first person Jack saw as the hunting party
trudged up the road was Luthien, curled into her
favorite spot in the oak tree. Kit was sitting on an
upthrust root, practicing hitting a mark with stones.
The children heard them and looked up, and he
saw his son's face set in a scared frown and
Luthien's face grimed and streaked with tears.

"Lutie! What's the matter?" Merideth ran forward as the girl slid out of the tree and caught her
in her arms. "Is it your mother—Lutie—"

"No! No!" Luthien was sobbing again. "It's Sarah,
she's sick—she was bleeding and they made me

and Kit go outside. What is it? Is she going to die?''

"Oh honey, honey—" Merideth's eyes met Jack's in appeal. Kit was already leaning against him; he reached out and eased Luthien from Merideth's embrace to his. Once she would have started telling the girl it was all going to be okay, but not now. They would be lucky not to lose both mother and baby with no doctor or hospital care.

"I'd better go in and help them, Lutie—you'll be all right with Uncle Jack now. Okay?" The only answer was a long, shuddering sob, then silence as Merideth pulled free and hurried into the house.

The Reynolds were asking if there was anything they could do. Jack shrugged and shook his head.

"Well, we'll just be going then—" Mr. Reynolds murmured apologetically. "They'll be worrying about us at home. But we'll be praying for that poor child, and if there's any way we can help, you let us know!" He lifted his hand in a brief wave, then he and Jean turned to begin the two-mile hike that would take them home.

Yes, you pray . . . thought Jack, with a pang of mixed scorn and envy for those who could still believe in a God made in the image of man. *And what do I believe*? Something in him strained for vision, as the fools who had been flash-blinded by looking at the detonations struggled to see.

Ron had disappeared as they neared the house, but Joel and Brian were still standing in the yard. Brian had his arm around his lover's shoulders; he was talking, low-voiced, freckled face creased anxiously. Joel stood rigid. Jack could see the white around his eyes.

"No man, you can't tell me it gonna be okay! She's losing the baby, ain't she? Man, you know, she got like a sister to me, and the baby—well we were like a family, weren't we? We was gonna be like fathers to that kid, two daddies to take care of it in this crapped-out world!"

Jack held Kit and Lutie more tightly as Joel's words tore at his own never-healing fear. He had to take care of the children—if he couldn't do that, he wasn't a father—he wasn't a man! He should have realized that Joel and Brian would feel that way too. . . .

They heard the creak of the screen door and stiffened. Alice came out, wiping her hands on the towel tied around her waist. There were shadows beneath her eyes. Jack saw a smear of blood on the towel.

Alice took a deep breath of the cooling air. "Well, we lost the baby, but Angela was trained as a nurse, thank God, and we've stopped the bleeding. I think Sarah will do all right now."

Joel glared at her. "Is that all you gonna say? The baby—that was a human life there—another human life that's gone."

Alice's face hardened and she met his stare. "Joel, I don't think it would have lived even if she'd carried it to term. Maybe it was all she went through or maybe it was radiation that did it—" she stopped a moment. "It was a life, maybe, but I don't know if you'd call it human—" She spoke harshly, but her eyes were dilated with pain. "Believe me, it was better this way!"

Joel gasped and Jack saw him go gray beneath the dark skin. "No . . ." he said softly, and then "No!" again in the beginning of a wail. "God you hear me? You stop this now! You hear me?" He shook his fist at the sky; his cheeks were shiny with tears. "Why'd you do this, God—You tell me, *why?*"

"Joel, come on now—there's nothing we can do here—come on home . . ." Brian's voice cracked. He put his arms around Joel and this time the other man did not resist him. But as they stumbled up the path to their cabin, Jack could still hear Joel echoing Job's unanswered cry which was also his own—"Why, Lord, why?"

"I know an old lady who swallowed a fly—I don't know why she swallowed a fly, perhaps she'll die!

"I know an old lady who swallowed an icicle—it froze her insides and she fell off her bicycle—"

The children's giggles became laughter as Joel invented new misadventures for the old lady. His guitar accompaniment was precise and cheerful, displaying the expertise that had made Joel a favorite at taverns all around Clear Lake.

Jack found himself relaxing, almost for the first time since Sarah's miscarriage. It had been a week, and now they were celebrating her recovery. Intellectually, they had all known that abortions and birth defects were to be expected. But Jack had seen the thing that came out of Sarah's immature womb, and the reality was harder to rationalize away. He told himself that once the worst of the radiation had decayed and the weather stabilized, healthy children would be born. But he remembered the rotting vegetables in the garden and wondered.

"I don't know why she swallowed the fly—perhaps she'll die!"

It was only on the punchline that Joel's voice faltered, but the children were singing so loud you hardly noticed. His eyes met Jack's and slid away. Old songs, old stories—so many things from Before were booby-trapped now.

And yet the children were laughing. Kit's freckles stood out against his pale face and Lutie's curls bounced as she swayed. They had gathered miner's lettuce and lambs-quarter and wild onions for a salad, and Alice and Merideth had made a cobbler with a can of peaches and some of the carefully hoarded flour. There was the meat of a pig that

had ventured too close to the garden. It was enough
to make a feast, especially when they had Joel's
music.

Angela was helping with the dinner, but Helene
crouched in the corner near the fireplace as if she
hoped no one would notice her. He had to admit
she looked better than she had when she arrived—
she was even managing to put back some of the
weight she had lost. But her brown eyes still gazed
out at the world in dumb apology. Damn the
woman! Was she trying to make him feel guilty, or
did his discomfort come from the feeling that perhaps all of them should apologize for having
survived? The tortoise-shell cat was curled in her
lap, purring. Jack hoped it was some comfort.

"All right everybody—soup's on!" announced
Alice. The room was too small for all of them to sit
at one table. Jack took the plate she handed him
and went back to his seat against the throw pil-
lows on the mattress that served as a couch, leaning against the madras-covered pine boards of the
wall.

The food was good. Merideth had not lost her
touch with spices, even though the peppercorns
must be used sparingly until they could dry more
from the valley's pepper trees. But she was making
progress with wild herbs, and somebody on the
coast had begun to extract salt from the sea and
trade it inland. As the hot food warmed his stomach,
the room itself seemed to brighten. The California
Indians had never starved, and if they learned to
use the resources of the land and barter their
specialties, neither would they. It might even be a
good sort of world. . . .

And then across the room he saw Sarah's thin
face, and remembered the unripened fruit in the
garden, distorted as the fruit of her womb. What
was the point of survival if they were the last?

And Sarah was talking to Merideth and Angela

and smiling. Angela's lips turned up primly and the other two laughed. He wondered what she had said—she had an unsuspected dry humor that had once or twice caught him on the raw. He wondered how the women could laugh. They were the lifebearers. Even better than he did, they *knew* the horror of what had happened to the world.

Joel reached over and offered him the clay pipe. Jack took it, drew in a deep lungful of the sweet smoke, and handed it back again. These days, pot was one of the most useful crops in the area, especially since before the War it had usually been grown in protected places or indoors. When they ran out of anesthetics, at least they had one anodyne, as well as the raw materials for rope and sacking in the long-fibered stems.

Jack shook his head. This wasn't the time to think of everything in terms of its usefulness. It should be enough to pass the pipe back and forth and let the smoke's sweet veil insulate him from the world. They finished that pipe and filled another, and when that one was done Jack felt too mellow to need more. Joel picked up his guitar again and began to play softly. Fragments of melody emerged, were modulated, and disappeared again into the opalescent bath of sound in gentle evocation of a world that was gone.

After a while the air of the room began to seem too close—a reaction, perhaps to those weeks when they had been cooped up inside. Jack got to his feet and wandered out onto the porch. His body was still relaxed from the pipe, but his skin had become acutely sensitive, and the coolness of the night air was like a caress.

Unguided, his feet found the path up through the pasture. He moved slowly, each deep breath bringing its own inebriation of scent the darkness had set free. The full moon was shining serenely, its pearly surface unmarred by the violence that had racked its greater sister below. Suddenly Jack pulled off his shirt and lifted his arms, turning, bathing himself in that pure light.

There was music near him—for a time it seemed one with the music of Joel's guitar, as if the night were singing to itself and he were part of the song. Then Jack realized that the sound was coming from the garden.

He was still too stoned to be worried, but he moved toward it, trailing his shirt through the damp grass. The song ceased as he came closer, but through the fence he could see something in the midst of the tomato plants, shapeless and still as stone. Wood creaked as he leaned on the fence. The shape moved and he saw a face white in the moonlight and the glitter of dark eyes.

Helene . . . A sharp comment came to mind, but the night was too peaceful. "Singing to the moon?" he asked instead.

"Oh—I guess so." Helene laughed softly. "There's something healing in the rays of the moon. The plants feel it too. I always used to open the curtains so that the moonlight could reach my houseplants. Maybe it can get through easier now. I feel something, like a power trying to find words. The moon is so beautiful!" She tipped back her head and closed her eyes so that her round face mirrored the moon in the sky.

Something in him realized that this was the first friendly conversation he had ever had with her, and wondered. But it didn't matter now. Jack followed the direction of her gaze.

"It doesn't look changed at all. I wonder what the folks at Jefferson Base think, looking down? Are they glad to be safe or sorry they're cut off from us all?"

"They have their shops and their gardens, and I read that the asteroids have all those minerals they could use," Helene answered him. "I think they'll find a way to survive . . ."

"Maybe they'll build the ships we were too cheap to fund and go on—" Jack said then. "The dangers they'd face are no worse than here. Maybe they'll build floating worlds where they can live forever, and travel until they find a new earth and a new sun . . ."

For a long time they stayed silent, watching the Queen of the Night sail slowly across the sky. The black flanks of the hills lay stretched in sleep; in the garden, moonlight enchanted the leaves. The prayer Jack had not been able to make before slid easily away and was received by the glowing air.

After awhile he began to feel cold and put on his shirt again. Down in the house Merideth must be in bed by now, waiting for him.

He stepped away from the fence and started to wave goodnight to Helene, but she did not move. Whether she were entranced or asleep, he did not want to disturb her. Half-way down the hill he looked back and saw her still there, an anonymous dark shape in the moonlight, as if the earth itself had found a voice to speak to him.

It was an odd fancy, but he was almost to the house now. He thought of Merideth in the big double bed in the loft, and remembered how they had made love the whole night through when they first moved up here. His body quickened with a warmth he had not felt for a long time and he hurried inside.

Merideth stirred drowsily as Jack stripped off his clothes and crawled into the bed beside her.

"Oh, you're all cold!" She opened her eyes and he grinned.

"I was outside, looking at the moon. Need a warm wife to get my circulation going again—" He pulled her close so that her head nestled in the hollow between his shoulder and his chin. He could feel the softness of her breasts against his chest and he moved his hand down her back, cupping her firm buttocks and drawing her against him. She shivered for a few moments, but did not pull away. Then her warmth took the edge off his chill and she relaxed against him.

"That was a good dinner . . ." he whispered into the crisp waves of her hair. "But I'm still hungry."

"Mmnn?"

He squeezed her buttock, then slipped his hand across the top of her thigh and down, probing for the softness there. He began to kiss her neck, her ear. She rolled her head away and he found her lips.

"Hmmm?" he echoed after a little while. He was hard already. He listened to her quick breathing in the darkness and bent his head to kiss her again.

"No." Merideth pulled away. Not understanding, he bent farther and found her breast, tonguing her nipple until it grew as hard and sensitive as his penis was now.

"Oh—" she gasped, "Oh Jack, we can't. It's my fertile time and I don't dare—not yet—Jack, please!"

She pushed at him and shocked, he let her go. His entire body was throbbing, clamoring to release into her softness all his passion and fear and to create something new! She was wet; he knew that she wanted him—he reached for her again.

"Jack, it's too soon! We don't know what's still in the air and the soil. If I got pregnant now we don't know what it would do. My God, Jack—" she added brutally, "do you want me to have a monster like Sarah's?"

Jack rolled away from her, breathing hard. She had been laughing with the other women at dinner. How could they laugh if they were really living with this fear? He didn't understand.

"Jack—oh damn! We talked about this before. In a few days it'll be okay, and God knows how much

I want you!" Merideth was crying. "Look, honey, let me get you off at least—" Her hand brushed down his belly, reaching for his penis.

But the passion had already left him, more quickly than it had grown. "Never mind." He turned onto his side with his back to her and tried to calm his breathing.

After awhile he heard small sounds that told him that Merideth was trying to relieve her own tensions as she had offered to do for him and he smiled sourly. She had said she wanted him, but she didn't understand that he had been after something more than sexual release. For a moment he had felt the power to make something beautiful in the midst of this hell they were living through. But the opportunity was gone.

Jack dreamed that he went up the hill to work in the garden, and under the leaves of the cabbages something began to move. He tore open one of the largest with a pitchfork. A round white face was looking up at him with an infant's body curled beneath it.

"Hello, father—" the thing said. It had a high, fluting voice. The other cabbages stirred, more faces appeared, echoing the greeting.

"You are their father and I am their mother—" said Helene, who had suddenly emerged from the midst of them. Jack began to shake his head.

"We are the new generation of life on the earth—" sang the infants.

"No!" Jack cried, "oh no!" and fled into the darkness of sleep once more.

"No, Kit—dividing ten sixteenths by four is not the same as multiplying it, even though you multiply in both operations. You have to turn the four upside down, see—and—"

"Aw Dad, why do we have to learn this stuff

anyway? There's no colleges left to go to, and no money to count anymore!" Kit wailed.

Jack looked at his son in frustration, then at Luthien and the two younger Reynolds children, wondering if any of them understood. The parents had agreed that they should give the children some kind of schooling, and Jack was the only one with a graduate degree. He was beginning to think that somebody who had just gotten out of high school could have done a better job. Someone young enough to at least remember what the problems were.

The kids were waiting for him. Jack cleared his throat and searched for words.

"You don't just use arithmetic for counting money. Suppose we want to build another house—"

"Like for Angela and Helene?" asked Luthien eagerly.

Jack grimaced. He had brought the children outdoors into the shade of the big walnut tree on the hill where they could get a bit of breeze. He had forgotten that you could see right over the fence into the garden where Alice and Helene were working, sunhats bobbing as they moved. Did *everyone* assume that the women would be staying here?

"Angela and Helene will need a house to live in wherever they go," he answered neutrally. "Say they were down in the Valley and they wanted to build a wall. The boards should be all the same height, but if they measured by laying them side by side they'd get tired pretty fast. And they'd have to know how many they were going to need. If they measured how wide the boards were and divided the length of the wall they were building by that number, they would know exactly how many boards they would have to have." He frowned at them all. "Do you understand?"

"The Indians didn't do math and they got along all right—" Kit said, still rebellious.

"We aren't Indians!" Jack exploded.

"If we were Indians, Kit, we wouldn't have had the War . . ." Luthien added patiently.

Jack stared at them. The parents had agreed that he should just teach the basics for now. Why burden the children with the history of a world that was gone? But maybe they had been wrong, Jack thought suddenly. Maybe if the kids learned what had happened in the past they wouldn't make the same mistakes again.

If there is any 'again' . . . he thought grimly. *If enough of us survive to breed future generations who will need to know . . .* The night of the full moon he had found the capacity to hope again—for an hour or two—but the memory of it was poisoned now by Merideth's rejection. And yesterday Joel and Ron and Brian had headed south to see if they could find some new parts for the generator, and who could say if they would make it back again?

The children were whispering. Jack coughed and stared them down.

"Okay, everybody, pick up your slates. I want you to do the next five exercises here—can you all see the book? All right. You get busy now, and I'll check your work when you're done. . . ."

He leaned back against the trunk of the tree, shifting position until he was comfortable. The play of sun and shadow through the leaves was hypnotic. Eyes closed, he could hear the scratching of stone markers on slate and the murmur of women's voices from the garden.

"You should thin the mulch on the string beans— there's not enough drainage in that corner—" Helene's voice had that note of apology that always annoyed him, but Alice didn't seem to mind.

"Do you think that's the problem? I wondered if they were getting too much sun."

"Well, that's what he said—" Helene stopped abruptly. "Maybe you could try it with just half the vines and see . . ." she corrected herself.

There was a short silence. Then Alice cleared her throat. "Helene—what were you going to say? I know you used to be a whizz with houseplants, but this is a vegetable garden on a mountainside. *Who* said the mulch should be thinned?"

Who indeed? Jack grimaced silently. Maybe Alice was finally realizing what a weirdo this woman was.

"The plants—the Spirit of the bean plants—" Helene answered almost too softly to hear. Then she rushed on. "Alice, I don't really know what it is—that's just how I think of it. It's like a bright light shining, and the words come to me."

Now that she had started, the words cascaded out. *Oh brother!* thought Jack, listening. *Carrots with wings and halos—this is all we need!*

"When I sit down and get quiet the visions come, and there's Something behind them—it *wants* to communicate, and it's so *happy* when I listen!" said Helene breathlessly. "I used to sing to my plants, you know, Before, and I knew they were listening. But this is *much* stronger. The plant spirits are supposed to be *joyful*, but they were terrified by the War. They're supposed to be like blueprints, so everything will grow right, but it's all *changing*, and they don't know what to do!"

"And they want *us* to help them?" Alice laughed painfully. Jack could not tell whether she believed Helene. "We're the ones who did it to them!"

And to ourselves, Jack thought bitterly. The woman was talking nonsense, of course, but something in him deeply wished it were true.

"They need us to love them . . ." said Helene very quietly.

The sharp thwap of a rifle shot tore the air, then another, then silence that rang in Jack's ears. Heart lurching, he jumped to his feet. Slates clattered as the children followed him. Merideth! That was her .22—she had taken it with her that morning when she herded their goats down to the good grass by the stream.

He began to run.

Halfway down the trail to the creek he saw Merideth coming toward him, trailing the gun. Her face was smeared with tears.

"Merideth! I heard the shots. Are you all right? What was it? Oh, darling—" He reached her and she fell against him, shaking with sobs. He held her tightly, patting her back with the automatic rhythm he had learned when Kit was teething years ago.

"Merideth, sweetheart, are you hurt?" he asked as she quieted. "Was it a boar or a dog?"

"Oh Jack," her upturned face twisted, "it was a man! He was filthy—at first I didn't even know what he was. Then he grabbed Buttercup and started to drag her away. I shouted at him and he made a sound just like those dogs, Jack—just like the wild dogs! And I shot once to scare him off and he let go of the goat and came for me and then I shot *him!*" The words came in a rush and she was clutching Jack's shirt and crying. "I didn't mean to—I didn't, Jack, but I was so scared!"

Jack held her to him, rocking her, murmuring soft reassuring phrases that had no meaning anymore.

Merideth's anguish dissolved the barricades Jack had built around his own soul. *You! Help her—help us all!* cried that part of him that logic did not rule. *Even if we don't deserve it—oh God, we don't deserve it! We do it to ourselves!*

"How could they do it?" Joel turned to each of them, but no one could answer him. "How could people let it happen? How?" He collapsed onto the

bench beside the fireplace and covered his face
with his hands. He and Ron and Brian had gone
farther south than anyone from the Valley had
been since the War. Sarah eased down and put her
thin arms around him, but he stayed rigid.

Jack turned to the other two men. "What happened to him?"

"I don't know. We had to go all the way to San
Rafael—" Ron answered slowly. "We got jumped
by one or two gangs along the way, but we handled that. Joel did his share, and it didn't seem to
bother him too much."

"They're releasing people from the shelter camps,"
Brian cut in. "They say it's because the country's
safer now, but I think they were having trouble
getting in supplies. People with homes in Santa
Rosa have been making them into little forts with
whatever they can find. The town's under martial
law, and everyone carries a weapon there now."

"Yeah—I was goin' to talk to you about that—"
said Ron. "We may be getting some strays. We
should think about some kind of defense—deadfalls
to block the road, maybe—and weapons training
for everyone here."

"And what about the Reynolds and the Bellinis?"
exclaimed Alice. "Are we just going to hole up and
let them be raped and murdered by whoever comes
along?"

"She's right," Jack nodded. "We have to work
together up here or none of us will survive." It
sounded sanctimonious, but he did not know what
to say. For a moment he had glimpsed something
he could not put into words.

"It'll be harder—the land widens out down there.
Maybe we could rig some kind of warning system—"
Ron began.

"God damn you!" Merideth exclaimed, "While
you were away I killed a man. I don't ever want to
do it again! What are you trying to turn us into—

one of your goddamned guerilla armies? Well I
won't! I'd rather let them kill me than live that
way!" She was weeping with pain and rage.

"You may just do that, lady," Ron answered
with a deadly quietness. "But are you going to make
that choice for *him?*" He pointed to Kit, who was
standing wide-eyed in the doorway. "Are you going
to just stand there and wring your hands when
they bash his head against the wall? Well, I'm not
going to stick around here to see. You can go to
hell your own way!" He turned abruptly and stalked
toward the door, brushing past Helene, who gasped
as if he had hit her and lurched out of his way.

Jack stared after him. What was happening? They
had been getting ready to celebrate a safe return,
and now it was all falling apart. His head pounded
and he shook it, trying to think.

"Why did you have to go and do that?" Brian
said slowly. "You know what Ron's like! He's a
pro—you shouldn't have insulted him. What *are*
we going to do when they come charging up the
road? Put up a 'No Trespassing' sign? And they're
gonna come, everybody—I saw them, I heard what
they were saying out there. Ron's the only one
here who knows fighting. You're crazy to let him
walk out this way!"

"Oh come on now, Brian—" Jack stepped between him and Merideth, whose face was redden-
ing dangerously. Alice shepherded the children
outside. Helene had backed all the way into the
corner by the stove and Angela was standing in
front of her protectively.

"Well, what are *you* doing to save us?" Brian
turned on him. "You stay at home safe when the
rest of us go out and risk our asses, and now that
your woman's having hysterics you want everybody to sugar-coat the world? You haven't been
there, you haven't seen what it's like Outside!"

Jack's fists clenched and he forced them open

again. He had to be calm, to stop this, but the blood was pounding in his head and the words burst free—

"I faced the dogs with the rest of you, and so did Merideth! It was a group decision for me to stay here this time—What do you want me to do, run down the hill right now and tell them all where to go? All right—" He reached for his hat.

"Jack, what are you doing?" screamed Merideth. "You're rattling your horns like a damned billy-goat because you think he insulted you? What the hell is that going to prove? You're as bad as they are—put that wretched hat down!" She grabbed his arm.

He turned on her, his anger finding a focus at last. "Well what does it matter what happens to me? You won't sleep with me—you're afraid to have children, and maybe you're right. But if there aren't going to be any new generations, then what does it matter if we kill or are killed now? If the plants die, if the children die, then what are we hanging on for anyway?" He shook off her grip and they stood glaring at each other, ignoring the others.

"There were bones . . ." Joel said suddenly. "Just bones. They musta hit the refineries in Richmond and the firestorm went straight across the Bay. There was a car—I guess they was headin' north when it happened and the car just turned into an oven. Two grown and a child and a baby barbe-cued like ribs before they could run. And the dog . . ." he was sobbing soundlessly, "and the god-damned family dog . . ."

Helene moaned and stumbled past Angela and out the door. *Let her go*, thought Jack, and the sooner she went for good the better it would be. But his eyes were still on Joel, who stood up stiffly, not even noticing that Sarah was crying and trying to hold onto him.

"Joel—" Brian spoke softly and stepped toward him, but Joel did not seem to see. Jack shivered. This was something worse than the fury that had shaken them all. But still he watched, as if something had frozen him there, and then suddenly Joel wrenched open the door of the pot-bellied stove and reached in.

Brian leaped for him, but Joel snatched out a log and swept it in a flaming arc before him. Jack caught the odor of scorching flesh, but Joel seemed to feel no pain. He jabbed at Brian with the brand.

"Don' you understand?" he said softly. "We all supposed to burn. I'll burn, and you'll burn and the whole world gonna burn up!" he giggled. "And then we all be pure! All go to God then, because we all gonna be burned clean!" He whirled, trailing fire in a bright circle around him, leaped, and touched the flame to the madras bedspread tacked to the wall.

Merideth grabbed a pillow and ducked past him, beating at the flames that flared across the thin cotton to attack the wall. Jack was starting after her when Joel's shirt caught fire.

Jack snatched at the blanket that covered the couch and leaped for Joel, trying to get it around him to smother the flames. Sarah had the tap on full blast and was splashing the wall; Brian tripped over her and they all went down, rolling Joel over and over in the blanket until the madness left him and he began to scream.

Jack smelled the stink of the burning on Merideth when they finally fell into bed. He supposed he must smell the same. But Angela had taken charge of Joel, and now he was settled as comfortably as possible on the couch with strips of Aloe Vera laid over his burns. They had been afraid he would go into shock, and the danger was not yet over, but there was nothing more they could do. Alice had put both children to bed in the trailer, while the adults took shifts watching by Joel. All of the adults except Helene . . .

She can rot out there in the garden, for all I care, Jack thought tiredly. *Maybe she'll do some good that way!* His muscles twitched with weariness and reaction. He was almost, he thought, too tired to sleep. And when sleep came at last, it was haunted by dreams.

He thought that he was digging graves in the garden when Kit whistled that someone was coming. Jack felt a great weariness. In a little while he would have the holes dug deep enough so that they could all fall into them and rest . . .

But the intruders were still coming—an army of worn and bitter people from the camps, men and women and children snarling like wild dogs, and followed by the animate seared bones of those who had died by fire.

Helene was leading them. He should have expected it—he had cast her out and now she was returning, her loose flesh quivering on her bones. Jack ran down the hill shouting at them to stop, to go away. He reached for his bow, but it was not there, and he remembered that they had thrown their weapons away.

The attacking rabble had rifles and guns and bows and garden tools honed into crude spears. Their chanting crashed against Jack's ears; he felt the vibration of their feet shaking the ground. They came on and he tried to grapple with them, but they pushed past him as if he had been invisible.

Up the hill and into the garden they rushed, with Helene leading them. When they got there she stopped and lifted her flabby arms. It was a curious, hieratic pose—Jack had seen it in some art book, in his other lifetime Before.

And then Helene brought down her hands, and her body solidified and darkened until she was

like a great image made of stone, and all of her
followers swung down their weapons and jammed
them into the freshly turned ground.

The earth quivered. Rifle stocks and spear hafts
trembled, bulged, and began to put out leaves and
branches that flamed with green. Green flared in
every direction, radiating from that still figure in
the garden toward the horizon, where it rose into
an inpenetrable hedge around the land.

And a gentle sun shone, for a dome of mist formed
from the breath of the new trees to screen its rays.
And Jack stood in the midst of the garden with his
wife and child. . . .

Jack woke to the warm security of Merideth's
arms wrapped around him. Her head was pillowed
on his chest so that his beard mingled with the
crisp waves of her hair. The square window beside
the bed was already glowing with the light of a
new day.

He lay very still, holding at bay the horde of
worries that would swarm into his consciousness
as soon as he admitted he was awake. Then Kit's
whistle tore the silence.

"Come on! Come to the garden! Come see!" The
boy's voice, rough as if he were already running,
trailed away.

Merideth jerked upright, staring, the chill air
pebbling her arms with gooseflesh. Jack rubbed
his eyes and met her gaze

"He doesn't *sound* as if anything is wrong . . ."
she said doubtfully.

Jack nodded, though he dared not believe her.
His stomach muscles were already tensed. What
was it now? He did not think he could bear any
more.

He found his voice. "We better go see . . ."

It was quicker to pull on their hooded ponchos
than to fumble with shirts and jeans. Naked under

their robes, they stumbled down the ladder from the loft.

Angela looked up from the couch where Joel lay sleeping. "Yes, he's alive—why do you think I'm still sitting here?" Seeing Merideth's face she relented a little and went on. "His pulse and breathing are both good. You two go find out what the problem is out *there!*" She pointed to the door.

Outside the sky was brightening, but the sun had not yet breasted the hills. The air was still crisp, and dew from the long grass washed their bare legs as they ran. Luthien was pulling her mother along ahead of them. Brian was almost there. Even Ron was coming down from his hill.

Puffing, Jack came to a stop by the open gate of the garden. Something was different there. No one spoke, but somewhere nearby a bird summoned the morning with a clear, piping call. Maybe that was it—so many of the daybirds had died . . . He tried to slow his breathing. Merideth was staring; his gaze followed hers.

He saw Helene sitting in the middle of the garden— *still* sitting, as if she had not moved since the night before. Like Buddha beneath his Bo Tree, she had refused to move until—until what? Jack blinked, realizing that he had been distracted.

But from what? His body signaled fear. He saw nothing threatening, yet he felt the pressure of strangeness all around him, as months ago he had sensed the deadly radiation sifting through the sky. But this was a different kind of fear. The light grew. It was only daylight, surely, but when had the light of dawn ever hurt his eyes?

But he had been distracted again! *Look at the garden*—he told himself. *If something has happened it's there*—

The garden . . . Well, what had he expected to see? The dark leaves of the sprawling vines of zucchini and crook-neck squash glistened with dew.

The slender bean poles were garlanded with the lighter green of runners with their velvet leaflets and bulging pods. The corn patch looked normal—silk tassels peeping out of the long swathed ears quivered in the early morning breeze, and the lacy tops of the carrots showed up nicely against the earth's deep brown.

But there was nothing wrong there . . .

Helene sat still, a melon clasped in her arms as if it had been a child. She was smiling.

Nothing wrong!

Jack's heart thudded irregularly. He took a breath, trying to remember how long it had been since he had worked in the garden. While the other men were away he had been doing much of their work, and perhaps he had avoided the garden because Helene was usually there. But even if the plants had been healthy already there was no way they could have grown so much since he had seen them last.

Merideth was kneeling beside one of the tomatoes, cupping a glowing fruit reverently in one hand.

"I read once about a place called Findhorn . . ." Alice spoke so softly she hardly disturbed the air. "They said the Spirits of Nature talked to the people there, and though their garden was planted on sand, everything grew and grew! I think Helene hears them too . . ."

Jack remembered that Helene had said something like this, last week, when—a memory of exasperation blurred his sight. Helene was just one of those hysterical women who used to keep Swamis in Cadillacs. Was he going to be taken in?

Or perhaps this was all part of his dream . . .

Jack blinked as the bright colors faded, and his eyes smarted with loss. His vision was filled by a stray memory of a hillside of manzanita he had seen after a fire, the little leathery leaves gone and the tough shrubby branches seared and black, like the bodies Joel had seen in that car. And yet, looking closer, Jack had seen those scorched branches budding new shoots of bright green.

Joel's fire burned us all—Jack thought then, *but has he killed or cleansed?* His breath caught and he could not feel his heartbeat. For a moment there was no Time. *"Choose—"* the word distilled in his consciousness and he did not know where they came from. *"Choose what you will see!"*

Jack rubbed at his eyes, but it was all a blur, and he was shaking too badly to stand. *I can't see—I don't know what's true*—he answered. *You! Help me!* He did not know if it was weakness or something else that forced him to his knees. He groped for support and felt his hands plunging deep into the soil, felt moist-smooth-gritty-rich-*life* speak through his naked skin and to his soul.

Slowly he opened his eyes. At eyelevel around him he saw the garden, and every leaf was outlined in light. Brightness flickered in a network of radiance that patterned each plant—each being— for looking up he perceived the bright shadow of each of the other humans there. Perhaps it was the dawn, said his retreating scepticism, but he had never seen such a light in the rising sun.

Perhaps it was all a snare and a delusion. He would never have proof that the intellect could understand. But his hands had their own knowledge; as he had known Merideth, their first time together; as his touch had recognized the flesh of their newborn son. His fingers closed in the earth that he had hated, then relaxed, caressing, surrendering.

Maybe the tortured world outside these hills would one day overwhelm them, but if the life he felt in this garden could become a fertile seed underneath the ashes of the world, then there was hope. Surely it would be better to live with hope's illusion than to starve the spirit waiting for certainty.

And Helene? came a last objection. *Are you going to learn to love her, too?*

Jack made himself look at the woman who sat in the center of the garden. He saw the soft and sloppy body that had disgusted him. And he saw a rooted strength that made him afraid. He understood now how she had survived and why they needed her. Helene's words were clumsy, but she *listened* . . .

And you, his thoughts went on, *you can talk the sun down, but what do you know?*

Merideth touched his shoulder, and suddenly Jack's awareness expanded. He felt her and Helene and the others as he felt his own limbs. All the legends he had loved fused with reality.

His hands in the earth were trembling.

I know that all of us . . . and the zucchinis and the soil and the sky . . . are all one thing . . .

Consciousness expanded, containing and contained. Jack lifted his head. Behind his closed lids he saw a blaze of light.

I know that from the consuming fire the Phoenix is reborn.

I've never met Esther Friesner, but then, with her savage wit, I might not survive an encounter. For anyone who's ever dealt with politicians of any stripe, this story will be a delight. For the rest of you, take our word for it: There are plenty of contemporary politicians whom it would be well to send campaigning in the 13th District.

PRIMARY
by Esther M. Friesner

The sealed black van glided noiselessly through the streets of the 13th District. Noiselessly being, of course, a relative term. The insulation of the passenger compartment was such that the four riders could hear nothing of the machine's robot-guided progress to its preset destination, and as there was nothing human in the nighted streets outside—nothing sentient, for that matter—to bear witness to any sound generated, it was as good as saying no sound existed.

"If a candidate falls in the primary and no one is there to hear him, does he make a sound?" Wayne Irons asked brightly. He touched the blue button on his armrest and the panel opposite him lifted, showing total blackness. "Excellent. We can be sure of a good turnout once we cross over."

Seated beside him, Tanya Jones squinted at the screen. "Good turnout? No one's there!"

"Ah! No one's *here*, you mean. But the 13th

171

District, you will find, is not to be gauged by appearances alone. They come back through on Election Day; that's all I care about."

"Don't we know it," snarled Calvin Baird. He was what Irons thought of as a splinter Democrat, and like all splinters, a candidate for removal with a hot needle. It was largely due to his last-minute entry into the primary race that Irons now found himself in the uneviable position of incumbent forced to tread the campaign trail in what should have been a rubber-stamp election.

In his corner of the van, Ng Ti remained aloof from the others as he reviewed all his campaign manager had told him earlier that evening. Strapped to his thin body was a moneybelt packed with scrip, and under his conventional three-piece suit was a silk tunic, hose, a heavy gold and topaz neckchain, and a foot-long dagger of whose proper management he hadn't the vaguest notion. Still, Harry was the best manager money could buy. Ng Ti understood money very well.

The van came to a halt and a red light switched on in the passenger compartment. A small chute flopped open from the panel just behind the autopilot's forward section. Irons took the initiative, as senior politico, to withdraw the little touchbox inside and key in further instructions.

"Gentlemen—and lady—" Tanya Jones curled her luscious nether lip at him. "Sorry, I mean *Madam*. I have instructed our chauffeur to remain here, taking all protective action needful, for a period of twenty four Earth-hours. At the expiration of this time, the van will stay here, but with selective defenses activated, for an additional hour, after which it will return to home base. To get in, you just lay your hand on the grille plate beside the door. Those of you who return *with* hands, of course, ho, ho."

"Shut up, Irons. You won't scare us off." In the

fluorolight of the passenger compartment Baird looked like a choleric frog. "We've made it this far down the trail, and we're racing you to the bitter end."

"Well, this race has hardly been the show of party solidarity I'd hoped for," Irons replied cheerily enough. He knew just the right tone to use which, when combined with his boyish good looks, would aggravate Baird into seeding a new ulcer.

"Solidarity! If that means backing an idiot just because he's a Democrat, count me and my people out!"

"How true. Your people prefer to back a psychotic just because he's a Democrat."

"Gentlemen, gentlemen, please," said Ng Ti, rising gracefully with hands outspread. "Let us forget out differences, if only for the moment. As soon as the primary campaign is over, whichever of us is victor must be backed by the rest. Bitterness and in-fighting will be just what our rivals desire. The hardest part of this campaign will be preparing for the next, which is the one that counts."

"You said it, honey." Tanya Jones nodded her auburn streaked head solemnly. "Those Republicans are tough mothers. Remember '03? Brother Yin uncovered their arms cache just in time."

The others remembered it well. Although they had been little more than children at the time, Brother Yin's famous suicide mission in the name of democratic principles and the two-party system had been instrumental in removing low-yield nukes from the campaign trail as well as guaranteeing mutants the vote.

"Jee-zus," said Tanya as Irons gallantly handed her out of the van. "This place doesn't look like it's been touched since Little 'Geddon Day." It was dark, but the moon was in its third quarter, light sufficient to see the shells of ancient buildings and the piles of rubble where rats and roaches held their midnight frolics. "What is it, some kinda monument? Y'know, a historical district?"

Baird uttered a disgusted growl. "The 13th District's as close as you can come to Ground Zero and still have something left standing. Any fool knows that. Don't you know a goddam thing about history? Or can't you read anything longer than your customers' credit card numbers?"

Tanya lavished a long, tantalizing stroke on her own thighs. "At least I got something the people want to buy," she purred. "Nobody down in the 6th bothered asking me to read a damn thing. Nobody in the 11th or the 9th neither."

"The first thing I'm going to get through Council is an election reform bill," said Baird. "Those three Districts had maybe twelve voters apiece, tops, but they still count as heavily as Districts with populations in the thousands! the only reason you took them was because while we pounded the pavements, you pounded the mattress!"

"You'da done it if there'da been any takers, sweet stuff," Tanya sneered. "And it wasn't easy." Politics, she had learned, was indeed what they say.

"A thousand pardons, gentles," came a velvety voice from the shelter of one of the ruined buildings. "Are you seekers after the true realm?" Soft golden light radiated outward to form an ellipse through which stepped a tall young man dressed all in white. Fine blond hair streamed down his back, where a quiver of arrows hung. When he spoke again, the points of his ears twitched ever so slightly.

Irons stepped forward and cut a fancy bow. "Noble lord of Elfin," he said, "we are honored to find one of your race awaiting us. We are the candidates, whose coming was foretold you by the wizard Sleipgar."

Behind him, Tanya giggled, Baird gagged, and

Ng remained impassive, only noting to himself that thus far Harry's notes were reliable.

"That is so," answered the elf. "Since you come into the true realm not to remain, but merely to behold, you are granted freedom with all its privileges and perils. But you must return to this curve of the great shell after one turn of the middle sun. To stay longer, not adapted to the realm's nature, would mean your deaths. Enter and be free." He stepped aside and made a sweeping motion with his slender arm.

"Come along, kiddies, the first bus for Lala-Land is now boarding," said Irons. He stepped through the golden ring. The others followed. Last of all came the elf.

"God," said Baird. It was fortunate for him that none of his adherents were there to overhear him. Mention of a Supreme Being was equivalent to vestigial belief in same, and to a hard-core atheist, that was blasphemy. However, had any of Baird's prime backers been present, no doubt the marvelous landscape now stretching away to an infinite horizon would have moved them to quasi-deification too.

"The realm is fair," said the elf. "My own woodland portion hereof is not without its dangers, but its beauty makes up for it, I think. Will it please you to come there with me?" He slipped his arm around Tanya's narrow waist. She looked up into his feline eyes and turned on everything she had. She hadn't gotten out of the cathouse and onto the power trail by missing her cues.

"*Love* to."

"But—" Irons held up a cautionary hand—"she must decline. You do understand, my lord of Elfin?"

"Quite so." He frowned, but withdrew. "The Bards of Law did rattle through it just last week. The candidates must traverse the realm unescorted, each separate from the others. In that case, it would be best were I to depart now. May the fortunes of Treveri go with you all."

Tanya tried to hiss directions for a rendezvous after her rivals were gone, but the elf feigned not to hear. With those ears, it had to be pretended deafness. Irons chuckled. "You won't find a more honorable race in the 13th District than the elves, Madam Jones. And yet, on Earth, that kid was brought in to the school Supe's office five times for cheating on exams, cutting classes, selling teachers to the 8th District, you name it. And when election day rolls around and he has to spend a full twenty-four hours on our side of the passage ring, he'll regress back into as acneous a little twerp as ever. But a twerp with the franchise, a voting twerp, and as such not to be scorned. Shall we begin our campaign?"

They were standing on the brow of a grassy hill. All directions looked equally appealing from that vantage point. To the east, a turreted city beckoned. To the west, a tawny desert. North held the promise of a romantic darkwood, whither the elf-cum-twerp had headed, and the south was all smooth grasslands and rolling plains. (These directions, like silence, being relative, for three suns shone in that alien sky, and did not all invariably rise from the same point each morning.)

Baird struck out for the city without waiting to discuss the matter. *Cities are where the power lies,* he thought. *All I have to do is get the king, or whatever the hell they've got here, on my side, he orders everyone to vote for me on primary day, and they'd better listen up, you bet.* He wondered whether the king was as much of a twerp in the real world as Irons claimed of the elf. He knew how to speak to twerps in disguise. No matter how far they got from their original wormy selves, the ghost of self-worthlessness never left them. They were easily cowed if you yelled at them loud and long enough. Push the right buttons and they were in your pocket. Baird had big pockets.

"See you back at the van, toots!" cried Tanya with an airy wave.

"She'll never catch that elf, you know," Irons commented for Ng's benefit as they watched her fly down the hillside and make for the forest. "Once they hit the woods, the trees swallow them up. But maybe she'll find a wizard's camp and get to do some campaigning there. It doesn't hurt to get a wizard on your side. Madam Jones is, I would wager, woman enough to sway the mage vote. Lonely old geezers. Well, Ng, what's yours?" He indicated the remaining choice of plain or desert.

Ng Ti calmly shed his civilized clothes and stepped out of the tweed coccoon a magnificent creature. Irons had to whistle. "You've done your homework." He undid his own street clothes and emerged in similar finery. "So have I."

Ng Ti removed a thick wad of scrip from his moneybelt and passed it to Irons. "Your campaign fund is low," he stated with the sureness of a man rich enough to hire reliable spies. "During the last primary, two of the four candidates did not return from this District. Whether I win or lose, I will still retain enough influence to facilitate my many business dealings. Even though as the party's candidate, and possible victor in the coming election, I would no longer have the bother of using middlemen, still, the fortunes of politics are of less moment to me than the business of survival. I look to you, as a survivor of the last campaign, for advice, even though in doing so I add to the chances of my political demise."

Irons counted out the scrip and tucked it away. "Advice? Two bits, for this price: Don't go into the desert and don't count on buying your way out of everything. Now if you'd like some more . . ." He smiled a guileless smile and extended an empty palm.

"Many thanks," said Ng Ti, ignoring both. He had acquired his vast wealth and influence by following two bits of advice of his own distillation: Don't tell your rival the truth and don't believe he'll tell it to you. This in mind, he headed straight for the sandy wastelands. Harry's report claimed there were uncounted oases and desert strongholds to be found there, complete with huge concentrations of voters in various guises. Of the plains, Harry knew less.

Irons watched his last competitor go and enjoyed a long, self-satisfied laugh. They'd forced this primary on him. They'd turned down his suggestion of a coalition platform. They'd each wanted all or nothing. They were each about to get it.

At the city gates, Calvin Baird caused a stir in his outre rig-out. A man of the people, he clung to denim and leather with a vengeance. Although most of Earth's cattle had perished during the modified nuclear disaster of Little 'Geddon Day, thus putting leather beyond the reach of the common man, it still carried symbolic oomph. Of course, that was on the other side of the golden ring . . .

"Beggars to the Nightsoil Gate!" snapped the pikeman, leveling his weapon at Baird's chest. A caravan of silk-robed merchants paused in their bribe-haggling with the other gate guard to watch.

"I'm no beggar!" roared Baird. His face creased and turned a rich purple when angry; he was almost always angry. "I'm a Democratic candidate, damn you, and I've got an appointment with your king!"

The pikeman slowly lowered his weapon. The light of uncertainty came into his eyes. The Bards of Law, sent by the great wizard Sleipgar, had passed this way some time earlier, reminding all the non-native population in the realm of the impending elections. A good turnout at the polls was urged—nay, demanded. He himself would have to abandon his post and lose one night's turn in the military brothel in order to vote, but better to lose one night than your whole hide. The king had said—

"Pass." He waved Baird through.

Twerp, thought Baird. *You're all a bunch of twerps here. Gutless twerps playing hidey-hide from responsibility on the outside. While we've been sweating to rebuild civilization, you're tucked in here dicking away with little tin spears. Well, once I'm elected, that's all going to be changed.*

All the way up the awesome sweep of the Nine Hundred Kings' Highway, Calvin Baird was escorted by dreams of forcing these bubbleheads back to reality, sending troops through the golden ring if need be, herding the malingerers home, sealing the dimensional gate that had opened on Little 'Geddon Day. If it took a nuke to be the opening key, would he hesitate to use the same means to lock and bolt the shimmering door?

Calvin Baird did not have the makings of hesitancy in his soul. To ideate was to act. He gave the royal palace guards the same short shrift he'd given the pikeman, and recalling what the Bards of Law had sung, they swallowed his abuse and let him through. The king's major domo, used to bent backs and clasped hands, got sharp words and plain speech. At last, at the end of a trail of bristling retainers, Calvin Baird stood before His Majesty, King Hiermon the Silent, fourth of that royal line.

"I am Calvin Baird, Democratic candidate." Baird stood with arms folded across his pigeon chest, using all the force of his personality to quell a king whose throne could have seated three Calvin Bairds comfortably. Three Calvin Bairds would still not have been sufficient to heft the great iron broad-axe at His Majesty's splayed feet. It was supposed to be there for purely ceremonial reasons, but there were times, there were times . . .

"Welcome, Calvin Baird," intoned King Hiermon. "As the wizard Sleipgar decreed, so be you welcome. Now go. I am weary." He did not look at all weary.

"In a minute," said Baird. "First of all, I'd like to explain my political position to you. It'll save us both a lot of time and make your choices easier on primary day. Do you have any whatchamacallits? Scribes? Heralds? Town criers? Maybe we should get them in here and take down my statement so they can relay it to the people."

"Today is the swine market," the king said. His eyes were closed, but since the lids were as veined with wine as the whites, sometimes it was hard to tell. "Go there. You have leave to stand upon the central block and declare whatever madness strikes you. Thus have I, and my fathers before me, ever shown our forbearance."

Calvin did not like this idea too well. He insisted on the scribes and criers. The king crooked his left pinky—the one permanently sheathed in gold and pointed at the end for convenient tooth-picking— and the room filled with men. They were rather sturdier than Baird imagined scribes and criers would be, and not one of them had brought a pencil.

"In the name of my fear of the wizard Sleipgar, you may speak. Your words will be taken to the people. But recall the wizard's own wisdom: Respect the might of wizards and the patience of kings."

"Yes, sure. Very well. First of all, I promise you a return to the values that made our country great. There'll be no more of this let-George-do-it attitude. Everyone works, and everyone works hard!"

King Hiermon the Silent nodded. It was good when the people worked.

"No more special privileges, believe me, and no more excuses! Elect Irons and it'll be four more years of political fudging. Elect Jones and civilization will degenerate into only doing what feels good. Elect Ng and the rich will grow even fatter with stolen prerogatives that are the right of every man!"

"Stop," said the king. He conferred momentarily with his major domo, who explained *political fudging*, *degenerate*, and *prerogatives* in simpler language. "I have heard enough. You are a fool. We will await the other candidates. Do not go into the swine market."

"Why, you blown-up little twerp, who the hell do you think you're talking to?" It was time to assert himself, to make this little worm aware of what was real and what was make-believe. It was time for yelling, loud and long. "I've got my eye on you, boy, don't think I don't. I'll remember you, no matter what kind of adolescent slime-ball you turn into once you're through that cockamamie portal. I'll see you, and I'll fix it so that you'll be sporting a beard a mile long before you get to crawl back to this sickie world and play Prince Ugly again! King or not, we're both citizens of the United States of America, and that doesn't give you the right to keep me out of your goddam pig market!"

King Hiermon's major domo was shaking. He whispered something into the king's right ear, but the king only edged his left foot half a length forward. This move sent the ceremonial axe crashing to the floor. The assembled scribes and criers leaped at the sound and pinioned Calvin Baird's leather and denim sheathed limbs. As he struggled and spat obscenities, the harried major domo scuttled up to him.

"Mr. Baird—" he began.

"—freedom of speech! And if he—"

"*Mr. Baird!*" One of the scribes—or was it a

crier?—backhanded Baird to get his attention. "Mr. Baird, you seem to have made a little mistake. His Majesty is not one of us."

"Ungh?" Baird's lips were starting to puff already. "He nah Deboc'at?"

"His Majesty, may he live a thousand years to spew on the graves of his enemies, is a native of this dimension. There are many such, you know. Or . . . didn't you know?"

The scribes and criers dragged Baird from King Hiermon's sight. Halfway out of the throne room he howled, "Wheah a' they tagimme? Wheah?"

The major domo sighed and murmured, "It won't be the swine market, Mr. Baird," then hurried back to his post at the king's side. "How may I serve Your Majesty?" he cooed in soothing tones.

"Summon the scribes and criers," said King Hiermon. "Issue a royal decree. All those of your people currently living as my subjects are to vote— What's not a Democrat?"

"Republican, Majesty."

The forest surrounded Tanya like an especially pesky and determined lover. There was no way out, and she was no longer sure of which way was in. She was fed up with the merry chatter of squirrels, nauseated by the thick reek of pine needles, and tired of twisting her strap-heeled feet on tree roots.

"Come out, you—you—elf!" she hollered. "Here, elfie! Oh, damn." She leaned against an evergreen's scaly trunk and got a gummy streak of resin down the back of her slinker. Her curses escalated.

An animal like a mink with opalescent wings hovered a handspan from her eyes. She yelled at it. It squeaked and fell dead at her feet. Tanya stared.

A young woman burst from the covert and pounced upon the hapless beast with a yip of triumph, a thin blowpipe still in her hand. She tore off the wings, gutted the quarry, pressed her lips to its opened belly, and had the pause that refreshes. Only then did she politely offer Tanya a sip.

Tanya accepted, first raising the still-warm corpse to her hostess in a toast. *What the hell. Easier than what I had to swallow in District 8. And I didn't even win District 8!* She lapped at the blood and smiled. "Delicious. Uh, you old enough to vote, Dear?"

Later, surrounded by the huntress' tribe, Tanya delivered an impassioned speech on the subject of the body human and the unnatural restrictions post-nuclear-whoops society had placed upon it. The warrior women sat in unmoving ranks and heard her out in stony silence. She only got a reaction when she entered the home stretch and declared, "What's the first thing those old fossils in power do after *they* push the button? Blame it all on—on a climate of moral laxness. And who gets the blame for *that?* Women! Mama Eve probably couldn't even reach that stupid fruit unless Adam gave her a boost. And guess what he was up to while holding the ladder? Sisters, I can see you've got clout around here. If you start spreading the word about my Habeas Corpus ticket, by primary day I'll bet we could mobilize a bloc of votes that'll swing the 13th District right over to—"

The oldest woman present unfolded her legs from the tailor posture and stood up. One by one, the others followed suit. One by one they walked from the cozy oak grove where Tanya had been preaching. Gaping, she watched them go until only the young huntress she'd first met was left:

"What's the matter? I say something wrong? Don't you women *want* the freedom of your bodies? Take it from me, it's fun."

The young woman shook her head. "You didn't

say anything wrong. Chieftess Caroo was impressed by your speech, Madam Jones. We forest Amazons are indeed influential. Not even King Hiermon's troops can stand up to us here in our realm. By leaving now, our Chieftess has signified her provisory approval of you. She and the Elders will be back to inform you officially."

"For real?" Tanya was all grins. *Maybe I won't stir up voting reform. Sure, why borrow grief? One vote to a District, and the candidate who gets the majority of each District's popular vote gets the whole District. And carrying the 13th will give me four, and that means I'll get the nomination. Heck, the system works!*

Chieftess Caroo returned. "It is good that women wield power," she said solemnly. "But the sword is not the only way. The woman who rules must be strong. Are you that woman, Jones? Are you strong?"

"Just try me!"

"Yes," said the Chieftess, and she gave her followers a signal. It was not as tradition-bound or formalized as King Hiermon's repetoire of body language, but it served its purpose, namely the immediate release of the tribe's mascot, a cantankerous she-bear. One snarl alerted Tanya Jones, one glimpse of forest Amazons swarming up friendly trees to get out of the way convinced her, and when the bear hove into sight through the rapidly vanishing crowd, Tanya did not stand around to ask whether they expected her to wrestle it, slay it, or taste it. She ran. She ran straight and true, tore out of the forest, stumbled up the familiar hill, and shot through the golden portal like a Robin Hood Special. On the other side, she crouched panting in the pre-dawn light while a friendly rat crept up to study her. She chucked a brick at him.

The cushioned comfort of the robo-van tempted her. She paused to consider the portal—there was no reason she could not go back through and make a fresh start—but it was a short pause.

"Politics!" she snorted as she put her hand on the grille plate. She meant it to sound like an obscenity, but any tonal nuances were lost in the shrill whine of the van's cell disruptor, which had strict instructions *not* to let anyone back in until twenty-four hours were up. It had remembered; Tanya had not. Perhaps it was just as well. The best politicians have always had long memories.

Tanya slipped down to cool amid the rubble of District 13.

"Well, I'll be *proud* to vote for you, Mr. Ng, just *proud*," said the camel-driver, pocketing the scrip. "And tell you what, we merchants get around plenty. I'll pass the word on you in every market-place from Silin to Vashac. And—and, hey, I've got friends who owe me favors. I'll offer to call 'em quits if they vote your way."

"Thank you," said Ng Ti, this time not ignoring the open palm. "That will be most agreeable." As he counted out the additional scrip he said, "If you do not mind a random observation, you and your fellow merchants do not seem to speak with the same—fulsome style of the other inhabitants."

The merchant chuckled and stroked his plush black beard. "That's because we're the heart and soul of what really makes this dimension tick, brother. Money. Trade. Pretty-pretties. When we came through the portal the first time, we didn't know what we'd find. We just wanted an out from the mess back stateside. Well I'll tell you, it may've sent some of those gog-eyed dreamers straight to heaven when they saw what kind of place this is—hot and cold running unicorns—but the na-tives wouldn't have let one of 'em start playing wizards and lizards here; until Bob Kingman spoke up."

"Ah." Ng Ti knew the name well. The wonders of District 13 had no sooner been discovered than a financial nobody named Robert Kingman had built an empire overnight. The foundation of it was precious stones and metals imported from nowhere on Earth. For Ng Ti, Kingman Enterprises had always been a living myth to which wise men aspired. Bob Kingman was long dead, but his descendants continued to run the family business. What a shame that Solarex Industries (Ng Ti director, chairman, owner, kahuna squared) had swallowed it only last year.

"Yeah, Kingman was the man who asked the natives the Big Question: What's in it for you if you let these weird kids pop through the portal and stay awhile? And he gave 'em the answer, too: Earth goods. So we make money, the natives make money, and the rest of 'em have a good time." He tightened the girth on his lead camel and gave the oasis one last look. "Hey, why don't you join up with us, Mr. Ng? We're heading for Piun, the biggest city in this part of the desert. You'll get a whole lot more votes there than you will oasis-hopping."

Ng Ti accepted graciously. The journey to Piun was short and pleasant. They only stopped once more en route, to take a midday meal in the shelter of another oasis. The *carte du jour* consisted primarily of sheep's eyes.

"I feel I may be frank with you," said Ng to his host. "One of the least appealing aspects of this campaign has been the need to sample the local delicacies of each District and feign enjoyment." He allowed the staring bowlful to pass him by. "I have eaten odder things, particularly in District 8."

"Yeah, we've sure heard about them," said the merchant, popping another peeper into his mouth.

"One of the saddest aspects of Little 'Geddon

Day was its aftermath. People were compelled to resort to certain inappropriate means of survival. It is unfortunate that the people of District 8 have continued these regrettable culinary practices long after the need has passed, perhaps making a present virtue of a past necessity."

Ng enjoyed the last lap of his desert trip thoroughly. His merchant guide was lavish with advice and helpful hints for dealing with the voting population of Piun. "If you lean forward in your saddle, Mr. Ng, you can just see the city towers now." They arrived not long after. At the gate, Ng Ti slithered down from his camel and shook the merchant's hand while the other merchants and caravan personnel gathered around.

"I cannot thank you enough. Your hospitality and advice have been priceless."

"No they haven't," said the merchant, and he proceeded to present Ng Ti with an itemized bill for transportation, food, luxury items (*one bowl of sheep's eyes; imported*), professional counsel, and sightseeing ("... you can just see the city towers ..." etcetera). The total had been converted from the native currency to scrip, the conversion surcharge thoughtfully appended. Not that it mattered.

"Are you mad? I haven't this much on me!" Ng Ti was no longer his impassive self.

"You don't? Oh dear. The law is quite clear on the subject of bad debts, I'm afraid. But don't worry!" The merchant rubbed his hands together. "You'll find I'm a very easy master. I never sell any of my slaves without good cause."

"*Slaves?*" Ng was livid. Some of the merchant's previously acquired slaves came forward to persuade him to lower his voice. One look at their narrow eyes convinced him. "You can't be serious," he whispered.

"I have no choice, Ti. Law's law. I've got you the

same way you got Kingman Enterprises for Solarex Industries; all legal."

"But I can't stay here longer than twenty-four hours. I have not been physically altered to bear the subtle environmental differences of this dimension!"

The merchant waved away Ng's objections. "I've got a friend in Piun, a leech who can take care of that little matter. And while he's at it, maybe he can make one more minor alteration. I've been having troubles in the harem. I need a man with heavy executive skills to manage things." Seeing Ng's horror-struck face, he quickly added, "Oh, no, no, don't worry. You'll be *chief* eunuch!"

Ng Ti fell to his knees in the sand and clasped the merchant's knees. "Is there no other way?" he moaned.

The merchant's smile was mostly hidden by his beard. He turned to his slaves. "Bring parchment."

When Ng Ti emerged from the golden portal he was a free man, entire, and poorer by one megacompany. Stuck in his belt next to the useless dagger was his duly notarized copy of the contract transferring control of Solarex Industries to a young merchant who would no longer have to rely on the chancy income of camel drives. Now there was truth to the lie Ng had told Irons earlier: It didn't matter whether he won or lost the primary. He had other worries.

By the clear light of Earth-noon, Ng saw Tanya Jones' body sprawled near the van. Prudently he sat down some distance away from the self-defending vehicle to wait for the twenty-four hours to elapse. As he sat, he thought he saw a human figure coming toward him. At first he imagined it was either Irons or Baird, but as the person neared he saw that it was an unidentified male/normal— lean, muscular, and very scruffy.

"Hey, brotherman," came the greeting. "You look

rugged. What's eating you?" Then the visitor's eyes fell on Tanya's body. He assumed a look of deep commiseration. "Oh. Hey, too bad. She your woman?"

"She is nothing to me," said Ng.

"For true?" The young man slapped his hands together with glee, all traces of sympathy gone. He slung her body over his shoulder. "Well, thanks lots. Things're getting thin over on my home turf, but this'll save me some sweat, let me tell you. Maybe we oughta give this agriculture stuff a whirl. Still, old ways, best ways."

"Stop!" cried Ng. "What are you doing? Where are you taking Madam Jones?" All of the frustration and humiliation he had undergone on the other side now surfaced as unthinking rage. Or perhaps having come so close to losing his manhood, he now felt compelled to show that he still possessed it.

"Huh? You said she wasn't nothing to you, brotherman. I'm taking her back with me to District 8's where."

"In a sheep's eye you are!" With a wild cry, Ng Ti threw himself at the young man, his drawn dagger brandished in a thoroughly amateurish way.

"Oh boy," sighed the hunter, sliding the body from his shoulder. There was nothing at all unprofessional in the way he held his own knife.

"I'm sorry, Mr. Irons, but the law is plain," said the Registrar, her hands folded neatly on the desk. "The candidate with a clear majority of Districts is the one to carry the Party nomination."

"*What?*" For the first time since his smug return from the realm, Wayne Irons lost his temper. "I'm the only candidate left *alive*, dammit! Are you telling me that one of the others carried the 13th District? Well, so what? Are we going to run a corpse against the Republicans?" Only now did

Irons regret that he had spent his twenty-four hours in the realm hiding out in a shepherd's cot on the grasslands. Until this moment he had believed that main survival would be his trump card in carrying off the nomination.

The Registrar gave him a frosty look. "Each of the official candidates had three Districts. The 13th was the deciding one, and it was taken by a write-in candidate. According to the electoral laws, we must now have run-offs between the two of you in all the Districts."

"God damn it, if I've got to go back on the trail—if I've got to go back to kissing babies, or whatever the hell it was I kissed in the 4th District—then I want a word with the dark horse bastard responsible!"

"Gladly, Mr. Irons," came a voice. A golden ellipse, smaller than the ever-open portal, opened and closed behind the Registrar's desk and a tall, white-haired man in flowing blue robes stepped through. He carried a silver wand, with which he touched the Registrar once, gently. Her eyes glazed over.

"Vote . . . for . . . Sleipgar," she intoned.

"That's not fair!" shrieked Irons. The wizard offered a benevolent smile.

"Please, Mr. Irons, I had hoped to encounter more Party solidarity from you. Remember, this is merely a primary. The real contest is yet to come." He reached into his robes and brought out a frog. Irons gasped to see that the beastie had the face of one of the rival party's most formidable candidates.

"You see? Even with all of my powers invoked, the transformation was incomplete; nor is it permanent. I foresee a rough campaign, dear colleague." The wizard Sleipgar slowly shook his head. "Those Republicans are tough mothers."

Tough mothers being, of course, relative.

Ian Watson's story is just downright beautiful. In his cover letter, he—as almost everyone did when they'd finished their pieces—expressed some hesitancy and doubt, admitting that, in the end, ". . . it's the story that emerged from me . . . I suspect it mightn't quite be what you were looking for, being more shamanistic than realistic (though the business of junking old nuclear submarines by burying them in a convenient desert is a recent serious proposal). . . . And it does offer an element of hope . . ." But, as you'll see, it was exactly what I was looking for.

WHEN IDAHO DIVED
by Ian Watson

"Gather round, elders, wives and juniors! Gather round, brothers and sisters of the tribe! Listen to the tale of how I piloted the sand submarine named Idaho down to the deep cave of treasure and bones.

"So you have heard it all before? Well, you will hear it once more . . ."

In the century following the end of the world, when skies were always grey, when plants grew flimsily, when birds fell from the air, when even the rattlesnake lost the voice in his tail, when wild dogs were our food, and we were theirs, the last tribe of the family of man made its way out into this desert land. For all the rest of the earth had become a deadly desert, but here, where the dunes

191

roll and the salt-pans glisten, was merely desert pure and simple: clean desert as it had always been.

Sores sprouted on our bodies, and strange thoughts moved inside our minds: strong dreams and nightmares. The sicker we became and the thinner with hunger, and the more we glowed in the dark with fever-heat such as only the rattlesnake was able to perceive in earlier times, the more so did the minds of some of us children grow fierce with new senses; and of all I was the fiercest, though my legs were rickety and my chest was patched with red spiders' webs.

In those days, children pointed the way to safe pools and edible roots, pulling their puzzled ailing elders by the hands. And I pointed farthest of all, deep into the desert, which seemed a wild and foolish way to walk; but it was clear and clean to me.

The journey was too late for all but one of the grown-ups of the last tribe of people; but we children knew which of those who fell were safe to eat, and which parts of which ones: the liver of one, the brain of another, the heart of a third. What parts we did not eat fell to the lot of the mongrel packs on our heels; and many hounds died of what they ate, or became enfeebled and could not follow us onward.

Only seven of us arrived here: six children, and young Gabriel's Grandad whose eyes had melted many years before when a sun suddenly rose in the north. Gabriel's Grandad never seemed to know how to die—as though this was a skill he had lost along with his eyesight.

And so we came at last to this dry valley in the very heart of the belly of the desert, where we found to our joy this metal village where in later years you were bred from our loins and now dwell.

What a person knows with full familiarity, a

person cannot see with the eyes of fresh perception; so I will say how our home seemed to us when we first arrived; and how it sounded to the ears of Gabriel's Grandad.

Side by side along the valley floor stood seven mighty cylinders, all jet-black, with winged towers on top of each to enter by. These are our long-houses now.

When we told their shape and size and structure to Gabriel's Grandad, he answered madly that they were called submarines; that they were made to swim beneath the seven seas—a sea being a pool of salty water as wide and as deep as the sky.

You've never seen such a thing as a sea, my tribe. No more have I. So what were these mighty vessels, which Gabriel's Grandad said were made for swimming beneath the seven seas, doing here standing in a line in middle-desert? Had the great winds of the end of the world, of which our parents had talked, picked those submarines out of the pool called the Pacific and carried them here and set them all down so neatly together?

"Not so!" wheezed Grandad. He recollected—so he claimed—that submarines had been buried in this empty desert many long years ago, to get rid of them safely without harm to fish or water. They were 'active,' he said, and their activity could rot a man's testicles. The great winds of the end of the world must have uncovered them all, so that the seven submarines appeared like a village planted on the valley floor. Or perhaps other winds since had done the work, funneling down and scooping out our valley.

We advanced. By piling up sand in a ramp for several hours, then using blind Grandad as our ladder, we were able to scramble up on top of one of the submarines and gain access by way of the 'cunning tower,' the clever high entrance door. We descended and explored the crowded darkness

within, which wasn't as dark to our eyes as it
might have been to our dead parents' eyes; besides,
mushrooms and fungi glowed on furniture and
tubes and walls.

We found shelter. We found food: those fungi
and mushrooms. We found water. We had found
our new homes.

We traced the word-shapes that our ancestors
once used, and which we discovered within this
'submarine and the others, upon Grandad's palm;
and he told us the names of our new longhouses:
names such as Kentucky and Idaho.

But Grandad wasn't able to tell us a great deal.
It was as though those words told him what he
had forgotten, namely how to die; and he did so
soon after. So we ate his best parts.

Yet Grandad's best parts did not last long, nor
for that matter did the fungi and mushrooms growing in our seven fine sanctuaries. We ate our way
through the lot; and hungered again, and our minds
grew fierce.

It came to me, in this glowing state of being,
that Grandad had been mad these many long years,
and that what he had said about the origin of
these 'submarines' was nonsense. He was of the
old days; he had no vision. It was obvious to me
that these great hulls had *dived*, for they were of
the right shape to thrust themselves sinuously
through other matter with as little hindrance as
could be. But though our ancestors were crazy and
caused the end of the world, no one could have
been crazy enough to carry these vast hulks for the
weeks and weeks (or even years) it would have
taken to bring them here, just to pile sand over
them. Nor could any possible wind have borne
them all the way from the Pacific Pool. Therefore
the submarines must have dived right here, down
through the sands of the desert; and here was their
real home and harbor. Rocks jut out of the desert,

but the great pools of sand in between might sink as deep as the core of the world.

And why should these vessels dive down through this part of the desert if there was not something rich and rare beneath to seek?

Grandad had mumbled at times concerning the caves that men had dug during the last days before the end of the world, before the false suns burned and the wild winds blew and the sky became grey for years: caves filled with meat and drink, with forever-food and fresh water. The people of old must have dived to such caves in these submarines, down through the sand and the earth to the deep safe places.

And maybe our ancestors weren't all dead! Maybe we weren't the only remaining tribe of man! Maybe deep below our feet lived men and women who could be our new parents or servants, or new brothers and sisters.

Could a submarine take us down below the ground to the caves of our ancestors?

Oh that was a wild and glowing time, a hungry time, a yearning time, a time of bright visions and fierce wishes; especially for me.

And as I sat there alone within Idaho, starving, I conceived—not as you conceive, brothers and sisters, sons and daughters; but I conceived within my mind. I conceived a power such as never before nor ever since has been conceived.

I went to the room in the midst of Idaho where there are seats to sit in and many handles and little jutting metal fingers to push and pull and twist. I sat me down. The power burgeoned within me. I grasped handles. I snapped the metal fingers up and down. And Idaho awoke.

I know you do not fully credit this, my juniors. I know that you whisper behind my back that this is simply a 'myth' of how we came to be as rich and prosperous and populous as we are today; and how many do I count of us here today, crowded into this mighty steel hall of the self-same Idaho. This hall, which Grandad named the 'missile compartment'? Nigh on two hundred souls! Oh I know that your voices buzz behind my back; for I hear them buzz, saying that all our forever-food and other riches were already stored here in Idaho and its six companions when we children first arrived. But I tell you: it was not so! It was just as I say!

Idaho awoke under my hands. Idaho moved. Idaho tilted and dived, down through the sand, down through the earth.

After awhile Idaho leveled off, and traveled. I know not for how long. Time had stopped.

Eventually Idaho also stopped. Its metal heart quit thumping, its lungs ceased to pant softly, its blood no longer pounded.

I climbed up through the cunning tower and discovered that Idaho was at rest in a huge stone chamber many times its size, where lights burned brightly. The mouths of several well-lit tunnels led away, but Idaho was too huge to have entered the chamber by any of these mouths. Yet behind Idaho the chamber wall was flawless—apart from ancient marks of cutting and chiseling. Nevertheless Idaho had slipped through.

Many things were stored in that first chamber; and many more things in other chambers, to which the tunnels led. There were enormous stocks of sealed forever-food, boxes of fine garments, stores of seed, barrels and bottles of drink, tools, knives and axes, neat bundles of stitched bound paper covered with meaningless word-shapes, enigmatic devices of all shapes and sizes wrought in metal and glass.

I found many skeletons, too, the bones of our ancestors lying about on the floors. But though many still had leathern skin and muscle-string and hair attached, these bones did not whisper anything to me.

A month and more I must have spent in filling Idaho with the plunder of these chambers, enough to last us many lifetimes. I sensed that my small band of sisters and brothers would not starve in the meantime, however long I took; for did I not say that time stood still? Yet while I worked I also feasted and slept and put on weight.

Finally I retired back into that room in the midst of Idaho and felt for the power again; and the power duly came to me.

Idaho carried me and my cargo back. Idaho rose and surfaced once more here in our desert as though it had never been away.

My brothers and sisters fed; they drank. A tiny lump of forever-food fills the belly wonderfully, does it not? Presently we increased and multiplied.

And that is how it was, when Idaho dived.

So you have heard all this before? And you wonder why, if this was so, the power has never come to me a second time and Idaho has never dived again?

Listen, elders, wives and juniors, sisters and brothers of the tribe! I am old; and until now there was no need for the power. Yet I feel that the power is near me once more. I feel it waiting for my hand to grasp it.

I tell you that there is nowhere else in this world for us to live except here amidst these sands. Yet now that the all-grey skies of yesteryear have cleared, the sun beats hot upon us by day, the moon shines cold by night. Every day it is too cold and too hot. And I know that two hundred mouths, even the little mouths of our golden babes held in your arms as you hear me, will gobble many lifetimes of forever-food before many more years pass by. What then, my tribe, what then?

Do you challenge me to dive Idaho down again underneath the earth to the same chambers of plenty? Do I hear that?

The power, oh my tribe, may only be used once in one direction.

But it can be used again—in another direction!

Consider the sun by day, the moon by night! Those are *places* afloat in the sky, of fire and of ice. Consider the thousand smaller twinkling lights in the black sky, which first showed themselves to us when the sky-blanket fell into threads!

The power tells me that we must go to one of those lights in the sky! Idaho will take us all up there, to fields of green and to bubbling streams, to plains of skipping game beasts and pools of fat fishes. It will take us all to a new living-place, as once it took me to the caves of treasure and bones; and it will take us timelessly.

Do not doubt! For here you are all gathered together; and did you not know that the cunning tower is closed? Nothing will leave by it now, not even a breath of air, till I say it is safe.

Now I shall go to the room of handles and metal fingers, to steer us to a star.

Let me through! Do you not feel the floor beneath our feet begin to tilt? Upward, yes a little upward!

Let me through, I say!

Why are you all staring at me so? Why are you hemming me in so tightly? What is this harm you mean me? What folly is this, what madness?

I repeat: the power is upon me! This is the time! Can you not feel Idaho quivering to rise? Do you not wish to tell your babes' babes the tale of how Idaho *flew*—to a star in the sky?

You are fools, fools. Alas, my tribe, you are fools.

And now you will eat my brain and my heart and my liver. But first of all you will eat my tongue, which spoke to you, saying all these things.

Craig Shaw Gardner says succinctly, "Okay, here it is, my submission to Afterwar. *The story comes from spending too much of my life in bars." Being a teetotaler, I spend almost no time in bars—just enough to browbeat Gardner into writing this story. Whatever works, works. However, after you read this, you might have second thoughts if the author invites you out to have a few. . . .*

BAR AND GRILL
by Craig Shaw Gardner

He'd walk right out of this place, and he'd never come back here again.

Paddy would say sure, sure, how many times have you said that? But this time was different. Sometimes he had trouble making up his mind, but now, well—

He belted back the shot and felt the fire burn his throat, then spread to his shoulders and arms, his neck and legs and crotch, then his head. God, the stuff was good here. It was like pouring a little bit of summer down your throat every time you took a drink. He didn't know what was in it, and he was a little afraid to ask, but he'd miss it as much as anything, once he was gone.

His fingers rubbed the knuckles of his synthetic hand. A nervous habit, something he did more and more, another reason to get out of here.

The soft silver felt cool, even in here. He wished the air conditioning didn't break down so often. He snapped two sets of fingers, one new, one flesh and blood. His timing was still perfect. No degeneration at all.

The heat was fading from behind his eyes. Maybe it was time for another drink.

Fabric rustled at his side. He turned to see Jeanette sit at the next stool. She was wearing something long and complicated, with a whole series of ruffles down the skirt. The dress was an intense shade of blue, almost violet, and she'd pinned a pink flower on the strap that covered one shoulder.

He smiled when he realized what it was. A prom dress. He wondered where Jeanette had found it. Bandages peeked from behind her corsage where the replacement hadn't quite knit with her flesh yet. Were the flowers there to hide the scars or show them off? With Jeanette, he was never sure.

The jukebox in the corner was playing "Tennessee Waltz." He asked Jeanette if she'd like to dance.

"Why, Vinnie, I'd love to." Her smile lit up her whole face, the half that was silver and the half that wore a deep tan. Her face had startled him the first time he saw it, but now it warmed him when she looked into his eyes, like the sun and the silver moon shining on him all at once. She really was quite beautiful.

Paddy had a big dance floor here, but people rarely used it. Vince and Jeanette whirled around the floor alone, two people wrapped in a world of music. He slowed the pace and she rested her head on his shoulder. Vince took a slow breath. The smoky, too warm air of Paddy's place tasted sweet in his lungs. His heart beat in his ears, and he could feel Jeanette's heart pounding where he held her against his chest. Two hearts were a different kind of music, but somehow they went along with the jukebox just fine. Vince closed his eyes and smiled. Every once in a while, they got it just right in here. This was the way to live.

He had heard about this place long ago, months before he learned it wasn't just another story. There were a lot of stories that made the rounds, after all; stories just as impossible as this place was, stories that somehow kept people going, day to day.

They had stories here, too, but they were different.

Vince thought about how he first stumbled on this place. Oh, he'd followed rumors here, but they had been dead wrong in a couple of crucial details. He'd been about to give it up, just like all those other stories he'd followed before, when he saw the red neon.

He tried the door and it opened. It didn't open for everybody. Or so Paddy said.

It was dark inside, but it was a different darkness from the night. There were a few, scattered lights in the place. Everything in the room, tables, chairs, people, was a soft silhouette. But the first thing you saw as you entered the room was the bar. It was quite long, stretching the entire length of the not-too-tiny interior. And the top edge of the bar was lit by two strips of neon, one red, one blue, that ran the whole length of the thing and made the bottles and glasses behind the bar sparkle like Christmas lights.

Vince walked towards the bar. The stories were right. It looked like something from a long time ago.

"And what have we here?"

Vince froze with the voice. It was a thick Irish brogue, like a cross between Pat O'Brien and Barry Fitzgerald in all those old movies about happy priests. "A newcomer to Paddy's, are you?"

Vince stared across the bar. The voice was definitely male, but the speaker didn't look much like a man. At first glance, he looked as if he was made all of metal, like some badly designed robot from a 1950s science fiction film.

"And aren't I a sight, you're saying to yourself?" the cross between Gort and Robbie continued. "Well, you're in Paddy's now, and it's Paddy you're staring at, and if you're going to keep that up, the least you can do is sit down and have a drink at the same time."

There was some soft laughter from the shadows in the room, one woman's voice rising above the rest. Vince sat at an empty stool, and a drink appeared before him.

"The house specialty," Paddy explained as he turned away. Vince took a sip.

It was like nothing he'd ever tasted before, warm and dry and smooth, like the best parts of whiskey, wine and water all swallowed at the same time. He stared at the glass.

"Pretty amazing, isn't it?" Vince looked at the man on the next stool. "We come into this place for a hundred different reasons, but that's what we stay for."

Vince nodded. "What's in this stuff?"

"Paddy's joy juice?" The other man laughed. "Paddy won't talk, and no one else knows. Most likely it's sunshine mixed with the blood of virgins." The other man drained a glass of his own.

"Sam," the other man said, extending his hand. Vince introduced himself, and they shook.

"You want to hear about Paddy's?" Sam asked after a moment's silence.

Vince glanced at the talking metal man, now down at the far end of the bar. "I'd just like to know about Paddy," he whispered. "Just what is he, anyway?"

"What all of us will become, one of these days," Sam replied. "He just wears it a little more proudly than the rest of us."

Vince finished his drink. Paddy appeared before

him to refill his glass. The efficient machine, Vince thought. He asked about the cost, but Paddy said not to mind, they never took money here anyway.

Sam toasted the newcomer. As their glasses clinked together, he added, "The door back there is open. You can leave any time you want."

And then Jeanette had sat down on Vince's other side. Her face had been all her own then, and as beautiful in its way as it was now.

Vince felt the weight of her head against his shoulder, listened to the rustle of the prom dress as they moved across the floor. He could dance forever with her like this. The jukebox played "As Time Goes By."

He remembered their first night together. He hadn't felt that way about anybody since Margaret. Funny how he hardly thought about Margaret anymore.

And that first night: Sam had told a long story about living in the suburbs and traffic jams. Vince laughed along with the others, but his eyes were on Jeanette. And she returned the kindness, her eyes drifting back to his again and again. Her eyes were very dark in the dimly lit bar, but the neon gave them a hint of electric blue.

He could stay here, Paddy said. They'd find him a room. Vince had been very drunk by then. Parts of Paddy's body reflected light, and Vince became fascinated by the neon patterns that danced along the chrome.

But he hadn't gone to his room that night, he had gone to hers.

Beautiful Jeanette. They undressed each other in the dim light, their hands propelled by awkward passion. Her dress fell away, revealing small breasts, a narrow waist, and a patch of silver skin stretched across her stomach.

Vince's fingers stroked the silver patch before

his mind knew what they did. Cool and soft, almost like skin. He raised his eyebrows in a question.

"Didn't Sam tell you?" The corners of Jeanette's mouth threatened a frown.

Vince shook his head. The motion made him feel drunker than before.

"I told him I didn't want to know."

"Oh, not now!" she whispered, and held his head in both her hands. She kissed him, hard, as if she didn't want either of them to speak again. He kissed her in return, more gently, and felt the tension leave her body. They held each other close on the bed.

In the night, he dreamed.

He met Margaret in a park. She was very happy to see him, the way it was when they were first together, not like it was towards the end. He guessed they were supposed to meet there, because Margaret carried a picnic basket. She led him out from among the trees onto a great expanse of lawn. The lawn seemed to go on forever, lush and full, the green of four-leaf clovers. Green the way grass used to be.

They found a level spot and Margaret spread out the picnic things, drawing Vince down beside her. It was then he noticed that the sky was silver. Margaret talked about old friends, and what she and Vincent should do tomorrow. Vince found he had no appetite. He couldn't take his eyes away from the sky. The silver seemed to pulsate, as if the sky were a living thing. He could hear screams in the distance, and farther away than that there were explosions, so deep you felt them more than heard them. The silver above them was brightening, turning first to a molten glow and then to blinding white. A hot wind sprang up at Margaret's back, bringing the distant screams closer and closer still. And Margaret continued to smile and sip her iced tea, and talk about the weather the day before yesterday, and how Abby was having so much trouble with George these days. Vince wanted to scream at her, but it was so bright. The wind was so strong. Couldn't she see? Couldn't she?

He woke up, crying, in Jeanette's arms. She held him close and comforted him, saying simple words in his ear. "Now, now, now. There, there, there."

When he could talk, he told her about his nightmare.

"Now there," she said when he was done. "Here, at least for a little while, we can have better dreams."

She sent him to his own room later, and he slept. When he got up again, he went to the bar.

"And it's good to see you again, boy-o," Paddy said from across the bar. He pushed a plate of something brown and steaming in Vince's direction. "Here. You have to keep up your strength."

He ate whatever it was. It tasted vaguely Italian. Not bad, and it went with the drinks.

He looked around for Jeanette. His eyes had grown used to the light in there. He could make out a lot more faces, all but those in the shadow-filled corners. But no Jeanette. He had another drink and waited. She'd come.

But she didn't. He tried to pace his drinking a little better tonight, thinking, when Jeanette came, the two of them could get drunk together and do it all over again. So he sat at the bar and listened to stories. About one fellow who'd taken his kids to the zoo. He went on at great length, describing parrots and the monkey house, how his smallest had been fascinated by a baby giraffe, and his eldest had gotten sick on peanuts and caramel corn. It had all been sort of a game, the man said, keeping the kids happy, until he'd seen the tiger.

It was some distance away, sitting on the other

side of a moat in an enclosure full of rocks and dirt and a few small trees. But it was big, you could tell that even from far away. And every time it moved, you could sense its power.

The man said he'd never seen anything like that cat before. Even when the big orange and black beast rested, you could tell how strong it was, how fast it moved, how easily its claws could shred you to pieces.

The others around him nodded. They all remembered tigers.

Jeanette still hadn't come. Finally, Vince lost interest in drinking. He gave it up and went to his room. He imagined Jeanette could find him if she wanted to.

He couldn't sleep. Even with all that booze inside him, his eyes wouldn't close, his fingers wouldn't stop tapping the side of his bed.

Maybe he was afraid to dream.

His eyes snapped open. He had drifted off at last. But there was a noise, a pushing at the door, like someone fumbling with the lock.

"Who's there?" he called, his voice ragged with sleep.

The noise stopped. The room filled with the empty quiet.

He couldn't find Jeanette the following morning, either. Sam had said the door was open. He decided it was time to use it.

The jukebox played "Boogie Woogie Bugle Boy." Vince blinked. Sometimes he just drifted when he was out on the dance floor with Jeanette. She looked up at him and smiled. The Andrews Sisters bopped and scatted through the hidden speakers, doubling the pace of the music that had gone before. Vince and Jeanette kept on dancing slow.

Once he left this place, why hadn't he stayed away?

But he knew the answer. Where else was there? With his technical background, he was moderately employable. But that all depended on the season, and who wanted protection from whom, or who wanted the upper hand. One time, they even tried to set up a central government. But when he went out this time, there was nothing at all. Well, there was always the high risk stuff, but he kept his distance. He hadn't stayed healthy so long by being stupid.

So he drifted back to Paddy's place. Maybe it was because he couldn't work. But he'd been out of work before.

Jeanette was at the bar when he came in. She turned to him and smiled. It took him a minute to recognize her. She had changed in the weeks he was gone.

Half her face was silver now. Her features were the same, but new fabric stretched over her muscle and bone. Half her flesh was gone.

Her hand touched her silver cheek when she saw the way he looked at her. He closed his hand over hers and drew her to him.

Kissing her was strange. Her flesh was warm, the silver cool. It made his own lips tingle.

"I'll tell you about it now," she said.

He went and got a drink.

Ella sang "A-Tisket, A-Tasket" on the jukebox. Vince paused and lifted the silver hand from where it clasped Jeanette's waist. He could have left then, when she told him. But he needed her so badly. There's a price you pay for everything.

And Jeanette had told him the price at Paddy's Bar and Grill.

They only let healthy people into Paddy's. The skin cancers, the falling hair, the pale faces that said there was something wrong inside, they never made it beyond the door. If you stayed at Paddy's, you came from good stock.

Because that's what they needed here. They gave you everything, food, drink, companionship. No one had to work here, or worry about accidental exposure. And all they wanted in exchange was an occasional body part.

Vince had seen them from time to time, even worked under them as a tech. Once, you might have called them power brokers, although now there didn't seem to be any power left. No matter. If they couldn't fight over the pie, then they'd fight over the crumbs. And they were never sick, never weak, never had cancers or failing bowels or loose teeth or any of a thousand ailments that seemed to have taken over the world.

Or, if something did get to them, they had replacements. They had to be healthy and human. It might be a very small game they were playing, but there were very strict rules.

"Why?" Vince said when Jeanette was finished.

She smiled. "Why do any of us do anything? Why, when old rules don't work, do we make up new ones?"

Vince shook his head. "No. Why do you stay here?"

"I remember a Sunday afternoon," Jeanette replied after a moment's thought, "when I was six."

She took a swallow from her drink. They'd both been drinking for awhile by then.

"I remember one Sunday aftenoon, in the family room, my two sisters and I were watching TV. I grew up in Tiffen, Ohio. We had a split-level house, not very big, but it seemed gigantic to me when I was six. Well, the three of us, my sisters and I, were watching some silly old movie, a costume thing, where all the women wear these incredibly flouncy dresses and all the men jump around in tights. But we were all watching this movie, and my sisters, who were both older than I, were playing a game at the same time. And part of me wanted to play that game, but part of me was fascinated by the tv, with all those beautiful women and dashing men.

"It didn't seem like much at the time, but I remember it so well now. Maybe my sisters were keeping me out of their game on purpose, which made me want to join them all the more. But somehow, I was upset and excited and fascinated by the silly movie all at the same time. I remember pacing back and forth between my sisters and the TV.

"And then my father came in. I think he sized up the situation right away, because he looked at me and asked me how the movie was. And then he said, 'Netty, why don't you sit on my lap and we can watch it together.'

"So I did. I don't remember much more about the movie. I laughed a lot and clapped my hands when the good guys won. But I remember the feel of daddy's pant leg under my hand, the smell of the old wool sweater he wore, and just how safe and warm I felt."

She stopped and looked at Vince, tears running from her human eye. He took her hand.

"You two all right?" Sam stood over the table.

Vince looked up. "Yeah. We're talking."

"I heard you going on about Paddy's secret earlier." Sam pointed to the bottle on the table. "Well, drink up. That way they'll never get your liver." He laughed and turned away.

Jeanette and Vince left together a few minutes later. There was a wildness to their lovemaking this time, a force that said this is animal, this is flesh and blood and sweat and semen. This is not machine.

Later, as Vince slept, he dreamed.

He and Margaret were in a supermarket, one of the really big ones they used to have, where only half the aisles were full of food and the rest held lawn chairs, cosmetics, magazines, and personal banking. He turned to say something to her, and was surprised to see that one half of her face was silver. He meant to ask her about it, but just then they reached the end of the aisle, and Margaret pushed the cart over to a cooler filled with cuts of beef. Behind the cooler stood a butcher. Vince realized with a start that it was Paddy, wearing a white apron. Margaret recognized Paddy, too, and waved to him. Paddy waved back, and Vince saw that, instead of metal hands, each of Paddy's wrists ended with a long, sharp knife.

Margaret reached out a hand for Paddy, and he reached out a knife for her. Vince ran to grab Margaret and pull her away, but there was something wrong with his hand as he touched her shoulder. The flesh was limp and lifeless. As he tried to flex his fingers, bones ripped through, exposing muscle, tendons, knuckles. Vince looked again. No, it wasn't bone that tore his hand from the inside out. His hand was filled with shards of metal.

Vince woke with a scream. He was all alone, in a room that he didn't recognize.

He looked at his hand. It was whole, but it was silver.

Vince didn't remember the next few minutes too clearly. Somehow, he got dressed. Somehow, he made it down to the bar.

"Look what they've done," is all he could say.

"Ah." Sam came up behind him. "Initiated at last. Welcome to Paddy's."

"How could they do this?"

"It's not so bad. You'll get used to it."

"Why did they take my hand?" Vince found himself grabbing Sam's shirt with both hands, real and silver. He let go to stare at the new one.

"Look," Sam's voice had an angry edge to it, "you'll get used to it." He unbuttoned his shirt. His chest and stomach held half a dozen scars. "I'm an inside man myself. You're lucky. You can admire their handiwork. I don't know what's gone in here and what's still mine."

Vince turned away. Why had he ever come here in the first place? Numbly, he walked over to the bar. Paddy was in the middle of a story.

"And did you ever see the way Jim Rice swung a bat? Ah, there was a man who knew how to use what he had. The sound of it, when he hit the ball just right, and you knew it was out of the park."

"Paddy!"

The metal man turned to Vince. "And could you be using a drink, boy-o?"

Vince held up his artificial hand. "Look at this!"

"Ah, so the lad's developed a sign of grace, now."

Vince grabbed at Paddy's chrome. Up close, he could see silver flesh underneath.

"Why?" he asked.

"Ah, now don't go mournin' your losses. It's a form of kindness, really. You get fed here, and plenty to drink. You're among friends, and you can talk about things that really matter. Once in a while, of course, there's a small inconvenience, but you don't remember it. And your new parts, why they're almost as good as the old. And take it from Paddy, once they wear out, they replace them free of charge."

Paddy pointed to the door. "Out there, boy-o, everybody's slowly dyin'. But who's to say you and I might not live forever?"

Vince clenched his new hand into a fist. "Who's to say you were ever alive in the first place?"

Paddy turned away from him to address the other customers at the bar. "Now, as to this matter of Jim Rice."

Vince cleared the bar in a single move. He clung

desperately to Paddy with his human hand, searching for a grip on the chrome. He flailed at the thing with his silver hand, again and again and again.

Jeanette looked up at him, a question in her eyes. He had stopped dancing. The jukebox played a heavily orchestrated version of "Some Enchanted Evening." Violins swelled to every side.

"Are you all right?" she asked.

"Sure. Just thinking again."

She hugged him, then disengaged herself. "I'll be over at the bar if you need me."

He watched her walk away.

They had calmed him down that night, and he'd stayed calm after that. Sam had it right. Sure, Vince had a new hand, but it worked just as well as the old one. He could still leave here if he wanted to, the door was right there. Now Sam, if he was outside and something failed inside him, he was out of luck. But if Vince's hand stopped working, why, he still had another one, and he could always come back here and they'd fix him up good as new. Why, look at Paddy. He probably didn't have a single thing on him that hadn't been replaced three times. Nah, Vince had nothing to worry about.

The door was right over there.

Jeanette laughed, over at the bar. The Thousand and One Strings faded away, and Sinatra came on singing "One for My Baby, and One More for the Road." Vince walked across the dance floor. The door was open. Maybe there was something else out there, some new way to start over that he hadn't found yet. He'd looked a long time before he found this place. Some of the other stories out there might be true.

He snapped both sets of fingers in time to the music. No degeneration yet. The door was right over there. Well, why not? He should get out of here while he still could, before they took away anything else. There was a whole world out there. Sure, a lot of it was unlivable, but there had to be someplace better than this.

Paddy was telling some long sports story at the bar. Jeanette looked up from her drink and smiled. Sam whispered something in her ear, then laughed softly to himself.

Vince snapped his fingers. The door was open. But first he needed another drink.

Carolyn and I go back a ways. This fine Cherryh story comes to you via my powers of persuasion (read: blackmail). Blackmail, of a sort, figures in the plotline, as well. As does a very old, very tired deep-space probe which, despite its ultraclear message and the intentions of its builders, is misunderstood.

POTS

by C.J. Cherryh

It was a most bitter trip, the shuttle-descent to the windy surface. Suited, encumbered by lifesupport, Desan stepped off the platform and waddled onward into the world, waving off the attentions of small spidery service robots: "Citizen, this way, this way, citizen, have a care—do watch your step; a suit tear is hazardous."

Low-level servitors. Desan detested them. The chief of operations had plainly sent these creatures accompanied only by an AI eight-wheel transport, which inconveniently chose to park itself a good five hundred paces beyond the shuttle blast zone, an uncomfortably long walk across the dusty pan in the crinkling, pack-encumbered oxy-suit. Desan turned, casting a forlorn glance at the shuttle waiting there on its landing gear, silver, dip-nosed wedge under a gunmetal sky, at rest on an ochre and rust landscape. He shivered in the sky-view, surrendered himself and his meager luggage to the irritat-

ing ministries of the service robots, and waddled
on his slow way down to the waiting AI transport.

"Good day," the vehicle said inanely, opening a
door. "My passenger compartment is not safe
atmosphere; do you understand, Lord Desan?"

"Yes, yes." Desan climbed in and settled himself
in the front seat, a slight give of the transport's
suspensors. The robots fussed about in insectile
hesitance, delicately setting his luggage case just
so, adjusting, adjusting until it conformed with
their robotic, template-compared notion of their
job. Maddening. Typical robotic efficiency. Desan
slapped the pressure-sensitive seating. "Come, let's
get this moving, shall we?"

The AI talked to its duller cousins, a single squeal
that sent them scuttling; "Attention to the door,
citizen." It lowered and locked. The AI started its
noisy drive motor. "Will you want the windows
dimmed, citizen?"

"No. I want to see this place."

"A pleasure, Lord Desan."

Doubtless for the AI, it was.

The station was situated a long drive across the
pan, across increasingly softer dust that rolled up
to obscure the rearview—softer, looser dust, occasionally a wind-scooped hollow that made the transport flex—("Do forgive me, citizen. Are you comfortable?")

"Quite, quite, you're very good."

"Thank you, citizen."

And finally—*finally!*—something other than flat
appeared, the merest humps of hills, and one anomalous mountain, a massive, long, bar that began as
a haze and became solid; became a smooth regu-
larity before the gentle brown folding of hills hardly
worthy of the name.

Mountain. The eye indeed took it for a volcanic
or sedimentary formation at distance, some anom-

alous and stubborn outcrop in this barren reach, where all else had declined to entropy; absolute, featureless, flat. But when the AI passed along its side this mountain had joints and seams, had the marks of *making* on it; and even knowing in advance what it was, driving along within view of the jointing, this work of Ancient hands—chilled Desan's well-traveled soul. The station itself came into view against the weathered hills, a collection of shocking green domes on a brown lifeless world. But such domes Desan had seen. With only the AI for witness, Desan turned in his seat, pressed the flexible bubble of the helmet to the double-seal window, and stared and stared at the stonework until it passed to the rear and the dust obscured it.

"Here, Lord," said the AI, eternally cheerful. "We are almost at the station—a little climb. I do it very smoothly."

Flex and lean; sway and turn. The domes lurched closer in the forward window and the motor whined. "I've very much enjoyed serving you."

"Thank you," Desan murmured, seeing another walk before him, ascent of a plastic grid to an airlock and no sight of a welcoming committee.

More service robots, scuttling toward them as the transport stopped and adjusted itself with a pneumatic wheeze.

"Thank you, Lord Desan, do watch your helmet, watch your lifesupport connections, watch your footing please. The dust is slick. . . ."

"Thank you." With an AI one had no recourse.

"Thank *you*, my lord." The door came up; Desan extricated himself from the seat and stepped to the dusty ground, carefully shielding the oxy-pack from the doorframe and panting with the unaccustomed weight of it in such gravity. The service robots moved to take his luggage while Desan waddled doggedly on, up the plastic gridwork path to the glaringly lime-green domes. Plastics. Plastics that could not even originate in this desolation, but which came from their ships' spare biomass. Here all was dead, frighteningly void: Even the signal that guided him to the lakebed was robotic, like the advisement that a transport would meet him.

The airlock door shot open ahead; and living, suited personnel appeared, three of them, at last, at long last, flesh-and-blood personnel came walking toward him to offer proper courtesy. But before that mountain of stone; before these glaring green structures and the robotic paraphernalia of research that made all the reports real—Desan still felt the deathliness of the place. He trudged ahead, touched the offered, gloved hands, acknowledged the expected salutations, and proceeded up the jointed-plastic walk to the open airlock. His marrow refused to be warmed. The place refused to come into clear focus, like some bad dream with familiar elements hideously distorted.

A hundred years of voyage since he had last seen this world and then only from orbit, receiving reports thirdhand. A hundred years of work on this planet preceded this small trip from port to research center, under that threatening sky, in this place by a mountain that had once been a dam on a lake that no longer existed.

There had been the findings of the moon, of course. A few artifacts. A cloth of symbols. Primitive, unthinkably primitive. First omen of the findings of this sere, rust-brown world.

He accompanied the welcoming committee into the airlock of the main dome, waited through the cycle, and breathed a sigh of relief as the indicator lights went from white to orange and the inner door admitted them to the interior. He walked forward, removed the helmet and drew a deep breath of air unexpectedly and unpleasantly tainted. The foyer of this centermost dome was business-like—plastic walls, visible ducting. A few plants struggled for life in a planter in the center of the floor. Before it, a black pillar and a common enough emblem: a plaque with two naked alien figures, the diagrams of a starsystem—reproduced even to its scars and pitting. In some places it might be mundane, unnoticed.

It belonged here, *belonged* here, and it could never be mundane, this message of the Ancients.

"Lord Desan," a female voice said, and he turned, awkward in the suit.

It was Dr. Gothon herself, unmistakable aged woman in science blues. The rare honor dazed him, and wiped away all failure of hospitality thus far. She held out her hand. Startled, he reacted in kind, remembered the glove, and hastily drew back his hand to strip the glove. Her gesture was gracious and he felt the very fool and very much off his stride, his hand touching—no, firmly grasped by the callused, aged hand of this legendary intellect. Age-soft and hard-surfaced at once. Age and vigor. His tongue quite failed him, and he felt, recalling his purpose, utterly daunted.

"Come in, let them rid you of that suit, Lord Desan. Will you rest after your trip, a nap, a cup of tea, perhaps. The robots are taking your luggage to your room. Accommodations here aren't luxurious, but I think you'll find them comfortable."

Deeper and deeper into courtesies. One could lose all sense of direction in such surroundings, letting oneself be disarmed by gentleness, by pleasantness—by embarrassed reluctance to resist.

"I want to see what I came to see, doctor." Desan unfastened more seams and shed the suit into waiting hands, smoothed his coveralls. Was that too brusque, too unforgiveably hasty? "I don't think I *could* rest, Dr. Gothon. I attended my comfort aboard the shuttle. I'd like to get my bearings here at least, if one of your staff would be so kind to take me in hand—"

"Of course, of course. I rather expected as much—do come, please, let me show you about. I'll explain as much as I can. Perhaps I can convince you as I go."

He was overwhelmed from the start; he had expected *some* high official, the director of operations most likely, not Gothon. He walked slightly after the doctor, the stoop-shouldered presence that passed like a benison among the students and lesser staff—*I saw the Doctor*, the young ones had been wont to say in hushed tones, aboard the ship, when Gothon strayed absently down a corridor in her rare intervals of waking. *I saw the Doctor.*

In that voice one might claim a theophany.

They had rarely waked her, lesser researchers being sufficient for most worlds; while he was the fifth lord-navigator, the fourth born on the journey, a time-dilated trifle, fifty-two waking years of age and a mere two thousand years of voyage against—aeons of Gothon's slumberous life.

And Desan's marrow ached now at such gentle grace in this bowed, mottle-skinned old scholar, this sleuth patiently deciphering the greatest mystery of the universe. Pity occurred to him. He suffered personally in this place; but not as Gothon would have suffered here, in that inward quiet where Gothon carried on thoughts the ship crews were sternly admonished never to disturb.

Students rushed now to open doors for them, pressed themselves to the walls and allowed their passage into deeper and deeper halls within the maze of the domes. Passing hands brushed Desan's sleeves, welcome offered the current lord-navigator; he reciprocated with as much attention as he could devote to courtesy in his distress. His heart labored in the unaccustomed gravity, his nostrils accepted not only the effluvium of dome plastics and the recyclers and so many bodies dwelling together; but a flinty, bitter air, like electricity or dry dust. He imagined some hazardous leakage of the atmosphere into the dome: unsettling thought. The hazards of the place came home to him, and he wished already to be away.

Gothon had endured here, during his further voyages—seven years more of her diminishing life; waked four times, and this was the fourth, continually active now for five years, her longest stint yet in any waking. She had found data finally worth the consumption of her life, and she burned it without stint. *She* believed. She believed, enough to die pursuing it.

He shuddered up and down and followed Gothon through a seal-door toward yet another dome, and his gut tightened in dismay; for there were shelves on either hand, and those shelves were lined with yellow skulls, endless rows of staring dark sockets and grinning jaws. Some were long-nosed; some were short. Some small, virtually noseless skulls had fangs which gave them a wise and intelligent look—*Like miniature people, like babies with grown up features*, must be the initial reaction to anyone seeing them in the holos or viewing the specimens brought up to the orbiting labs. But cranial capacity in these was much too small. The real sapient occupied further shelves, row upon row of eyeless, generously domed skulls, grinning in their flat-toothed way, in permanent horror—provoking profoundest horror in those who discovered them here, in this desolation.

Here Gothon paused, selected one of the small sapient skulls, much reconstructed: Desan had at least the skill to recognize the true bone from the plassbone bonded to it. This skull was far more delicate than the others, the jaw smaller. The front two teeth were restructs. So was one of the side.

"It was a child," Gothon said. "We call her Missy.

The first we found at this site, up in the hills, in a streambank. Most of Missy's feet were gone, but she's otherwise intact. Missy was all alone except for a little animal all tucked up in her arms. We keep them together—never mind the cataloging." She lifted an anomalous and much-reconstructed skull from the shelf among the sapients; fanged and delicate. "Even archaeologists have sentiment."

"I—see—" Helpless, caught in courtesy, Desan extended an unwilling finger and touched the skull.

"Back to sleep." Gothon set both skulls tenderly back on the shelf; and dusted her hands and walked further, Desan following, beyond a simple door and into a busy room of workbenches piled high with a clutter of artifacts.

Staff began to rise from their dusty work in a sudden startlement. "No, no, go on," Gothon said quietly. "We're only passing through; ignore us. —Here, do you see, Lord Desan?" Gothon reached carefully past a researcher's shoulder and lifted from the counter an elongate ribbed bottle with the opalescent patina of long burial. "We find a great many of these. Mass production. Industry. Not only on this continent. This same bottle exists in sites all over the world, in the uppermost strata. Same design. Near the time of the calamity. We trace global alliances and trade by such small things." She set it down and gathered up a virtually complete vase, much patched. "It always comes to pots, Lord Desan. By pots and bottles we track them through the ages. Many layers. They had a long and complex past."

Desan reached out and touched the corroded brown surface of the vase, discovering a single bright remnant of the blue glaze along with the gray encrustations of long burial. "How long—how long does it take to reduce a thing to this?"

"It depends on the soil—on moisture, on acidity. This came from hereabouts." Gothon tenderly set it back on a shelf, walked on, frail, hunch-shouldered figure among the aisles of the past. "But very long, very long to obliterate so much—almost all the artifacts are gone. Metals oxidize; plastics rot; cloth goes very quickly; paper and wood last quite long in a desert climate, but they go, finally. Moisture dissolves the details of sculpture. Only the noble metals survive intact. Soil creep warps even stone; crushes metal. We find even the best pots in a matrix of pieces, a puzzle-toss. Fragile as they are, they outlast monuments, they last as long as the earth that holds them, drylands, wetlands, even beneath the sea—where no marine life exists to trouble them. That bottle and that pot are as venerable as that great dam. The makers wouldn't have thought that, would they?"

"But—" Desan's mind reeled at the remembrance of the great plain, the silt and the deep buried secrets.

"But?"

"You surely might miss important detail. A world to search. You might walk right over something and misinterpret everything."

"Oh, yes, it can happen. But *finding* things where we expect them is an important clue, Lord Desan, a confirmation— One only has to suspect where to look. We locate our best hope first—a sunken, a raised place in those photographs we trouble the orbiters to take; but one gets a *feeling* about the lay of the land—more than the mechanical probes, Lord Desan." Gothon's dark eyes crinkled in the passage of thoughts unguessed, and Desan stood lost in Gothon's unthinkable mentality. What did a mind *do* in such age? Wander? Could the great doctor lapse into mysticism? To report such a thing—would solve one difficulty. But to have that regrettable duty—

"It's a feeling for living creatures, Lord Desan. It's reaching out to the land and saying—if this were long ago, if I thought to build, if I thought to trade—where would I go? Where would my neighbors live?"

Desan coughed delicately, wishing to draw things back to hard fact. "And the robot probes, of course, do assist."

"Probes, Lord Desan, are heartless things. A robot can be very skilled, but a researcher directs it only at distance, blind to opportunities and the true sense of the land. But you were born to space. Perhaps it makes no sense."

"I take your word for it," Desan said earnestly. He felt the weight of the sky on his back. The leaden, awful sky, leprous and unhealthy cover between them and the star and the single moon. Gothon remembered homeworld. *Remembered homeworld*. Had been renowned in her field even there. The old scientist claimed to come to such a landscape and *locate* things by seeing things that robot eyes could not, by thinking thoughts those dusty skulls had held in fleshly matter—

—how long ago?

"We look for mounds," Gothon said, continuing in her brittle gait down the aisle, past the bowed heads and shy looks of staff and students at their meticulous tasks. The work of tiny electronic needles proceeded about them, the patient ticking away at encrustations to bring ancient surfaces to light. "They built massive structures. Great skyscrapers. Some of them must have lasted, oh, thousands of years intact; but when they went unstable, they fell, and their fall made rubble; and the wind came and the rivers shifted their courses around the ruin, and of course the weight of sediment piled up, wind- and water-driven. From that point, its own weight moved it and warped it and complicated our work." Gothon paused again beside a further table, where holo plates stood inactive. She waved her hand and a landscape showed itself, a serpentined row of masonry across a depression. "See the wall there. They didn't build it that way, all wavering back and forth and up and down. Gravity and soil movement deformed it. It was buried until we unearthed it. Otherwise, wind and rain alone would have destroyed it ages ago. As it will do, now, if time doesn't rebury it."

"And this great pile of stone—" Desan waved an arm, indicating the imagined direction of the great dam and realizing himself disoriented. "How old is it?"

"Old as the lake it made."

"But contemporaneous with the fall?"

"Yes. Do you know, that mass may be standing when the star dies. The few great dams; the pyramids we find here and there around the world— One only guesses at their age. They'll outlast any other surface feature except the mountains themselves."

"Without life."

"Oh, but there is."

"Declining."

"No, no. Not declining." The doctor waved her hand and a puddle appeared over the second holo plate, all green with weed waving feathery tendrils back and forth in the surge. "The moon still keeps this world from entropy. There's water, not as much as this dam saw— It's the weed, this little weed that gives one hope for this world. The little life, the things that fly and crawl—the lichens and the life on the flatlands."

"But nothing *they* knew."

"No. Life's evolved new answers here. Life's starting over."

"It certainly hasn't much to start with, has it?"

"Not very much. It's a question that interests Dr. Bothogi—whether the life making a start here has the time left, and whether the consumption curve doesn't add up to defeat—But life doesn't know that. We're very concerned about contamination. But we fear it's inevitable. And who knows, perhaps it will have added something beneficial." Dr. Gothon lit yet another holo with the wave of her hand. A streamlined six-legged creature scuttled energetically across a surface of dead moss, frantically waving antennae and making no apparent progress.

"The inheritors of the world." Despair chilled Desan's marrow.

"But each generation of these little creatures is an unqualified success. The last to perish perishes in profound tragedy, of course, but without consciousness of it. The awareness will have, oh, half a billion years to wait—then, maybe it will appear; if the star doesn't fail; it's already far advanced down the sequence." Another holo, the image of desert, of blowing sand, beside the holo of the surge of weed in a pool. "Life makes life. That weed you see is busy making life. It's taking in and converting and building a chain of support that will enable things to feed on it, while more of its kind grows. That's what life does. It's busy, all unintended, of course, but fortuitously building itself a way off the planet."

Desan cast her an uncomfortable look askance.

"Oh, indeed. Biomass. Petrochemicals. The storehouse of aeons of energy all waiting the use of consciousness. And that consciousness if it arrives, dominates the world because awareness is a way of making life more efficiently. But consciousness is a perilous thing, Lord Desan. Consciousness is a computer loose with its own perceptions and performing calculations on its own course, in the service of that little weed; billions of such computers all running and calculating faster and faster, adjusting themselves and their ecological environment, and what if there were the smallest, the most insignificant software error at the outset?"

"You don't believe such a thing. You don't reduce us to that." Desan's faith was shaken; this good woman had not gone unstable, this great intellect had had her faith shaken, that was what— the great and gentle doctor had, in her unthinkable age, acquired cynicism, and he fought back with his fifty-two meager years. "Surely, but surely this isn't the proof, doctor, this could have been a natural calamity."

"Oh, yes, the meteor strike." The doctor waved past a series of holos on a fourth plate, and a vast crater showed in aerial view, a crater so vast the picture showed planetary curvature. It was one of the planet's main features, shockingly visible from space. "But this solar system shows scar after scar of such events. A many-planeted system like this, a star well-attended by debris in its course through the galaxy— Look at the airless bodies, the moons, consider the number of meteor strikes that crater them. Tell me, spacefarer: am I not right in that?"

Desan drew in a breath, relieved to be questioned in his own element. "Of course, the system is prone to that kind of accident. But that crater is ample cause—"

"If it came when there was still sapience here. But that hammerblow fell on a dead world."

He gazed on the eroded crater, the sandswept crustal melting, eloquent of age. "You have proof."

"Strata. Pots. Ironic, they must have feared such an event very greatly. One thinks they must have had a sense of doom about them, perhaps on the evidence of their moon; or understanding the mechanics of their solar system; or perhaps primitive times witnessed such falls and they remembered. One catches a glimpse of the mind that reached out from here . . . what impelled it, what it sought."

"How can we know that? We overlay our mind on their expectations—" Desan silenced himself, abashed, terrified. It was next to heresy. In a moment more he would have committed irremediable indiscretion; and the lords-magistrate on the orbiting station would hear it by suppertime, to his eternal detriment.

"We stand in their landscape, handle their bones, we hold their skulls in our fleshly hands and try to think *in* their world. Here we stand beneath a threatening heaven. What will we do?"

"Try to escape. Try to get off this world. They *did* get off. The celestial artifacts—"

"Archaeology is ever so much easier in space. A million years, two, and a thing still shines. Records still can be read. A color can blaze out undimmed after aeons, when first a light falls on it. One surface chewed away by microdust, and the opposing face pristine as the day it had its maker's hand on it. You keep asking me about the age of these ruins. But we know that, don't we truly suspect it, in the marrow of our bones—at what age they fell silent?"

"It *can't* have happened then!"

"Come with me, Lord Desan." Gothon waved a hand, extinguishing all the holos, and, walking on, opened the door into yet another hallway. "So much to catalog. That's much of the work in that room. They're students, mostly. Restoring what they can; numbering, listing. A librarian's job, just to know where things are filed. In five hundred years more of intensive cataloging and restoring, we may know them well enough to know something of their minds, though we may never find more of their written language than that of those artifacts on the moon. A place of wonders. A place of ongoing wonders, in Dr. Bothogi's work. A little algae beginning the work all over again. Perhaps not for the first time—interesting thought."

"You mean—" Desan overtook the aged doctor in the narrow, sterile hall, a series of ringing steps.

"You mean—before the sapients evolved—there were other calamities, other re-beginnings."

"Oh, well before. It sends chills up one's back, doesn't it, to think how incredibly stubborn life might be here, how persistent in the calamity of the skies— The algae and then the creeping things and the slow, slow climb to dominance—"

"Previous sapients?"

"Interesting question in itself. But a thing need not be sapient to dominate a world, Lord Desan. Only tough. Only efficient. Haven't the worlds proven that? High sapience is a rare jewel. So many successes are dead ends. Flippers and not hands; lack of vocal apparatus—unless you believe in telepathy, which I assuredly don't. No. Vocalizing is necessary. Some sort of long-distance communication. Light-flashes; sound; something. Else your individuals stray apart in solitary discovery and rediscovery and duplication of effort. Oh, even with awareness—even granted that rare attribute— how many species lack something essential, or have some handicap that will stop them before civilization; before technology—"

"—before they leave the planet. But they *did* that, they were the one in a thousand— Without them—"

"Without them. Yes." Gothon turned her wonderful soft eyes on him at close range and for a moment he felt a great and terrible stillness like the stillness of a grave. "Childhood ends here. One way or the other, it ends."

He was struck speechless. He stood there, paralyzed a moment, his mind tumbling freefall; then blinked and followed the doctor like a child, helpless to do otherwise.

Let me rest, he thought then, *let us forget this beginning and this day, let me go somewhere and sit down and have a warm drink to get the chill from my marrow and let us begin again. Perhaps we can begin with facts and not fancies—*

But he would not rest. He feared that there was no rest to be had in this place, that once the body stopped moving, the weight of the sky would come down, the deadly sky that had boded destruction for all the history of this lost species; and the age of the land would seep into the bones and haunt his dreams as the far greater scale of stars did not.

All the years I've voyaged, Dr. Gothon, all the years of my life searching from star to star. Relativity has made orphans of us. The world will have sainted you. Me it never knew. In a quarter of a million years—they'll have forgotten; o doctor, you know more than I how a world ages. A quarter of a million years you've seen—and we're both orphans. Me endlessly cloned. You in your long sleep, your several clones held aeons waiting in theirs—o doctor, we'll recreate you. And not truly you, ever again. No more than I'm Desan-prime. I'm only the fifth lord-navigator.

In a quarter of a million years, has not our species evolved beyond us, might they not, may they not, find some faster transport and find us, their aeons-lost precursors; and we will not know each other, Dr. Gothon—how could we know each other—if they had, but they have not; we have become the wavefront of a quest that never overtakes, never surpasses us.

In a quarter of a million years, might some calamity have befallen us and our world be like this world, ocher and deadly rust?

While we are clones and children of clones, genetic fossils, anomalies of our kind?

What are they to us and we to them? We seek the Ancients, the makers of the probe.

Desan's mind reeled; adept as he was at time-relatively calculations, accustomed as he was to stellar immensities, his mind tottered and he fought to regain the corridor in which they walked, he and the doctor. He widened his stride yet again, overtaking Gothon at the next door.

"Doctor." He put out his hand, preventing her, and then feared his own question, his own skirting of heresy and tempting of hers. "Are you beyond doubt? You can't be beyond doubt. They could have simply abandoned this world in its calamity."

Again the impact of those gentle eyes, devastating. "Tell me, tell me, Lord Desan. In all your travels, in all the several near stars you've visted in a century of effort, have you found traces?"

"No. But they could have gone—"

"—leaving no traces, except on their moon?"

"There may be others. The team in search on the fourth planet—"

"Finds nothing."

"You yourself say that you have to stand in that landscape, you have to think with their mind— Maybe Dr. Ashodt hasn't come to the right hill, the right plain—"

"If there are artifacts there they only are a few. I'll tell you why I know so. Come, come with me." Gothon waved a hand and the door gaped on yet another laboratory.

Desan walked. He would rather have walked out to the deadly surface than through this simple door, to the answer Gothon promised him . . . but habit impelled him; habit, duty—necessity. He had no other purpose for his life but this. He had been left none, lord-navigator, fifth incarnation of Desan Das. They had launched his original with none, his second incarnation had had less, and time and successive incarnations had stripped everything else away. So he went, into a place at once too mundane and too strange to be quite sane—mundane because it was sterile as any lab, a well-lit place of littered tables and a few researchers; and strange because hundreds and hundreds of skulls and bones were piled on shelves in heaps on one wall, silent witnesses. An articulated skeleton hung in its frame; the skeleton of a small animal scampered in macabre rigidity on a tabletop.

He stopped. He stared about him, lost for the moment in the stare of all those eyeless sockets of weathered bone.

"Let me present my colleagues," Gothon was saying; Desan focused on the words late, and blinked helplessly as Gothon rattled off names. Bothogi the zoologist was one, younger than most, seventeenth incarnation, burning himself out in profligate use of his years: so with all the incarnations of Bothogi Nan. The rest of the names slid past his ears ungathered—true strangers, the truly-born, sons and daughters of the voyage. He was lost in their stares like the stares of the skulls, eyes behind which shadows and dust were truth, gazes full of secrets and heresies.

They knew him and he did not know them, not even Lord Bothogi. He felt his solitude, the helplessness of his convictions—all lost in the dust and the silences.

"Kagodte," said Gothon, to a white-eared, hunched individual, "Kagodte—the Lord Desan has come to see your model."

"Ah." The aged eyes flicked, nervously.

"Show him, pray, Dr. Kagodte."

The hunched man walked over to the table, spread his hands. A holo flared and Desan blinked, having expected some dreadful image, some confrontation with a reconstruction. Instead, columns of words rippled in the air, green and blue. Numbers ticked and multiplied. In his startlement he lost the beginning and failed to follow them. "I don't see—"

"We speak statistics here," Gothon said. "We speak data; we couch our heresies in mathematical formulae."

Desan turned and stared at Gothon in fright.

"Heresies I have nothing to do with, doctor. I deal with facts. I come here to find facts."

"Sit down," the gentle doctor said. "Sit down, Lord Desan. There, move the bones over, do; the owner's won't mind, there, that's right."

Desan collapsed onto a stool facing a white worktable. Looked up reflexively, eye drawn by a wall-mounted stone that bore the blurred image of a face, eroded, time-dulled—

The juxtaposition of image and bones overwhelmed him. The two whole bodies portrayed on the plaque. The sculpture. The rows of fleshless skulls.

Dead. World hammered by meteors, life struggling in its most rudimentary forms. Dead.

"Ah," Gothon said. Desan looked around and saw Gothon looking up at the wall in his turn. "Yes. That. We find very few sculptures. A few—a precious few. Occasionally the fall of stone will protect a surface. Confirmation. Indeed. But the skulls tell us as much. With our measurements and our holos we can flesh them. We can make them—even more vivid. Do you want to see?"

Desan's mouth worked. "No." A small word. A coward word. "Later. So this was *one* place— You still don't convince me of your thesis, doctor, I'm sorry."

"The place. The world of origin. A many-layered world. The last layers are rich with artifacts of one period, one global culture. Then silence. Species extinguished. Stratum upon stratum of desolation. Millions of years of geological record—"

Gothon came round the end of the table and sat down in the opposing chair, elbows on the table, a scatter of bone between them. Gothon's green eyes shone watery in the brilliant light, her mouth was wrinkled about the jowls and trembled in minute cracks, like aged clay. "The statistics, Lord Desan, the dry statistics tell us. They tell us centers of production of artifacts, such as we have; they tell us compositions, processes the Ancients knew—and there was no progression into advanced materials. None of the materials we take for granted, metals that would have lasted—"

"And perhaps they went to some new process, materials that degraded completely. Perhaps their information storage was on increasingly perishable materials. Perhaps they developed these materials in space."

"Technology has steps. The dry numbers, the dusty dry numbers, the incidences and concentration of items, the numbers and the pots—always the pots, Lord Desan; and the imperishable stones; and the very fact of the meteors—the undeniable fact of the meteor strikes. Could we not avert such a calamity for our own world? Could we not have done it—oh, a half a century before we left?"

"I'm sure you remember, Dr. Gothon. I'm sure you have the advantage of me. But—"

"You see the evidence. You want to cling to your hopes. But there is only one question—no, two. Is this the species that launched the probe? —Yes. Or evolution and coincidence have cooperated mightily. Is this the only world they inhabited? Beyond all doubt. If there are artifacts on the fourth planet they are scoured by its storms, buried, lost."

"But they may *be* there."

"There is no abundance of them. There is no *progression*, Lord Desan. That is the key thing. There is nothing beyond these substances, these materials. This was not a star-faring civilization. They launched their slow, unmanned probes, with their cameras, their robot eyes—not for us. We always knew that. We were the recipients of flotsam. Mere wreckage on the beach."

"It was purposeful!" Desan hissed, trembling, surrounded by them all, a lone credent among the quiet heresy in this room. "Dr. Gothon, your unique position—is a position of trust, of profound trust; I beg you to consider the effect you have—"

"Do you threaten me, Lord Desan? Are you here for that, to silence me?"

Desan looked desperately about him, at the sudden hush in the room. The minute tickings of probes and picks had stopped. Eyes stared. "Please." He looked back. "I came here to gather data; I expected a simple meeting, a few staff meetings—to consider things at leisure—"

"I have distressed you. You wonder how it would be if the lords-magistrate fell at odds with me. I am aware of myself as an institution, Lord Desan. I remember Desan Das. I remember launch, the original five ships. I have waked to all but one of your incarnations. Not to mention the numerous incarnations of the lords-magistrate."

"You cannot discount them! Even you—Let me plead with you, Dr. Gothon, be patient with us."

"You do not need to teach me patience, Desan-Five."

He shivered convulsively. Even when Gothon smiled that gentle, disarming smile. "You have to give me facts, doctor, not mystical communings with the landscape. The lords-magistrate accept that this is the world of origin. I assure you they never would have devoted so much time to creating a base here if that were not the case."

"Come, lord, those power systems on the probe, so long dead—What was it truly for, but to probe something very close at hand? Even orthodoxy admits that. And what is close at hand but their own solar system? Come, I've *seen* the original artifact and the original tablet. Touched it with my hands. This was a *primitive* venture, designed to cross their own solar system—*which they had not the capability to do.*"

Desan blinked. "But the purpose—"

"Ah. The purpose."

"You say that you stand in a landscape and you think in their mind. Well, doctor, *use* this skill you claim. What did the Ancients intend? Why did they send it out with a message?"

The old eyes flickered, deep and calm and pained. "An oracular message, Lord Desan. A message into the dark of their own future, unaimed, unfocused. Without answer. Without hope of answer. We know its voyage time. Eight million years. They spoke to the universe at large. This probe went out, and they fell silent shortly afterward—the depth of this dry lake of dust, Lord Desan, is eight and a quarter million years.

"I will not believe that."

"Eight and a quarter million years ago, Lord Desan. Calamity fell on them, calamity global and complete within a century, perhaps within a decade of the launch of that probe. Perhaps calamity fell from the skies; but demonstrably it was atomics and their own doing. They were at that precarious stage. And the destruction in the great centers is catastrophic and of one level. Destruction centered in places of heavy population. Trace elements. That is what those statistics say. Atomics, Lord Desan."

"I cannot accept this!"

"Tell me, space-farer—do you understand the workings of weather? What those meteor strikes could do, the dust raised by atomics could do with equal efficiency. Never mind the radiation that alone would have killed millions—never mind the destruction of centers of government: We speak of global calamity, the dimming of the sun in dust, the living oceans and lakes choking in dying photosynthetes in a sunless winter, killing the food chain from the bottom up—"

"You have no proof!"

"The universality, the ruin of the population-centers. Arguably, they had the capacity to prevent meteor-impact. That may be a matter of debate. But beyond a doubt in my own mind, simultaneous destruction of the population centers indicates atomics. The statistics, the pots and the dry numbers, Lord Desan, doom us to that answer. The question is answered. There were no descendants; there was no escape from the world. They destroyed themselves before that meteor hit them."

Desan rested his mouth against his joined hands. Stared helplessly at the doctor. "A lie. Is that what you're saying? We pursued a lie?"

"Is it their fault that we needed them so much?"

Desan pushed himself to his feet and stood there by mortal effort. Gothon sat staring up at him with those terrible dark eyes.

"What will you do, lord-navigator? Silence me? The old woman's grown difficult at last: wake my clone after, tell it—what the lords-magistrate select for it to be told?" Gothon waved a hand about the room, indicating the staff, the dozen sets of living eyes among the dead. "Bothogi too, those of us who have clones— But what of the rest of the staff? How much will it take to silence all of us?"

Desan stared about him, trembling. "Dr. Gothon—" He leaned his hands on the table to look at Gothon. "You mistake me. You utterly mistake me— The lords-magistrate may have the station, but I have the ships, *I*, I and my staff. I propose no such thing. I've come home—" The unaccustomed word caught in his throat; he considered it, weighed it, accepted it, at least in the emotional sense. "—*home*, Dr. Gothon, after a hundred years of search, to discover this argument and this dissension."

"Charges of heresy—"

"They dare not make them against *you*." A bitter laugh welled up. "Against *you* they have no argument and you well know it, Dr. Gothon."

"Against their violence, lord-navigator, I have no defense."

"But she has," said Dr. Bothogi.

Desan turned, flicked a glance from the hardness in Bothogi's green eyes to the even harder substance of the stone in Bothogi's hand. He flung himself about again, hands on the table, abandoning the defense of his back. "Dr. Gothon! I appeal to you! I am your friend!"

"For myself," said Dr. Gothon, "I would make no defense at all. But, as you say—they have no argument against me. So it must be a general catastrophe—the lords-magistrate have to silence everyone, don't they? *Nothing* can be left of this base. Perhaps they've quietly dislodged an asteroid or two and put them on course. In the guise of mining, perhaps they will silence this poor old world forever—myself and the rest of the relics. Lost relics and the distant dead are always safer to venerate, aren't they?"

"That's absurd!"

"Or perhaps they've become more hasty now that your ships are here and their judgement is in question. *They* have atomics within their capability, lord-navigator. They can disable your shuttle with beam-fire. They can simply welcome you to the list of casualties—a charge of heresy. A thing taken out of context, who knows? After all—all lords are immediately duplicatable, the captains accustomed to obey the lords-magistrate—what few of them are awake—am I not right? If an institution like myself can be threatened—where is the fifth lord-navigator in their plans? And of a sudden those plans will be moving in haste."

Desan blinked. "Dr. Gothon—I assure you—"

"If you are my friend, lord-navigator, I hope for your survival. The robots are theirs, do you understand? Their powerpacks are sufficient for transmission of information to the base AIs; and from the communications center it goes to satellites; and from satellites to the station and the lords-magistrate. This room is safe from their monitoring. We have seen to that. They cannot hear you."

"I cannot believe these charges, I cannot accept it—"

"Is murder so new?"

"Then come with me! Come with me to the shuttle, we'll confront them—"

"The transportation to the port is theirs. It would not permit. The transport AI would resist. The planes have AI components. And we might never reach the airfield."

"My luggage. Dr. Gothon, my luggage—my com unit!" And Desan's heart sank, remembering the service-robots. "*They* have it."

Gothon smiled, a small, amused smile. "O spacefarer. So many scientists clustered here, and could we not improvise so simple a thing? *We* have a receiver-transmitter. Here. In this room. We broke one. We broke another. They're on the registry as broken. What's another bit of rubbish—on this poor planet? We meant to contact the ships, to call *you*, lord-navigator, when you came back. But you saved us the trouble. You came down to us like a thunderbolt. Like the birds you never saw, my spaceborn lord, swooping down on prey. The conferences, the haste you must have inspired up there on the station—if the lords-magistrate planned what I most suspect! I congratulate you. But knowing we have a transmitter—with your shuttle sitting on this world vulnerable as this building—what will you do, lord-navigator, since *they* control the satellite relay?"

Desan sank down on his chair. Stared at Gothon. "You never meant to kill me. All this—you schemed to enlist me."

"I entertained that hope, yes. I knew your predecessors. I also know your personal reputation—a man who burns his years one after the other as if there were no end of them. Unlike his predecessors. What are you, lord-navigator? Zealot? A man with an obsession? Where do you stand in this?"

"To what—" His voice came hoarse and strange. "To what are you trying to convert me, Dr. Gothon?"

"To our rescue from the lords-magistrate. To the rescue of truth."

"Truth!" Desan waved a desperate gesture. "I don't believe you, I cannot believe you, and you tell me about plots as fantastical as your research and try to involve me in your politics. I'm trying to find the trail the Ancients took—one clue, one artifact to direct us—"

"A new tablet?"

"You make light of me. Anything. Any indication where they went. And they *did* go, doctor. You will not convince me with your statistics. The unforeseen and the unpredicted aren't in your statistics."

"So you'll go on looking—for what you'll never find. You'll serve the lords-magistrate. They'll surely cooperate with you. They'll approve your search and leave this world . . . after the great catastrophe. After the catastrophe that obliterates us and all the records. An asteroid. Who but the robots chart their course? Who knows how close it is at this moment?"

"People would know a murder! They could never hide it!"

"I tell you, Lord Desan, you stand in a place and you look around you and you say—what would be natural to this place? In this cratered, devastated world, in this chaotic, debris-ridden solar system— could not an input error by an asteroid miner be more credible an accident than atomics? I tell you when your shuttle descended, we thought you might be acting for the lords-magistrate. That you might have a weapon in your baggage that their robots would deliberately fail to detect. But I believe you, lord-navigator. You're as trapped as we. With only the transmitter and a satellite relay system they control. What will you do? Persuade the lords-magistrate that you support them? Persuade them to support you on this further voyage—in return for your backing them? Perhaps they'll listen to you and let you leave."

"But they will," Desan said. He drew in a deep breath and looked from Gothon to the others and back again. "My shuttle is my own. *My* robotics, Dr. Gothon. From my ship and linked to it. And what I need is that transmitter. Appeal to *me* for protection if you think it so urgent. Trust me. Or trust nothing and we will all wait here and see what truth is."

Gothon reached into a pocket, held up an odd metal object. Smiled. Her eyes crinkled round the edges. "An old-fashioned thing, lord-navigator. We say *key* nowadays and mean something quite different, but I'm a relic myself, remember. Baffles hell out of the robots. Bothogi. Link up that antenna and unlock the closet and let's see what the lord-navigator and his shuttle can do."

"Did it hear you?" Bothogi asked, a boy's honest worry on his unlined face. He still had the rock, as if he had forgotten it. Or feared robots. Or intended to use it if he detected treachery. "Is it moving?"

"I assure you it's moving," Desan said, and shut the transmitter down. He drew a great breath, shut his eyes and saw the shuttle lift, a silver wedge spreading wings for home. Deadly if attacked. *They will not attack it, they must not attack it, they will query us when they know the shuttle is launched and we will discover yet that this is all a ridiculous error of understanding.* And looking at nowhere: "Relays have gone; *nothing* stops it and

its defenses are considerable. The lords-navigator
have not been fools, citizens: we probe worlds with
our shuttles, and we plan to get them back." He
turned and faced Gothon and the other staff. "The
message is *out*. And because I am a prudent man—
are there suits enough for your staff? I advise we
get to them. In the case of an accident."

"The alarm," said Gothon at once. "Neoth, sound
the alarm." And as a senior staffer moved: "The
dome pressure alert," Gothon said. "*That* will con-
found the robots. All personnel to pressure suits;
all robots to seek damage. I agree about the suits.
Get them."

The alarm went, a staccato shriek from overhead.
Desan glanced instinctively at an uncommunica-
tive white ceiling—

—darkness, darkness above, where the shuttle
reached the thin blue edge of space. The station
now knew that things had gone greatly amiss. It
should inquire, there should be inquiry immediate
to the planet—

Staffers had unlocked a second closet. They pulled
out suits, not the expected one or two for emergency exit from this pressure-sealable room; but a
tightly jammed lot of them. The lab seemed a
mine of defenses, a stealthily equipped stronghold
that smelled of conspiracy all over the base, through-
out the staff—*everyone* in on it—

He blinked at the offering of a suit, ears assailed
by the siren. He looked into the eyes of Bothogi
who had handed it to him. There would be no call,
no inquiry from the lords-magistrate. He began to
know that, in the earnest, clear-eyed way these
people behaved—not lunatics, not schemers. Truth.
They had told their truth as they believed it, as the
whole base believed it. And the lords-magistrate
named it heresy.

His heart beat steadily again. Things made sense

again. His hands found familiar motions, putting on the suit, making the closures.

"There's that AI in the controller's office," said a senior staffer. "I have a key."

"What will they do?" a younger staffer asked, panic-edged. "Will the station's weapons reach here?"

"It's quite distant for sudden actions," said Desan. "Too far for beams and missiles are slow." His heartbeat steadied further. The suit was about him; familiar feeling; hostile worlds and weapons: more familiar ground. He smiled, not a pleasant kind of smile, a parting of lips on strong, long teeth. "And one more thing, young citizen, the ships they have are transports. Miners. Mine are hunters. I regret to say we've carried weapons for the last two hundred thousand years, and my crews know their business. If the lords-magistrate attack that shuttle it will be their mistake. Help Dr. Gothon."

"I've got it, quite, young lord." Gothon made the collar closure. "I've been handling these things longer than—"

Explosion thumped somewhere away. Gothon looked up. All motion stopped. And the air-rush died in the ducts.

"The oxygen system—" Bothogi exclaimed. "O *damn* them—!"

"We have," said Desan coldly. He made no haste. Each final fitting of the suit he made with care. Suit-drill; example to the young: the lord-navigator, youngsters, demonstrates his skill. Pay attention. "And we've just had our answer from the lords-magistrate. We need to get to that AI and shut it down. Let's have no panic here. Assume that my shuttle has cleared atmosphere—"

—well above the gray clouds, the horror of the surface. Silver needle aimed at the heart of the lords-magistrate.

Alert, alert, it would shriek, *alert, alert, alert—* With its transmission relying on no satellites, with its message shoved out in one high-powered bow-wave. *Crew on the world is in danger.* And, code that no lord-navigator had ever hoped to transmit, a series of numbers in syntaxical link: *Treachery; the lords-magistrate are traitors; aid and rescue—Alert, alert, alert—*

—anguished scream from a world of dust; a place of skulls; the grave of the search.

Treachery, alert, alert, alert!

Desan was not a violent man; he had never thought of himself as violent. He was a searcher, a man with a quest.

He knew nothing of certainty. He believed a woman a quarter of a million years old, because—because Gothon was Gothon. He cried traitor and let loose havoc all the while knowing that here might be the traitor, this gentle-eyed woman, this collector of skulls.

O Gothon, he would ask if he dared, *which of you is false? To force the lords-magistrate to strike with violence enough to damn them— Is that what you wish? Against a quarter million years of un-abated life—what are my five incarnations: mere genetic congruency, without memory. I am helpless to know your perspectives.*

Have you planned this a thousand years, ten thousand?

Do you stand in this place and think in the mind of creatures dead longer even than you have lived? Do you hold their skulls and think their thoughts?

Was it purpose eight million years ago?

Was it, is it—horror upon horror—a mistake on both sides?

"Lord Desan," said Bothogi, laying a hand on his shoulder. "Lord Desan, we have a master key. We have weapons. We're waiting, Lord Desan."

Above them the holocaust.

* * *

It was only a service robot. It had never known its termination. Not like the base AI, in the director's office, which had fought them with locked doors and release of atmosphere, to the misfortune of the director—

"Tragedy, tragedy," said Bothogi, standing by the small dented corpse, there on the ocher sand before the buildings. Smoke rolled up from a sabotaged lifesupport plant to the right of the domes; the world's air had rolled outward and inward and mingled with the breaching of the central dome—the AI transport's initial act of sabotage, ramming the plastic walls. "Microorganisms let loose on this world—the fools, the arrogant *fools!*"

It was not the microorganisms Desan feared. It was the AI eight-wheeled transport, maneuvering itself for another attack on the coldsleep facilities. Prudent to have set themselves inside a locked room with the rest of the scientists and hope for rescue from offworld; but the AI would batter itself against the plastic walls, and living targets kept it distracted from the sleeping, helpless clones—Gothon's juniormost; Bothogi's; those of a dozen senior staffers.

And keeping it distracted became more and more difficult.

Hour upon hour they had evaded its rushes, clumsy attacks and retreats in their encumbering suits. They had done it damage where they could while staff struggled to come up with something that might slow it . . . it limped along now with a great lot of metal wire wrapped around its rearmost right wheel.

"Damn!" cried a young biologist as it maneuvered for her position. It was the agile young who played this game; and one aging lord-navigator who was the only fighter in the lot.

Dodge, dodge and dodge. "It's going to catch you against the oxyplant, youngster! *This* way!"

Desan's heart thudded as the young woman thumped along in the cumbersome suit in a losing race with the transport. "Oh, *damn*, it's got it figured! Bothogi!"

Desan grasped his probe-spear and jogged on— "Divert it!" he yelled. Diverting it was all they could hope for.

It turned their way, a whine of the motor, a serpentine flex of its metal body and a flurry of sand from its eight-wheeled drive. "Run, lord!" Bothogi gasped beside him; and it was still turning—it aimed for them now, and at another tangent a white-suited figure hurled a rock, to distract it yet again.

It kept coming at them. AI. An eight-wheeled, flex-bodied intelligence that had suddenly decided its behavior was not working and altered the program, refusing distraction. A pressure-windowed juggernaut tracking every turn they made.

Closer and closer. "Sensors!" Desan cried, turning on the slick dust—his footing failed him and he caught himself, gripped the probe and aimed it straight at the sensor array clustered beneath the front window.

Thum-p! The dusty sky went blue and he was on his back, skidding in the sand with the great balloon tires churning sand on either side of him.

The suit, he thought with a spaceman's horror of the abrading, while it dawned on him at the same time he was being dragged beneath the AI, and that every joint and nerve center was throbbing with the high voltage shock of the probe.

Things became very peaceful then, a cessation of commotion. He lay dazed, staring up at a rusty blue sky, and seeing it laced with a silver thread.

They're coming, he thought, and thought of his eldest clone, sleeping at a well-educated twenty years of age. Handsome lad. He talked to the boy from time to time. *Poor lad, the lordship is yours. Your predecessor was a fool—*

A shadow passed above his face. It was another suited face peering down into his. A weight rested on his chest.

"Get off," he said.

"He's alive!" Bothogi's voice cried. "Dr. Gothon, he's still alive!"

The world showed no more scars than it had at the beginning—red and ocher where clouds failed. The algae continued its struggle in sea and tidal pools and lakes and rivers—with whatever microscopic addenda the breached dome had let loose in the world. The insects and the worms continued their blind ascent to space, dominant life on this poor, cratered globe. The research station was in function again, repairs complete.

Desan gazed on the world from his ship: it hung as a sphere in the holotank by his command station. A wave of his hand might show him the darkness of space; the floodlit shapes of ten hunting ships, lately returned from the deep and about to seek it again in continuation of the Mission, sleek fish rising and sinking again in a figurative black sea. A good many suns had shone on their hulls, but this one sun had seen them more often than any since their launching.

Home.

The space station was returning to function. Corpses were consigned to the sun the Mission had sought for so long. And power over the Mission rested solely at present in the hands of the lord-navigator, in the unprecedented circumstance of the demise of all five lords-magistrate simultaneously. Their clones were not yet activated to begin their years of majority—"Later will be time to wake the new lords-magistrate," Desan decreed, "at some further world of the search. Let them hear this event as history."

When I can manage them personally, he thought. He looked aside at twenty-year-old Desan Six and the youth looked gravely back with the face Desan had seen in the mirror thirty-two waking years ago.

"Lord-navigator?"

"You'll wake your brother after we're away, Six. Directly after. I'll be staying awake much of this trip."

"*Awake*, sir?"

"Quite. There are things I want you to think about. I'll be talking to you and Seven both."

"About the lords-magistrate, sir?"

Desan lifted brows at this presumption. "You and I are already quite well attuned, Six. You'll succeed young. Are you sorry you missed this time?"

"No, lord-navigator! I assure you not!"

"Good brain. I ought to know. Go to your post, Six. Be grateful you don't have to cope with a new lordship *and* five new lords-magistrate and a recent schism."

Desan leaned back in his chair as the youth crossed the bridge and settled at a crew post, beside the captain. The lord-navigator was more than a figurehead to rule the seventy ships of the Mission, with their captains and their crews. Let the boy try his skill on this plotting. Desan intended to check it. He leaned aside with a wince—the electric shock that had blown him flat between the AI's tires had saved him from worse than a broken arm and leg; and the medical staff had seen to that: the arm and the leg were all but healed, with only a light wrap to protect them. The ribs were tightly wrapped too; and they cost him more pain than all the rest.

A scan had indeed located three errant asteroids, three courses the station's computers had not accurately recorded as inbound for the planet—until personnel from the ships began to run their own observation. Those were redirected.

Casualties. Destruction. Fighting within the Mission. The guilt of the lords-magistrate was profound and beyond dispute.

"Lord-navigator," the communications officer said. "Dr. Gothon returning your call."

Goodbye, he had told Gothon. *I don't accept your judgement, but I shall devote my energy to pursuit of mine, and let any who want to join you—reside on the station. There are some volunteers; I don't profess to understand them. But you may trust them. You may trust the lords-magistrate to have learned a lesson. I will teach it. No member of this mission will be restrained in any opinion while my influence lasts. And I shall see to that. Sleep again and we may see each other once more in our lives.*

"I'll receive it," Desan said, pleased and anxious at once that Gothon deigned reply; he activated the com-control. Ship-electronics touched his ear, implanted for comfort. He heard the usual blip and chatter of com's mechanical protocols, then Gothon's quiet voice. "Lord-navigator."

"I'm hearing you, doctor."

"Thank you for your sentiment. I wish you well, too. I wish you very well."

The tablet was mounted before him, above the console. Millions of years ago a tiny probe had set out from this world, bearing the original. Two aliens standing naked, one with hand uplifted. A series of diagrams which, partially obliterated, had still served to guide the Mission across the centuries. A probe bearing a greeting. Ages-dead cameras and simple instruments.

Greetings, stranger. We come from this place, this star system.

See, the hand, the appendage of a builder—This we will have in common.

The diagrams: we speak knowledge; we have no fear of you, strangers who read this, whoever you be.

Wise fools.

There had been a time, long ago, when fools had set out to seek them ... in a vast desert of stars. Fools who had desperately needed proof, once upon a quarter million years ago, that they were not alone. One dust-covered alien artifact they found, so long ago, on a lonely drifting course.

Hello, it said.

The makers, the peaceful Ancients, became a legend. They became purpose, inspiration.

The overriding, obsessive *Why* that saved a species, pulled it back from war, gave it the stars.

"I'm very serious—I do hope you rest, doctor—save a few years for the unborn."

"My eldest's awake. I've lost my illusions of immortality, lord-navigator. She hopes to meet you."

"You might still abandon this world and come with us, doctor."

"To search for a myth?"

"Not a myth. We're bound to disagree. Doctor, doctor, what *good* can your presence there do? What if you're right? It's a dead end. What if I'm wrong? I'll never stop looking. *I'll* never know."

"But we know their descendants, lord-navigator. We. We are. We've spread their legend from star to star—they've become a fable. The Ancients. The Pathfinders. A hundred civilizations have taken up that myth. A hundred civilizations have lived out their years in that belief and begotten others to tell their story. What if you should find them? Would you know them—or where evolution had taken them? Perhaps we've already met them, somewhere along the worlds we've visited, and we failed to know them."

It was irony. Gentle humor. "Perhaps, then," Desan said in turn, "we'll find the track leads home again. Perhaps we *are* their children—eight and a quarter million years removed."

"O ye makers of myths. Do your work, space-farer. Tangle the skein with legends. Teach fables to the races you meet. Brighten the universe with them. I put *my* faith in you. Don't you know—this world is all I came to find, but you—child of the voyage, you have to have more. For you the voyage is the Mission. Goodbye to you. Fare well. Nothing is complete calamity. The equation here is different, by a multitude of microorganisms let free—Bothogi has stopped grieving and begun to have quite different thoughts on the matter. His algae-pools may turn out a different breed this time—the shift of a protein here and there in the genetic chain—who knows what it will breed? Different software this time, perhaps. Good voyage to you, lord-navigator. Look for your Ancients under other suns. We're waiting for their offspring here, under this one."

*David Langford has managed to insert his deter-
minedly British story into my purportedly American
project. When you read the piece, you'll see why.
Anyone who can devise a new use for what will by
then be "old" technology deserves to be among this
group. And certain of the technology, one may argue,
is American. The satellite system that is central to
Langford's piece may well be an outgrowth of Navstar,
our multi-unit Global Positioning Satellite network,
capable of providing 24-hour-a-day coverage from at
least four satellites that can calculate ground positions within 15 meters or less. I'm sure Navstar's designers never envisioned anything like this, though. . . .*

NOTES FOR A NEWER TESTAMENT
by David Langford

And in those days were signs and portents, and
prophesyings of woe unto the unrighteous; wherefore, in the eightieth year or thereabouts, when a
great and evil multitude did set itself against the
free people of Berkshire, the wrath of God (or
Goddess) waxed mightily, and—

I find this very difficult. Cristofer tells me his
precious books and fiche say that for high and
holy things you need the high style. When I try it,
the sentences just never will end. As for writing
that here in Royal Berkshire there are two hundred and seventy score of the allegedly faithful, or

possibly ten-score-and-three-score-and-ten score, well, there has to be an easier way.

The thing has happened, though, the thing he called Molnya. We need to write it down safely as a myth on the flyleaves and in the margins of these Acid Free Books. So my dear Cristofer says. Because it's too long after the Fall for us to cope with the "truth," and sure enough *I* don't believe a word of his patchwork explanation. (Squinting at those fiche through the burning-glass has burnt funny patches inside his head, I know, for all his talk about objective knowledge.) This way, maybe, the fear of God-or-Goddess will make our people nicer. Not that I can see much sign of it.

From the north they came, from evil waste places and wildernesses where sickness yet abides, even from Birmingham and the Midlands came they; and they were slayers of men and slayers of women, and a fire of wrath burned in their hearts, and the blackness of malice was in their eyes, and all manner of foul speaking lay like poison on their tongues, and in number they were a great multitude . . .

"Katrin darling," I can hear him saying, "you just need to stop tacking on those *ands*." That's the whole trouble; there's never any logical place to stop. Actually they were a sorry sort of destroying horde, three or four generations onward and far too many marches through the sick places. We take an interest in history, here in Berks—at least I do and Cristofer does, and quite a few Olders of the County Council even if the rest are all obsessed with potatoes, rapeseed, and chard. From the decaying papers and memories we put it together: the Army scattered just before the Fall as a survival measure, and got no leadership afterwards of course, so they carried on living off the land— meaning the rest for us. For a long while they'd been the North's problem, seeing as the South fell further (or was fallen on), but now . . .

From the north the news came before them, a pillar of cloud by day and a pillar of fire by night; four days' march from our land they were seen, below Banbury-that-was, and the beacons went up, and the people of Berkshire were sore afraid. Round green-shrouded Oxford in the Six-Hour-Exposure Zone, and southward and eastward across the Downs, the beacons flared high on the pylons of the old Grid, even on the holy pylons where once had pulsed the glory of 400,000 volts.

I absolutely refuse to translate 400,000 into so many score. Scores are bunk anyway. The years of our life are three score and ten, it says, and though we're nearly the healthiest people in the island, we barely average half that. (The Crab takes fewer year by year, but the plagues seem hardier.) Cristofer, always ready for a pointless argument, suggested the years were longer now. The fiche have addled his brain.

Anyone's brain would get addled by the stuff written down before the Fall. We only have dead peoples' word for it that volts are things of power that could move the dead images on the screens the simple folk pray to, and that never move now, no matter how finely crafted by the best of artists, the Invader and the Pacman and the rest. Dead people can be such liars. When Cristofer showed me stories about the whole world being destroyed from edge to edge, which plainly it was not, I asked him how he could believe the others about men on the moon (never women, and that's a sure sign of a patriarchal myth, eh?) or armed machines that watch us from the others side of the sky. "I have faith," he said in an odd, flat voice. You never get anywhere with Cristofer when he talks like that.

And the people were sore afraid, and they called on their gods, and the gods of the screens answered not. And they went up unto the palace of

the County Council, which in its greatness and
glory had two uncracked windows and most of a
roof, and there they asked how they should be
saved; and the Olders looked each to each, and
answered not. I may have to tone this down a bit:
The Council actually droned on at appalling length,
but there was a certain lack of content, as Cristofer
failed to make himself popular by mentioning. What
did he think he was, a mere librarian and record-
keeper, getting above himself just because the Curator of Relics (me) let him into her bed, disturbing
the lofty processes of debate, he should be out
weeding the fields, and so on? Poor dear, and him
with only one foot, too. (Congenital.)

Is it even possible to translate the geography of
all this into High Style? By now we'd heard from
rabbit-hunters on the fringes of the Chilterns that
Rickman's Army, scruffier than ever, was lounging
its way down the old A423, which runs southeast
from Oxford and crosses the Thames at Henley.
Rickman was the current leader—I don't know
how they choose their leaders, probably ordeal by
biting the heads off rats or something similar—
and h asked nothing more from life than free
food, women, and young boys for himself and, where
possible, his ragtag followers. So the rabbit- and
rat-hunters reported. We, meanwhile, were in the
clear patch of Berkshire just west of Windsor Forest,
at a safe distance from London-that-was to the
east, the remains of Strike Command HQ at High
Wycombe in the north, and the western chunks of
the county, Reading and beyond, which had paid
the penalty for making and storing the devices of
the Fall. Damn it, geography's boring. Cut it down
to this:

And those who snared food in the Chiltern Hills
told of the host which came straight as any arrow,
laying waste the small settlements and most abomi-
nably using the peoples thereof, nor did they spare

any by occasion of ages, or of sex or of ho[...]ness or poorness, sickness or health. (I may [...] detail here when the memories have got far e[...] away to blur into blue distance. How can peop[...]? But it seems they always have.) And the people were sore afraid . . . no, we've had that twice . . . were smitten with mortal terror, for that the evil was nigh unto them, a score and six kilometers north and east of what was the motorway called M4. And they said, Who shall aid us now?

Really those farmers fluttered around like frightened chickens, the Council not excepted. We should run away in a unified front, they said—at the pace of the slowest, no doubt, with Rickman famous for vindictiveness in the face of games like that. We should scatter and hide in the woods—but nobody wanted to meet the rabble alone. We should march to meet them, Cristofer suggested disgracefully, and fight with our rusty hoes and pickaxes at Henley Bridge. "Who will stand on either hand and keep the bridge with me?" he caroled, and his wooden foot seized up again and he nearly fell over.

Then he went all serious.

There was a way, he told the Council, while that old hag, the Chair, twittered away in a soft undercurrent of sound. Primitive, warlike creatures like Rickman's Army were known to be ever so superstitious. Therefore, while there was time, let the able-bodied minority of Royal Berkshire carry northwest the most awe inspiring totem of our culture, and place the same on Henley bridge where the invaders couldn't fail to see it and be blasted with supernatural terror. QED.

"Such a suggestion," he murmured while the Council members were still stunned and silent, "would of course require permission from the Curator of such relics . . ."

"Such permission would readily be granted," I

ııed. What else could I say? In bed last night he'd spent what seemed like hours conning me into this, all on the grounds that he had faith in a certain obscure something. I hadn't.

"The *Ark* . . . ?" said the Chair, wits beginning to function.

My predecessor, Marji, had explained the name to me. The Ark was a before-the-Fall thing from a magical land far to the west (you can believe that if you like), and was supposed to help ward off the Fall itself. Apparently it didn't, but it remained a potent-looking talisman, a more-than-man-sized cylinder with a pointed nose and little stubby arms, and the Free People of Berkshire paid lip-service to its powers of defence. Old Marji had substituted "Ark" for the old name "Cruse," which the then Librarian had told her meant a vessel, pot or bottle. A sacred vessel was an Ark. Years later Cristofer told me—its nominal keeper, a sort of low priestess—what he thought the vessel held.

"Cristofer," I'd said in bed last night, "it couldn't? Not another Fall?"

"Impossible. Well, anyway, I don't think so. After more than eighty years, if the fiche are right, the neutron source buzz buzz plutonium gabble gabble decay electronics contamination buzz-buzz-gabble . . ."

I tweaked him in a certain place to turn off the flow.

"Then it won't do any good, will it?" There was that story of someone who'd torn the heart from another Ark, and found it to be a tarnished metal egg, and when he broke it the shards had held the worst taint of sickness and the Crab, making his settlement another No-Go Zone . . . Too horrible. More to the present point, too slow to halt Rickman's Army.

Cristofer had told me then about the thing called Molnya. When I'd sorted out his meaning from the buzz-buzz-gabble (he gets drunk on those big words), I very nearly threw him out of bed. "Idiot! You'd believe anything. You found technical diagrams of that great ship called the *USS Enterprise* that flies around from galaxy to galaxy—why not call *them* for help, and they're just as likely to answer? Honestly, you've been squinnying at your fiche records and piecing paper-crumbs together until you've lost touch with the real world. It's all superstition. You can't believe in it."

He fondled my good breast gently. "Maybe it is all superstition. One thing I read in the old records, though, is that some superstitions work even if you don't believe in them."

But he had the good sense not to spout all this rubbish to the County Council. The Council in turn was slightly at a loss, not quite wanting to trust its own folklore but not quite able to dismiss it with that word. A persuasive fellow, Cristofer—never thought I'd fancy a skinny man two inches shorter than me, or seven when he stands on his other leg. Perhaps there's something in all these old books after all.

And on the morrow they bore the holy Ark to the appointed bridge; and a long journey it was, and grievous, and many fell by the wayside in great travail, and many cursed Cristofer in their hearts, and grew faint in their faith, and would fain turn back along the path whence they had come, and so on and so forth.

A fifteen kilometer walk is no joke, especially in the rain, over broken country, taking turns in the ten-person crew that carried the dead weight of the Ark in its rope slings. Cristofer hopped with rage because he couldn't take a hand, and was made even more morose by the weather (I knew why), until late in the day the soggy grey sky went watery blue with the halting of the drizzle. Most of the able-bodied of Berkshire were along, some hundreds of us, and the mud squelched between our toes.

We placed our sleek stainless-steel burden with more relief than reverence in the exact centre of Henley bridge, and retreated some way to wait out the damp night. A few miles further, Rickman's Army was reportedly idling. Cristofer alone limped onward to them, alone thanks to a fit of stupid heroics.

"Be reasonable, Katrin," he said. "I'm the persuasive one. They're so dim, it needs a traitor like me to persuade them to do the logical thing that's going to totally destroy our Berkshire morale."

"And afterwards?"

He cocked his head at me slyly. "Thanks to you, at any rate, they can't possibly deflower me." From the bridge I watched him hobble up the A423 into Henley, the fading sun picking out the white streaks in his hair, until he turned a corner and was gone.

And on the next morrow the cohorts of the ungodly came unto the bridge, and set eyes upon the holy Ark; and they laughed. Wherefore the hearts of the Berkshire folk were made cold as they watched from their camp; and many were troubled with doubt. And the host of the unrighteous cast from them into the Thames the body of one who lacked a left foot, and again did they make merry, and laid hands on the holy Ark of the Lord, and marched with it against the camp of Berkshire, where all were as if turned to stone. And a woman of that camp cried out—

(That's me. Observe my modesty: no mention of my name in this account, no faithful record of my so-careful timing and choice of words, "Let's get the hell out of here!")

—cried out, and fear went through our people; they turned and did flee, casting back glances of fear and of dread. Made strong in their folly and pride by this flight, they of the North came crying after, and they too ran, even the twelve men bearing the Ark ran with all their might, that Berkshire might be utterly discomfited, cast down and destroyed.

And in that hour the Lord smote the ungodly.

With lightnings smote he them, and with thunder she split their ranks; with terrible heat were they consumed and in light unbearable they perished. Yet though the trees were withered, and the grass was blackened, the Ark lay undefiled amid the smoldering dead; nor did harm come unto any person of Berkshire.

—I must admit, the style works quite naturally for the exciting bits. Of course it's exaggerated here and there. Two or three of our people had their eyes hurt, permanently, through looking back at the wrong moment (shades of Lot's wife). Some stragglers of Rickman's bully-boys escaped to tell the north how dangerous it is to invade the chosen land of Berkshire; while the Ark was, actually, rather singed—no longer could you read the PERSHING stencil that made Marji's Librarian think it was meant for Iran, wherever that is.

It's hard to kill someone as persuasive as Cristofer: We found him clinging to a willow-root halfway down the Thames to Maidenhead, still fully ten percent alive.

"I got deflowered after all," he muttered. "That Rickman was a right bugger." He perked up though, back in the tent with an admiring audience, when given the chance to explain about the thing called Molnya, which is Russian for lightning. (Librarians apparently knew things like this.) He garbled and buzzed for a while, throwing out words like "orbital weapon," "solar power," "satellite scan," and "energy beam" . . . "So when the Molnya system detected *that shape* moving cross-country at more than walking pace—" He shrugged and grinned evilly.

"Look," I told him, "I was there and I don't believe a word of what you're saying. That was the wrath of God-or-Goddess I felt on the back of my neck, none of your cheap pre-Fall myths."

He was still perhaps a mite delirious from the chill and shock, and I smiled on him as he lay there, smiled as I would on a favorite baby who was saying: "A working artifact from before the Fall, yes . . . gabble buzz priceless treasure, absolute proof, I'll get up there one day and bring it back to show you . . . I read in the old records, you harness a whole lot of swans to a chariot. . . ."

As keeper of a holy mystery, I could afford to smile.

David Drake takes us far into the future with this, our last tale, one of men (sort of) doing their jobs (more or less) in the same way (kinda) that perimeter guards and security men have done these jobs for thousands of years. Drake deserves extra thanks for reading some of the stories before publication (and laughing out loud while reading Primary) *and for helping me decide to run the stories chronologically, a conversation that went something like this: "Why don't you put yours first and mine last—then it'll be balanced . . . depressing at the beginning and at the end." Thanks, Dave, for all your encouragement and moral support.*

THE GUARDROOM
by David Drake

"Three kings," said Singer, and the alarm rang to scatter the guardroom's inevitable poker game.

All four guards came alert; but it was Cohen's turn to go out, and there was that awareness too in the glances of the others toward him.

"Never learn when to back off, will you, Cohen?" said Singer, whose body was as squat and powerful as a troll's. He gestured toward the cards which Cohen, the other long-time veteran, had thrown in without displaying. "It isn't a bluff every time."

Elfen, the youngest of them when he was recruited to the four-man guard force, chuckled and said. "He'll live longer, you mean?" He had folded his cards after the draw and now slid them into the pile.

Cohen, preparing to enter the transfer chamber, said, "Game stops when the alarm sounds," with an edge of irritation. The frown that wrinkled the veteran's high forehead was probably because he was about to go operational rather than because of the gibe about his cardplaying; but the poker game was a safe subject. "I could've been holding a full house, Singer."

Pauli, the fourth guard, snorted and reached for the cards Cohen had thrown in. Singer froze the pile with one hand and deliberately stirred his own cards and the rest of the deck together with the other. "Give 'em hell, buddy," he said to the man in the transfer chamber.

"Sure," said Cohen, "why should they be better off than everybody else?"

Then the circuits tripped, leaving the transfer chamber empty of what the other three men knew as Cohen: a guard, as they were, of the Citadel of Arborson.

"Been a long time since anybody's tried it," said Pauli—perhaps in regret, perhaps in hidden concern for the fact that he was next up on the rotation. Only one guard could be transferred at a time, while the number of intruders were in theory limited only by the population the Earth still managed to support. . . .

Of course, that theoretical number seemed still to be decreasing.

"Yeah," Elfen said, looser than the others because he was neither facing imminent duty nor closely bonded to Cohen—Singer had brought aboard and trained both the newer guards. "Back in my day, every full moon somebody'd get together a band to break into the Citadel of Arborson. Nobody's got any balls anymore."

"They've forgotten the trick of getting in," said

Singer, rifling the cards and appearing to look at them. "Not a matter of guts, just knowledge. And maybe metal."

"*We* knew how to get in, right enough," responded Elfen with a laugh. "It was just how to get out that was the problem."

Pauli grimaced toward the transfer chamber. "Some things don't change, do they?" he said.

The guardroom in Singer's imagination was momentarily infinite and featureless, a bleak expanse of dull ochre like the walls—themselves an electronic construct, as were the cards and all the other seemingly-physical objects within. Singer's massive hands shuffled cards that were as useful as they would have been if 'real' in some more material sense. "I wonder what they think they're going to find here," he remarked to the cards. "They can't have any conception of what Arborson was doing . . . of what a *scientist* was, for god's sake. Nobody in his own day believed he was more than a crank. Our day, Cohen's and mine."

"Well, so far as that goes," Elfen objected, "what do any of *us* know about Arborson—except that he's dead?"

"Do we know that?" Singer rejoined, rapping the cards on the tabletop to bring the deck into alignment. He looked up. Neither of the other guards spoke under his lowering gaze. Singer was the leader of the guardroom, in fact, if not officially. Arborson—if he were alive, rather than being dust or an electronic memory somewhere—did not involve himself in the affairs of the guards who carried out the orders he had programmed long ago.

Singer's face relented. He raised the reshuffled cards and asked in a mild voice, "Shall we play a couple of rounds of three-handed, then?"

Pauli sucked his lips and turned away. "Why don't we just wait awhile," he said, "until Cohen comes back."

So they waited, the three of them, until the alarm sounded again to indicate that Cohen would never come back.

Pauli jumped up with a curse or a prayer, headed for the transfer chamber instinctively because his eyes were shattered by tears and emotions beyond sorrow.

Pauli had been a warrior just short of thirty years old when he entered the guardroom, an advanced age that bespoke skill and toughness as clearly as did the scars overlying his body's more formal pattern of tattoos. There was a difference between the circumstances of his former life and what he was called on now to accomplish, however; and it may have been that the process itself was more a cause for his fear than was what—in addition to Cohen's body—he expected to find outside.

Singer stopped Pauli as he had earlier blocked his attempt to check the poker hand. Pauli whirled to glare at the big veteran who rose from his chair gripping the other's wrist.

"Singer, this is none of yours!" Pauli shouted. Anger had given him back composure of a sort, the hair-trigger readiness to strike, even pointlessly, here in the guardroom. "Back off and leave me go!"

"Sure, you've got the next call up," Singer said, easing his hold enough to defuse the situation without giving the smaller man a chance to make a break for the transfer chamber. "You can handle it, just like you did those calls before—hell, I trained you, didn't I? But now will you let me take care of *my* job, which a follow-up alarm damned well is?"

"What's that?" said Elfen, who had been watching the others struggle with an expression that was more nearly sexual than professional—though he was very good, no question of that, everything Arborson could wish if Arborson had desires. . . .

"I'm senior," Singer explained, using the interruption as cover to maneuver between Pauli and the chamber. "Cohen'd go if I weren't here." And very likely Cohen *would* have made the same split-second decision, had it been Singer out there on the ground; though they had not been friends during their long association, not until this moment when the association was finally terminated.

"Elfen, you're next up if there's a third call," the veteran added, an embellishment to establish the truth of what had gone before. That detail was unnecessary since Singer was already entering the transfer chamber, but it was better not to leave Pauli with the notion that his skill and courage was in doubt. God knew—but there was no god— that the kid would need skill, courage, and all his confidence the next time he did go out.

Maybe Arborson knew, since god did not.

And Singer felt his consciousness pass through the transfer chamber in a series of pin-prick intersections that ended with the breeze on his face and the light of the quarter moon by which he saw as clearly as he could have in sunlight before he became a guard at the Citadel of Arborson.

Singer stood in the first of the four external transfer booths, screened and safe from immediate detection by the intruders—barring hugely bad luck. Bad luck of one sort or another had met Cohen, though; and in any case, the guards liked to be free of the booth's constraints well before intruders were able to penetrate as far as the Citadel itself in the midst of the sprawling grounds. Cohen's failure had cost the remainder of the guard force that edge of time.

The veteran waited only a moment to be sure that there was some distance between the voices he heard and the alcove in which he was sheltered. The sounds were from far enough away that, though they were human, no words could be distinguished. Fair enough. He stepped through the black surface which was in reality an absence of light.

Singer moved quickly and, for a man of his size and bulk, very quietly; but just now, the rustle of oak leaves beneath his boots was not a matter of primary importance. He needed to learn as quickly as possible what had happened to Cohen.

Or rather, *how* it had happened.

The tell-tales in Singer's helmet indicated the external barrier had been breached almost in the center of its northern quadrant. He headed that way, knowing that Cohen would have acted to limit the incursion before he mopped it up.

He had been a rich man, Arborson, in his day, and the grounds of the Citadel were ample to sustain a population of rodents and the foxes that preyed upon them. There was not a great or as varied a number of birds as Singer would have liked, however; though god knew he'd not been a nature-boy before entering the guardroom. The migratory species were unable to leave after Arborson sealed the grounds behind the external barrier, so they died during the three years of brutal winter; and the change from parkland to increasingly dense forest had reduced the supply of seeds for the birds that required them.

There had been hummingbirds when Singer first met Dr. Arborson. Now the guard thought he missed those arrowing, hovering little forms more than anything else in life.

Since he was right-handed, Singer approached the breach clockwise to put the barrier on his left. Counterclockwise felt safer, though it was not: Singer *knew* and acted on that knowledge that nothing outside the barrier could harm him; but emotionally there was still a desire to keep his strong side to a world that was now beyond his conception.

There was forest of sorts on the other side of the barrier. The germ plasm of plants is far more malleable than that of animal life, and the sleet of radiation had hammered the genes ancestral to the growth outside. The barrier, transparent from within, was hedged with a thousand forms that no botanist of Singer's day would have recognized.

Most of the vegetation was of stunted shapes gnarling across piles of rubble where steel reinforcements retained a dangerous level of atomic warmth even when their structural strength had been oxidized away. There was one tall tree: a pine perhaps and a conifer surely, for cones swelled at intervals from the trunk all the way from the ground to the tip three hundred feet in the air. That height was needless since the giant would have towered above its competitors for light and air at a quarter of its present majesty, but it made an ideal post from which to overlook the sprawling black dome of the Citadel's external barrier.

Perhaps that was why so many of the intrusions into the Citadel grounds were made near the giant trunk, as was this one.

The apparatus piercing the barrier was a wooden frame covered by a mesh of hand-drawn wire. It looked unbelievably crude to have been sufficient for the purpose.

Ages before, there had been men who could carry forward the equations Arborson had published—before he chose to isolate himself on an estate whose defenses were solely physical until the long morning of miniature suns vaporizing stone and steel and bodies all across the world. There were governments then, too, or their semblance, and the sophistication of even a shattered world was quite high when all its resources were marshaled. Arborson's method of withdrawal seemed to offer the one real hope that civilization could survive the holocaust it had brought on itself.

The first intrusion through the barrier had been made with a stressed-wire tube that modified the size and shape of its rhomboidal meshes. Engineers dialed-in the mesh armor so that the fourth man trying to enter was not incinerated in the heart of the barrier as his predecessors had been. He died instead with a bullet through the brain as he squirmed out of the tube. The last of that particular party had been a woman. While her body twitched on the pile of a dozen of her friends, Singer had dragged the tube completely inside the barrier, his ears ringing with the muzzle blasts of his gun.

But later attempts—some of them, at any rate— had the benefit of knowing from the beginning what size and alignment of wires would screen intruders through the barrier. The guards still had advantages over the intruders, among them the fact that ammunition from within the Citadel was trustworthy long after parties of intruders had ceased to carry firearms except for show. Even so, not all the guards had made it through the early days. Singer had, and Cohen; and Cohen's body now was sprawled with an arrow so far through the back of his neck that its barbed point must have been deep in the leaf mold against which his face was buried. His hand was outstretched toward the mesh shield that he had intended to destroy before he hunted down the intruders.

Cohen had always been one to underestimate the competition. He'd been very good, though, good enough to last this long ... which meant that somewhere in the forest was someone even better.

The arrow itself gave the intruder away. It had slanted down from above when it struck and finished Cohen. Singer knelt, still as a stone, and quartered the treetops with his eyes the way Cohen should have done before assuming that the tube had been left unguarded. At last he found an oak trunk that was as thick above a major crotch as it was below, with a texture that was subtly wrong.

Singer peered carefully at the section of trunk, ten feet above the ground and twenty from the point at which Cohen lay. It was covered with inner bark, a robe woven of cambium and fastened artfully to conceal a human figure. The watcher had held his position after he made his kill instead of rushing down in a triumph that would have left him cold meat for an additional opponent.

If all of them were that good, then Pauli was going to get a chance to try his skills on them after all.

There were two choices, one of them a crossbow bolt of Singer's own into the intruder: a clout shot at twenty yards, but risky if the target were armored—and wasteful if it were not. Singer backed away, even more cautious than he had been when he made his final approach to the site of the intrusion. When he was well beyond risk of alarming the watcher in the tree by casual noise, he sped back toward the Citadel proper at a gliding lope.

Besides the watchman at the point they had entered—and hoped to leave—the Citadel grounds, the intruders had separated only two men as outliers. It was a pity that they had not guarded their backtrail closely, so that Singer could have eliminated more of their strength before dealing with the main body.

There were something less than a dozen intruders at the Citadel, their numbers confused by the way they crowded around the door they were attacking. That portal had never been satisfactorily repaired since the afternoon that a new recruit and Spannisky, one of the original guards, had both died before Cohen mopped up the party of intruders.

The outliers stood twenty yards deeper in the forest, out of sight of each other and the main body. The obvious danger of their position was lessened by the dog each man led, huge animals with the drooping stance of scent hunters. The hounds' noses were intended to do what the eyes of the men could not, warn of dangers in the darkness which moonlight could only emphasize in patches through the canopy. There was little undergrowth within the Citadel grounds this late in the summer, because the overspreading oaks absorbed most of the sunlight that could have nourished lesser vegetation.

One of the outliers stood with his back to a tree bole, stationary but too twitchingly nervous to remain unnoticed even if his hound were not casting between a pair of vole runs at the length of its short lead. The other man was pacing something less formal than a proper guard beat. He seemed to be of a mind that the dog was better able to give warning if it were allowed to roam—albeit in a twenty-yard circuit or less. The pacing man was as nervous as his fellow. He twisted his whole torso back and forth at rapid intervals, obviously terrified that something was creeping up behind him as he followed the hound.

Singer crept carefully into a position from which his exceptional night vision allowed him to see both outliers and the group battering at the Citadel with wedges and hammers besides. The leader of the intruders was huge, taller than Singer and perhaps as solidly muscular in the shoulders and chest. He wore a bark-cloth cape and over it a headdress of black fur. As Singer watched, the man turned from the doorway to the forest and called to the outliers. His fur covering was the pelt of something descended from a domestic cat, a beast that must have weighed twenty-five pounds in life. Now, its eyes replaced by bits of red glass and its jaws gaping—the skull had been retained as support—the cat glared angrily above the harsh face of the man who wore it.

The outlier with his back to the tree glowered as he shouted in reply. His fellow, the man starting at shadows as he paced behind his hound, did not respond to the leader's summons—save by spinning in almost a complete circle at the sound. Neither outlier left his post, so the call must have been meant as encouragement rather than summons. The intruders' speech was too alien for Singer to guess at the language, much less understand it.

This gang would almost certainly be able to gain entrance through the already-weakened section. That, and the way the attacking party kept itself together, gave Singer a workable strategy—though he wished, and not for the first time, that he could have a partner during operations.

But two hands would achieve what four could have made simpler. Singer circled silently through the light brush toward the outlier who kept in motion.

The dog made Singer's task easier because of the false security it gave its master. The outlier passed close to a huge oak as he made his rounds. Singer simply positioned himself behind that tree and waited with his crossbow cocked and poised in his left hand.

As the dog preceded its master down the track they had worn on previous circuits, its big head swung from side to side like a derrick loading freight. Singer, still as the trunk against which he waited, felt the dog's warm breath on his ankle as the animal moved on without taking notice.

The man himself walked by, left wrist wrapped with the end of a five-foot leash and the short spear in his right hand poised to stab. He twisted his head around to be certain there was no bogey approaching—nervousness and not expectation, so that he did not actually see the veteran guard looming behind him. Singer smiled and cut the outlier's throat with a knife whose blade the present age could not have sharpened, much less forged.

The dog turned when its master jerked the lead reflexively. The crossbow bolt broke both spine and windpipe before the animal could bay a warning.

Beast and man collapsed, thrashing at opposite ends of the leash that still connected them. To Singer, the *bang* of the bow-cord releasing was stunningly loud; but no one else within the Citadel enclosure remarked it.

Singer had to work very quickly now, though the door—even in its present damaged state—should give him some margin. He wiped the blade of his knife carefully before sheathing it, but he ignored the blood, which oozed in a bubbling seam from the outlier's throat when Singer lifted him in a fireman's carry. With the corpse's torso across the veteran's broad shoulders, one wrist and ankle gripped to keep the burden anchored, Singer set off at a lope that would bring him to another of the Citadel's entrances without being seen by the main body of intruders. The weight of the dead man made Singer more awkward, but it did not slow him significantly. He liked to feel the play of his muscles under stress.

The Citadel's doorways were unmarked against segments of the building's metal sheath, hidden except to sophisticated equipment. The current party had been guided by the damage earlier intruders had done. Without the guidance, well—the man Singer had just killed carried a stone-tipped spear, and there was not a scrap of metal on his body. It was scarcely credible that such a band could have woven the protective screen with adequate precision. Perhaps the external barrier was losing its effectiveness with the years.

Guards were not meant to worry about that, though it could be that no one else remained. Singer had a momentary vision of a tin can rusting slowly, retaining the appearance of a protective covering long after time had leached away the contents. Then the veteran's stride took him through the portal, which slid open at his approach as it was programmed to do.

The part of the Citadel entered through normal doorways was a bleak warren of conduit-lined halls to which only necessity could draw Singer. There were a few cabinets holding special-purpose tools and weapons beyond those of the kit a guard received when he went operational. Most of the interior was closed as firmly to the guards as to intruders who managed to penetrate the outer shell of the building by force. Singer sometimes believed that the interior 'rooms' were actually structural elements, supporting or capping the levels of the Citadel that held whatever reality Arborson retained. Once before, however, when he ran past on a mission of slaughter, a blank wall had become momentarily transparent. Singer had glimpsed a ballroom and dazzlingly-costumed humans. Under other circumstances, he would have assumed he was hallucinating—as perhaps he was.

None of the guards had any notion of where the physical reality of the guardroom might be. Perhaps it was not even part of the Citadel's structure.

The interior of the Citadel was humidity and temperature controlled, though even that could not prevent the primers of small-arms ammunition from degrading to the point that guns were useless. The dispenser spool of beryllium monocrystal that the guard snatched—wire so fine that spider-silk was coarse beside it—still had dull gleam of flawless, corrosion-free uniformity, however.

Singer carried it with him in his right hand as he ran down the pattern of long hallways with the corpse jouncing on his shoulders.

The fact that the intruders' efforts—and even their voices—were clearly audible on the inner side of the portal meant the guard had less time to prepare than he had hoped. The intruders had opened a visible crack between the door's two leaves and were now attacking the hinges. God knew whether or not folk so primitive could do real damage if they penetrated the shell of the building; but Arborson assumed they might . . . or at any rate, no one yet had told the guards that the progressive collapse of civilization had made their services superfluous.

Using the knife with which he had made his kill, Singer butterflied the corpse: splitting the breastbone the long way and then, with the body faced away from him and his knee on the spine, pulling back on the halves of the rib cage until bones cracked and the sides flapped with no tendency of their own to close over the organs trying to slip from the cavity. He strung the body from an armthick pipe running along the axis of the hall a few inches beneath the ceiling.

Singer's hands were slimy with blood and lymph, making the task of threading the wire through back muscles and twice around the spine even harder than the thin wire would have caused it to be. The Citadel had no washing facilities that the guard knew of, and the fact that he was working with a fresh corpse meant that an attempt to cleanse himself would be pointless in any case.

The beryllium filament had a tab on the end so that it could be tracked and handled without special equipment. The monocrystal itself was strong enough to suspend a locomotive, but the guard was very much afraid that a thread so fine would cut even the dense bone of spinal processes under the weight of the dangling corpse. The dispenser hissed as Singer used it to sever and tack-weld the loops he ran off while it automatically fused the new end of the spool into a tab.

Ordinary baling wire would have been better for the present job, thought the big man as he gently let the wire take the full burden of the dead man he had been supporting one-handed; but you use what you've got and the beryllium filament was perfectly satisfactory, despite a minuscule grating sound from the lolling corpse and a squeal from the pipe above.

That was half the job. Singer ran back in the direction by which he had entered. Along the walls quivered patches of torchlight that entered through widening cracks in the door that the intruders were forcing. The guard carried the wire dispenser and the knife which he had not had time to wipe and sheathe again. The light crossbow jounced uncocked from a spring tether on the right side of Singer's belt where it balanced the quiver of bolts on the left. He would need the missile weapon again; but for the moment, the knife would deal with anyone he met as he dashed among the trees on the next stage of his plan to preserve the Citadel—from men who might not be able to harm it, for a man who might for ages have been dead and dust.

How long had it been, anyway? The oaks within the external barrier were protected from lightning and the attendant possibility of fire, so their growth had been stunted by the dense equality of foliage and root systems. There was no way to estimate time's passage from their size. And as for the mad tangle of vegetation beyond the barrier—as well try to count the whorls of a storm cloud.

For now, time meant the minutes remaining before the intruders broke into the Citadel.

Singer tacked a loop of beryllium filament to a

fitting in the hallway before he stepped out of the building again. The door closed behind him, tugging at the dispenser. Even the tolerances of the Citadel's undamaged portals were not close enough to sever the monocrystal between their surfaces. With one end anchored immovably, the guard began to wind his lengthy snare among the oaks.

He drew loops of the filament around major trunks, tightly enough that the thin beryllium cut the outer bark and kept the segments of line between trees from sagging. The wire was so fine that, if he had wanted to, Singer could have sawed through the thickest boles with a steady pressure—severing the dense wood like a block of cheddar in a cheese slicer.

The trees were not his objective, of course. He strung his line at slants varying from eighteen to sixty inches above the ground: knee-height to neck of a man bolting between the trees.

The job required extreme care for all the haste. Not even Singer could see the strung filament which hung like the disembodied edge of a razor. If he fell against it, it would slice him to the bone or beyond—and that would keep him from completing his job.

Singer found the remaining outlier no greater problem than he expected. Fear had turned to restive loneliness in the half hour during which the man had been stationed with no company but a hound that was equally bored.

The patches of torchlight which the outlier could see from where he stood, backed still against the tree, were more fleeting and diffuse than those the same fires had flung within the cracking Citadel. It was toward those torches that the intruder turned at last and craned his neck, hoping for a glimpse of his fellows—as the dog tugged its lead in renewed interest and Singer, ten feet away in a thicket of bush honeysuckle, shot the man through the base of the brain.

The hound *woofed* in interrogation, tossing its big head from the slap of the crossbow to the sprawling collapse of the dead man to whom it was still tethered. Singer cared very little about the noise, now that he had strung a ragged line across what the intruders would think was their escape route, and he would have spared the dog if he could . . . but that was not one of the options that Arborson had permitted.

The guard's powerful forearm drew back on the bow's cocking lever while the dog, its flaring nostrils filled with the scent of death, yelped and sprang against its tether. Its last jump was toward Singer, straining so hard that it dragged along the corpse that anchored it. When the hound reached the limit of its attempt and crashed back to the ground, the guard put a bolt through its chest the long way.

Singer had no idea of how many men he had killed, either before the day Arborson hired him or after. He knew that he regretted none of them as much as he did the dog whose nostrils now sprayed bright pulmonary blood across the leaves on which it died.

Even that lengthy paired slaughter of man and beast went unnoticed by the main party in the moment of its own triumph. Metal shrieked from the direction of the Citadel, now out of the veteran's sight. Singer dared not creep closer and chance his own snare, but he flattened himself belly-down on the leaf mold. At the level of the moccasins and bare legs of the intruders, Singer could see them crowding to grip the levers they had wedged between the jamb and door leaves. The locking mechanism failed with a crash. The men gave a great shout and lurched forward, some of them tumbling onto all fours.

The leader with the catskin headdress was one of those who stumbled, though only to his knees. He rose now to his full great height, holding a torch forward in his hand. The bellow of fear from his men was louder even than their triumph of moments before.

Singer took the chance he was offered and snapped a crossbow bolt between the shoulder blades of the leader thirty feet away. The big intruder pitched forward without a sound, while the men he had commanded fled from the mutilated body of the fellow they thought was on guard behind them.

Even in flight, the survivors remained fairly well bunched. They would have been cold meat for an automatic weapon, but the beryllium razor they met at approximately waist height did quite well enough for Singer's purpose.

The wire was stationary and the victims ran slower than a sword could have been swung towards its impact. Even so, the edge the men struck was supernally sharp, and it was anchored with all of the ineluctable solidity of the Earth itself. Men screamed, and those who were able snatched out to free themselves from a gossamer tenuousness that lopped off the fingers terror flung against it.

For choice, Singer would have let the men on the wire wait for an hour or more before he exposed himself, but there was the last intruder yet to deal with—the one stationed at the break in the barrier. The noise of terror and confusion should not draw the watchman from his place even if he heard it; but dangerous as it was to count on an opponent doing the *wrong* thing, it was even more foolish to assume that someone under great stress would carry out each previous order as given.

Singer's time was short. He stepped from cover with his knife ready for use and his bow cocked against possibility.

The blade was enough. None of the men on the wire were by this point any danger to the guard, and only three of them really needed the quick stroke to finish the job. The filament had no barbs, but it cut with crystalline certainty even when a victim tried to withdraw from its invisible embrace. The intruders fumbled and lurched until they bled out. The one man who tore himself free, regardless of the pain, lay sprawled a few feet closer to the Citadel than the others. Those parts of him that had been between his ribs and the cup of his pelvis now lay in a liquid tangle beneath the wire which had skidded across bone as the intruder scooped himself free.

The guard used the dispenser's cutting jaws to sever the filament when he had disposed of the men on it. For choice, he would have clipped each segment of the lethal snare he had hung . . . but if Singer were to complete what was now his main task, he did not have time for those details. The irony was not lost on the guard as he strode toward the man who had led the intruders.

The leader had enough life in him to blink when Singer snatched away the catskin headdress. The man had been trying to lift himself or crawl, but his thick fingers had only marked the loam.

The brooch which held the leader's cape at the throat was an elaborate confection of garnets and bits of window glass in a matrix of bitumen. Singer unhooked it and pulled the bark-cloth garment away before he drew his bloody knife across the man's throat. A vein on the bald scalp spasmed as it emptied, and the eyes lost even the film of life they shared with the glass in the cat's sockets.

One to go.

Singer threw the cape across his shoulders and fumbled with the brooch until he had it fastened. The garment stank, but not nearly as much as did the catskin which had been, at least, imperfectly cured before it became a headdress. That mattered as little to Singer as it did to the dead man who once wore it. The guard tossed his helmet to the ground and put the catskin on instead before he set off to meet the remaining intruder.

This time when he ran through the forest, Singer did so with the deliberate intention of making noise. He flapped through brush too green to crackle and thumped heavily against tree trunks, bellowing wordlessly. His left hand gripped the cape to keep it from opening as he ran, because that would have exposed—among other things—the bloody knife he held blade to the thumb side in the other hand.

As the veteran burst into sight of the barrier, the wire-wrapped cylinder, and Cohen's body, his attention was focused on the intruder waiting in silence for another kill. Singer could not permit the other to know that, however—not until the intruder called to what he thought was his leader, below him and foreshortened by the angle. Singer leaped, his left hand outstretched—sure that he had taken the intruder completely by surprise.

The man's bowstring slapped his bracer as he sent an arrow down at Singer's chest. The point shattered on Singer's ceramic breastplate, but the bastard was very good and the shock of his reaction almost caused the guard to miss his grip on an ankle beneath the camouflaging drapery.

Almost. Singer was very good also.

They tumbled together, the Citadel guard's mass and momentum throwing his slighter opponent like a flail to the threshing floor. Tendons or the fibula cracked in the leg Singer held, and the bow sprang loose when the intruder hit the ground. The cape that had hidden the man fluttered from the tree to which it had been fastened. Without its shrouding, the scars on the intruder's torso and arms stood out sharply. He was missing an ear and the little finger of the hand with which he fumbled for the stone knife in his sash. Even stunned by the fall, the intruder's instincts were everything Death could have wished.

Cohen had picked the wrong time to get impatient . . . but without Cohen's body on the ground for warning, Singer wasn't sure that he couldn't have made as final a mistake himself. He punched the intruder in his jaw, using not his bare hand but the dagger pommel. Bone crunched and the wiry body went loose. The chest still rose.

The framework of the cylinder through which the gang had breached the external barrier was too heavy for even Singer to muscle it fully inside. He gripped a double handful of the wire sheathing instead and pulled on it. The meshes distorted from the precise rhomboids they had been. The currents induced in the barrier's heart ravened through the material: The wooden framework burst into flame and the wires, laboriously drawn and woven, blazed in showers of white sparks in the orange wrapper of the softer fire.

Singer tossed aside the portion of the shielding he held. By the time he next saw it, the metal would have rusted to a flush on the topsoil. Even the tetrahedral bonds of the beryllium monocrystal could, given time, be oxidized. Some day the filament would crumble at a breeze or a raindrop which, like normal light, penetrated the external barrier unimpeded. As ragged as this party of intruders had been, the Citadel itself might be dust before others gained access . . . unless the barrier failed first.

And again, the guardroom might precede the remainder of Arborson's constructs to oblivion.

Singer picked up the intruder whose breath whistled through a nose broken, it seemed, when he hit the ground. The man was smaller than the corpse

Singer had used to panic the others, but he was densely muscular and a fair weight. Size was valuable and Singer, a good big man himself, knew that as well as any did. The man who'd put an arrow into Cohen and missed Singer's own throat by a finger's breadth and a millisecond could afford to give a hundred pounds to just about anybody he met, though. Trained to use the weapons of the Citadel—bows better than his, blades better than his dreams, and all the other paraphernalia that remained when time overcame chemistry—the one-time intruder would become a worthy guard for Arborson or Arborson's tomb.

Singer carried the unconscious man back to the transfer booths in the cradle of his big arms, the gentleness a personal whim since he knew that the only requirement was that the subject being recruited remain alive.

The Citadel's front door still gaped, a body before it and a body dangling within. Its repair was no concern for Singer. The conditioning that Arborson's apparatus imparted to the guards locked them within certain strait parameters. Perhaps someone from a place that was not the guardroom would appear to repair the door and dispose of the intruders, men and dogs, whom Singer could not have left alive even if he had wished to do so. A division of labor: those who took care of the Citadel of Arborson ... and those, Singer and his fellows, who took care of attempts to break into the Citadel.

The big guard stepped through the immaterial curtain hiding the transfer booths. He could scarcely remember the first time he had done so, he and the three others who had hired themselves to guard Feodor Arborson less for the wages he promised than the possibility that the eccentric genius could provide survival in a world that teetered on the brink of a millenium and the abyss.

This much Arborson had provided: survival. He had never said that he was offering life.

The intruder gave a moan that suggested returning consciousness. Singer set him down in the second of the four alcoves. There were oak leaves on the floor, and dust; and among them, a dog-tag that had been Abraham Cohen's. In the first alcove, grating slightly under Singer's feet, was another bit of nickel steel that time had proven was not stainless. This one gave Singer's name, his church affiliation—none then and less than none by now—a serial number in an army that had not existed for thousands of years, and medical data, which had become pointless when Singer first stood in the transfer booth and died.

"Ready, one and two," he said aloud and felt the disorientation, familiar by now, as the apparatus of the Citadel scanned his being and stripped it away from his body.

The intruder in the second alcove fell silent, though his autonomic nervous system would keep his heart and lungs at work for minutes or even hours. What had been a man was brain dead, a machine running down.

In the other booth was the form that the Citadel had provided for Singer's soul to don like a cloak. It could not be said to have died, because it had never been truly alive; it was a simulacrum of humanity supplied as equipment, along with the weapons and the armor. It would not be preserved. An equivalent, like this one, with no more of the smells and aura of life than a billet of firewood, would be supplied at future need—as had happened more times than Singer could remember.

A titmouse hopped through the light curtain which it had learned was no real barrier. The bodies were of no interest to the bird however. It flew out again when its curiosity had been satisfied.

*   *   *

"Glad to see you, man," said Pauli to Singer, truthful in that as in most things. "And who is it we've got here?"

"Where am I?" demanded the intruder, wide-eyed and too shocked to be hostile.

"What's your name, friend?" asked the big guard as he turned to the newcomer who had exited the transfer chamber just behind him. "I'm Singer, that's Pauli and—" Elfen nodded his tattooed forehead "—Elfen." Singer offered his hand, hoping the gesture would translate. Language, like his present body, was a construct to the computer of which the guards were a part, but physical actions here had no import but that which the 'watcher' supplied from his own culture.

"My name's Kruse," the wiry recruit said, "but where *am* I?"

"Where?" repeated Elfen. "You're in the guard-room, wherever that is."

Elfen picked up the cards which lay stacked where he had left them. "Do you know how to play poker, Kruse?" he asked, holding the deck to the newcomer and rifling the edges.

"*What?*"

"Oh, don't worry," Singer said tiredly. "You'll have plenty of time to learn."

Here is an excerpt from Between the Strokes of Night *by Charles Sheffield, coming in July 1985 from Baen Books:*

Pentecost—A.D. 27698

The last shivering swimmer had emerged from the underground river, and now it would be possible to assemble the final results. Peron Turco pulled the warm cape closer about his shoulders and looked back and forth along the line.

There they stood. Four months of preliminary selection had winnowed them down to a bare hundred, from the many thousands who had entered the original trials. And in the next twenty minutes it would be reduced again, to a jubilant twenty-five.

Everyone was muddied, grimy, and bone-weary. The final trial had been murderous, pushing minds and bodies to the limit. The four-mile underwater swim in total darkness, fighting chilling currents through a labyrinth of connecting caves, had been physically demanding. But the mental pressure, knowing that the oxygen supply would last only for five hours, had been much worse. Most of the contestants were slumped now on the stone flags, warming themselves in the bright sunlight, rubbing sore muscles and sipping sugar drinks. It would be a little while before the scores could be tallied, but already their attention was turning from the noisy crowds to the huge display that formed one outer wall in the coliseum.

Peron shielded his eyes against Cassay's morning brilliance and studied each face in turn along the long line. By now he knew where the real competition lay, and from their expressions he sought to gauge his own chances. Lum was at the far end, squatting cross-legged. He was eating fruit, but he looked bored and sweaty.

Ten days ago Peron had met him and dismissed Lum as soft and overweight, a crudely-built and oafish youth who had reached the final hundred contestants by a freakish accident. Now he knew better. Peron had revised his assessment three times, each one upwards. Now he felt sure that Lum would be somewhere high in the final twenty-five.

And so would the girl Elissa, three positions to the left. Peron had marked her early as formidable competition. She had started ten minutes ahead of him in the first trial, when they made the night journey through the middle of Villasylvia, the most difficult and dangerous forest on the surface of Pentecost.

Now Elissa turned to look at him while he was still staring along the line at her. She grinned, and he quickly averted his eyes. If Elissa didn't finish among the winners that would be bad news for Peron, too, because he was convinced that wherever they placed she would rank somewhere above him.

He looked back at the board. The markers were going up on the great display, showing the names of the remaining contestants. Peron counted them as they were posted. Only seventy-two. The last round of trials had been fiercely difficult, enough to eliminate over a quarter of the finalists completely.

Peron wished he could feel more confidence. He was sure (wasn't he?) that he was in the top thirty. He *hoped* he was in the top twenty, and in his dreams he saw himself as high as fourth or fifth. But with contestants drawn from the whole planet, and the competition of such high caliber . . .

The crowd roared. At last! The scores were finally appearing. The displays were assembled slowly and painstakingly. The judges conferred in great secrecy, knowing that the results would be propagated instantly over the entire planet, and that a mistake would ruin their reputations. Everything was checked and rechecked before it went onto the board.

Peron had watched recordings of recent Planetfests, over and over, but this one was different and more elaborate. Trials were held every four years. Usually the prizes were high positions in the government of Pentecost, and maybe a chance to see the Fifty Worlds. But the twenty-year games, like this one, had a whole new level of significance. There were still the usual prizes, certainly. But they were not the real reward. There was that rumored bigger prize: a possible opportunity to meet and work with the Immortals.

And what did *that* mean? No one could say. No one Peron knew had ever seen one, ever met one. They were the ultimate mystery figures, the ones who lived forever, the ones who came back every generation to bring knowledge from the stars. Stars that they were said to reach in a few days—in conflict with everything that the scientists of Pentecost believed about the laws of the Universe.

Peron was still musing on that when the roar of the crowd, separated from the contestants by a substantial barricade of rows of armed guards, brought him to full attention. The first winner, in twenty-fifth place, had just been announced. It was a girl, Rosanne. Peron remembered her from the Long Walk across Talimantor Desert, when the two of them had formed a temporary alliance to search for underground water. She was a cheerful tireless girl, just over the minimum age limit of sixteen, and now she was holding her hand to her chest, pretending to stagger and faint with relief because she had just made the cutoff.

All the other contestants now looked at the board with a new intensity. The method of announcement was well established by custom, but there was not a trial participant who did not wish it could be done differently. From the crowd's point of view, it was very satisfying to announce the winners in ascending order, so that the name of the final top contestant was given last of all. But during the trials, every competitor formed a rough idea of his or her chances by direct comparison with the opposition. it was easy to be wrong by five places, but errors larger than that were unlikely. Deep inside, a competitor knew if he was down in ninetieth place. Even so, hope always remained. But as the names gradually were announced, and twenty-fourth, twenty-third, and twenty-second position was taken, most contestants were filled with an increasing gloom, panic, or wild surmise. Could they possibly have placed so high? Or, more likely, were they already eliminated?